THE MCMURDO RIFT

BRADLEY LEJEUNE

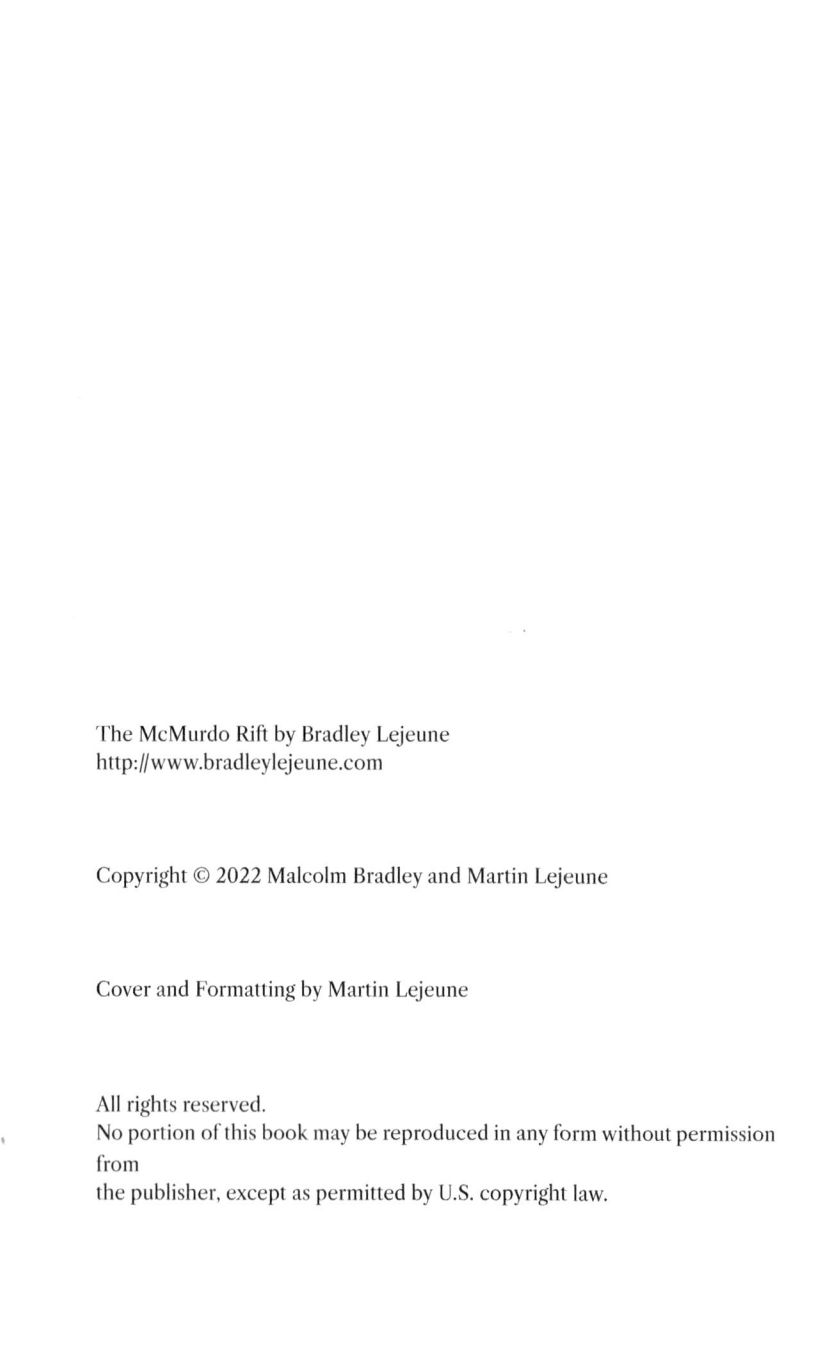

The McMurdo Rift by Bradley Lejeune
http://www.bradleylejeune.com

Copyright © 2022 Malcolm Bradley and Martin Lejeune

Cover and Formatting by Martin Lejeune

All rights reserved.
No portion of this book may be reproduced in any form without permission from
the publisher, except as permitted by U.S. copyright law.

Also In Series

THE MCMURDO RIFT

THE MCMURDO TRIANGLE

THE MCMURDO WAR

PROLOGUE

The Berlin TV Tower building loomed over the centre of Berlin where it had stood for hundreds of years, dominating Alexanderplatz below it. A space-age building from a time when man had first been reaching for the stars, it no longer towered over many of the modern corporate blocks around it, but the thought of it no longer being there was almost unimaginable, right up to the point that it wasn't.

The beam from the alien ship ripped straight through the silver ball—the proverbial olive on the cocktail stick—instantly vaporising much of it and toppling the iconic structure in a great gout of flame. It was only the latest instance of devastation to be visited upon a city that had seen so much during its history. A terrible new chapter had been written in the last three hours as attacking United Terran Colonies forces were joined in Earth's orbit by a much larger vessel.

The slow, lumbering Koru "mothership"—as it was becoming known among the Earth's defenders—was vast, a city-sized ship that dwarfed everything else in the battle. The purple beam fired by the enormous craft was like nothing used by any other combatants. Its width was not slowed down by anything that it attempted to cut through. It fired less often than any other weapon involved in the battle yet was responsible for much more than its fair share of the destruction, because nothing could slow it down.

Lieutenant Mark Franklin found himself banking sharply, first dodging a flying section of the Berlin TV Tower, then avoiding the beam. Wrenching hard on the flight stick of his dual-operation fighter as the vast streak of purple death seemed to try and pull him in, like it somehow had its own powerful gravity. The fighter shook uncontrollably for a terrifying moment, as if about to be ripped apart.

Then Franklin was free and climbing, his attention again on the Friend-or-Foe display in his tactical visor. There were a lot of little red dots on it and surprisingly few blue. Even worse were the larger red polygons and the far too innocent, green-coloured blob of the alien craft, indicated as "undetermined" on the key at the top right of the display.

Franklin climbed too far above the city buildings and yellow laser streaks flashed by his cockpit from UTC fighters, one briefly glancing mercifully off the front of the fuselage. A quick, diving barrel roll, and he was back among the safety of the buildings. "Safety" being a relative term. Flying in the twisting pathways between the structures required a constant adjustment of the variable vector thrusters. Before he had taken a hit earlier in the battle, it would have been handled by the fighter's onboard navigator and its superhuman reactions.

"Fuck," Franklin muttered. He hadn't been back to Earth in a long time and it was not the sort of homecoming he had wished for, to see his home planet's greatest city reduced to rubble around him while its few remaining pilots hid like rats.

Dammit, a week ago he hadn't even been a military pilot anymore. Instead, he worked on a very different mission among the mining communities below Olympus Mons on Mars. He reached out to touch a tiny picture that was gamely staying stuck to the instrument panel. It had been taken with a novelty retro camera just a few months ago and showed a smiling woman with eyes that were iridescent sapphire, even in the saturated, poor quality Instaprint picture.

Duty was an absolute shit, Franklin decided.

A yellow laser shot streaked overhead and obliterated a holographic billboard that was somehow still advertising long-lasting scent implants in the middle of a world-ending conflict. A two-hundred-foot-tall armpit belonging to a pretty young brunette flickered briefly before being replaced by a small ball of flame.

Cursing his lack of concentration, Franklin quickly spun with an almost blackout-inducing one-eighty to strafe his attacker. Using his short-range, powerful blue-beam laser, he disappeared backwards into the ball of flame, hoping that he didn't hit anything hard before he came to a stop. Half of the burning wreckage of his opponent's ship went past on his port side while Franklin caught a glimpse of the UTC pilot's shocked face as he hurtled towards his death.

Damn, the guy looked young.

"Great shot, that man," a voice cracked over the comms channel. It was Squadron Leader Arnold Philby, his clipped English accent serving to keep Franklin centred in the midst of all the madness. Only Philby could sound that chipper on the edge of defeat, his upper lip still stiff when all else was falling apart.

"We just need a few thousand more," Franklin acknowledged. For the first time in recorded history, Earth, as a planet, was going to fall. Even if they killed every UTC fighter, frigate, destroyer and cruiser in the enemy fleet, there would still be that vast alien craft. How would they ever destroy that? Not for the first time that day, Franklin wondered why the hell the usually aloof Koru had joined humanity's war.

Since our first meeting with them, the mysterious and enigmatic Koru had mostly ignored humanity for fifty years. It was almost rude. For all that they were a bipedal, uncannily humanoid species by appearance—save for leathery skin with chameleon-like properties, opaque eyes and a distinct lack of hair—their culture and individual personalities were more akin to that of ants and their regimented, colony-like approach. Well, if ants were to give off the vague air that they thought they were better than you.

The Koru had traded with humanity, but in a way that made it seem like they were humouring us, and otherwise mostly just stayed out of humanity's way. Fortunately, it was quite easy, as they occupied a sector of space that was already losing its value and economic interest to humanity by the time the Koru were encountered—beyond an area known as the McMurdo Nebula.

When many of the planets within the United Terran Colonies had attempted to secede from Earth's control, the Koru had, as expected, stayed out of things. At least until Earth had been about to win.

"Delta unit, new orders," came Arnold's voice over the comms. "Everyone is to rendezvous in low orbit. Coordinates coming through on Encrypt Channel 3. We are going after the Koru craft."

Franklin saw the new coordinates and felt sick to his stomach. They were being told to leave Berlin—all of Earth—to its fate. There had been so little time for an evacuation due to the progress of the invading fleet with the Koru Mothership backing it up. Just about every building that went down was taking lives with it, the smoke and the dust choking the air—higher and higher with every passing minute—rising like funeral pyres to its inhabitants. Now the fighters were supposed to leave the Earth's inhabitants to their fate so they could do what... die against the hull of that great, indestructible behemoth? It made no sense, yet orders were given by men and women who knew more of the overall picture than Franklin did.

Arriving at the rendezvous coordinates, the other fighters quickly turned from tiny specks into the craft occupied by his comrades, hanging there in loose formation in the cold blackness of space. Franklin looked back and couldn't help but notice how Earth, even under attack, still appeared mostly serene from orbit. The vast Koru ship, an ungainly-looking wedge with a vaguely shimmering dark grey hull, was flanked by more eye-pleasing but comparatively tiny and inconsequential-seeming UTC cruisers. Franklin had a sudden and unnerving sense of seeing those ships like dogs sitting at the feet of their master, and he wondered yet again what had made the Koru join the war so late. It seemed that they could have been decisive at any time with the firepower they now brought. Dammit, if they had the industrial and military might to build a ship like that, they likely could have wiped out humanity at any time they wanted. As far as Franklin knew, their military had not been aware that the Koru possessed anything like it. What, he wondered—more so even than the fall of Earth—was playing out here?

"So," Arnold's voice crackled with static, like the system was clearing his throat for him—his usual efficient tone having slipped a little, "this is it. We're going to throw everything at the big ship, ignore everything else. Our remaining capital ships are moving into position. Your role is to get up close under cover of their fire, see if there's any weak point that you can discover."

There were one or two exclamations over the general channel.

"It's a terrible idea," Arnold agreed, "it's desperate." There was a genuine tremor of emotion cutting through the clipped efficiency when he spoke again. "And if there was a spare fighter here that I could climb into, I would be right there with you. I can only apologise that this is not the case.

"Good luck, gentlemen."

"And women," came a gravelly female voice with hints of something Central American. Franklin smiled, remembering Jimenez from the hurried pre-battle briefing. She had the gung-ho confidence of someone who was either supremely skilled or totally insane. Perhaps both. Which would be nice.

"And gentlewomen," Arnold corrected.

Franklin glanced behind to his left, where a group of sleek, dangerous-looking Earth ships slid out of the Earth's shadow, straight and purposeful, bristling with antennae and weaponry. They might have filled him with more confidence if there had been more of them, but there were so few compared to what there had been only a few hours before.

"Here comes that cover," Arnold finished. A moment later, the remaining Earth forces opened up with everything they had.

As he sped towards the vast hulk, Franklin's fighter shook as it flew into blast waves. Most of the blasts were coming off the enormous hull of the Koru ship, which seemed to shrug off the missiles that detonated against it and the beams that tried to sear their way through with barely a scuff or a scorch mark on its surface, which was annoying.

He banked right, realising that if he got much closer he would be torn apart by the blast waves from his own side's ordnance well before he got close enough to identify any targets on the vast craft that might be worth shooting at. Other fighters around him seemed to be having the same idea and, thankfully, the UTC fighters that had chased them around Berlin had not come to the defence of the big ship, at least not yet.

Even as he continued to accelerate through the vastness of space, the enormous Koru craft continued to stay on his left. Eventually, he pulled his little fighter back on a direct course. Franklin's stomach sank as glanced over to see some of the most powerful weaponry humanity had ever deployed continue to detonate almost harmlessly against the surface, not more effective than a cat scratching at a door to be let in. It begged the question... what were they doing here in these little fighters? They were like gnats attacking a skyscraper.

When the surface of the enemy ship eventually came at him in the view from the front of his cockpit, it was quick. One moment a distant, vague, light-dotted greyness like the horizon on a cloudy day, suddenly those lights were whole sections of the ship, some of them firing smaller versions of the giant purple laser at Franklin and his fellow pilots. There was something oddly reassuring that it deemed the little fighters worth bothering with. That or they just needed the target practice.

The remains of the squadron were quite spread out, yet Franklin saw several of the tell-tale brief flashes that meant the end of another craft, the death of another pilot.

"Close as you can," Jimenez called out over the comms, which had been almost eerily quiet as the fighters had flown to their appointment with death. "Let's get in among those turrets and fuck some shit up."

One of the nearby dual-operation fighters—another just like his—dove simultaneously at an almost suicidal angle towards the surface, seeming to curve around the laser beam trying to kill it. Franklin knew for sure that it was Jimenez in that craft. Performing the same sudden high-g turn to avoid impacting in an underwhelming, vacuum-impacted fireball, he followed her as she unloaded on the turret.

At first, it seemed as resistant as the rest of the ship, until one of Jimenez's shots scored a direct hit on the small nozzle where the laser came from. A few moments later, the turret imploded and detritus—including little bodies—were sucked out into space.

"Good shot," Franklin said.

"Weapons are overheated," Jimenez panted back. "Take the lead, yeah?"

Franklin gunned his thruster to get in front of her. As soon as he had done so, something thumped into his back, sending his craft spinning in an ungainly forward roll. On the second revolution, he caught sight of Jimenez's crippled craft, which must have been the thing that had hit him. Still pretty much in one piece, it was spinning off at an oblique angle. He couldn't get clear enough eyes on the cockpit and called out as he wrestled with his thrusters, which were suddenly reluctant to respond. "Jimenez! You there, Jimenez?"

No response came and, without warning, his thrusters kicked back in, and shot him forward far faster than he would have expected. It took a moment for Franklin to realise that he had entered the Koru ship.

Everything was dark and Franklin's tactical visor was empty. It was as if he had suddenly dropped out of the universe altogether. If he was dead, then his fighter had come with him to the afterlife. In the dull glow from the cockpit's instrumentation, Franklin could just about make out the Instaprint picture on the panel.

He breathed her name into the darkness and his headset crackled a little static back at him. No other voices, however.

Belatedly, Franklin remembered the close manoeuvring beams on the front and rear of the craft and he switched them on. They smeared a grey-panelled wall with dirty yellow light. Using his variable thrusters, Franklin rotated left and right, revealing that he was in a vast, well... corridor, for want of a better word. Unlike most corridors he had come across, however, it was like a fifty-floor skyscraper lying on its side. Koru were generally shorter than humans, so maybe they were trying to make up for something with all of this.

Turning far enough to look behind, Franklin could see that he had entered through a gap where the turret had been, and some of its remains clung to the edges of the ragged hole.

He could go back through and fight his way across the ship's surface. Or... he could explore. At the worst he could, as Jimenez would have said, "fuck some shit up".

Electing to go right, Franklin came across a large set of bulkhead doors more than twenty feet across at the end of the space. The tranquillity was unnerving—the silent static on comms, filled by his breathing. The vast space was empty, save for a few pieces of floating debris from the imploded turret.

Franklin considered experimenting with his laser to try and blast through the bulkhead door. Suddenly the bulkhead opened, perhaps automatically triggered as he inched the ship nervously forward. Ever since he had got back into a dual-operation fighter after several years away from flying, he had been rediscovering the deft touch that had once made him the pride of his unit. Amongst all the terror and death, there was something reassuring in doing something well again. A guilty pleasure, but a pleasure nonetheless.

A faint, blue sheen hung across the opening. It was see-through, with tantalising hints of a space beyond, the bulkhead doors staying open as if inviting him to move forward. However, Franklin had some serious concerns about whether the front of his ship would burst into flame the moment he did so. His finger hovered in front of the trigger for a moment. In the end, he elected to let himself drift forward and saw that the vaguely transparent purple sheen crept along his hull without doing any damage. An atmospheric shield, perhaps. If so, it was another technology they had that humans did not.

The next space was even bigger than the last. Franklin's eyes were immediately drawn towards a bright, blueish light coming from the left. Turning towards the light, he noticed the bulkhead doors close behind the ship. Several small objects emerged out of the glow. Franklin tensed, ready to either fight or fire the thrusters and rocket past whatever they were. Each one was a roughly cube-shaped drone of some sort, less than half the width of his ship, and they drifted past, seemingly ignoring him.

Craning his neck, he saw the bulkhead doors open again as the drones disappeared through. Franklin thought their work was cut out for them if they were on damage control.

It was both a relief and a little insulting that he was so far being ignored, but Franklin decided not to wish away his good luck and pressed forward, searching for something vital looking to blow up. The light grew brighter as the space opened up into an almost mind-bogglingly vast area.

It took several moments for his eyes to adjust, as his brain began to take in what he was seeing. Even then, Franklin could not quite comprehend the astonishing sight before him.

"Philby... Are you seeing what I'm seeing?" said the fleet commander, Vice Admiral Maxwell, on the secure command channel.

He stood on the bridge of a small, stealth-painted ops ship some distance from the main part of the remaining Earth fleet. Arnold was, indeed, seeing it. He was having trouble believing it, though.

Great gouts of flame were coming out of the enormous Koru ship. The only craft the mysterious alien species had sent to join in the human war, the vessel that on its own had turned the tide and led the UTC fleet all the way to Earth—the centre of an empire. The ship began to spin, a slow, lumbering revolution caused by a spectacular eruption on the left side. He had sent his pilots to their death with no hope of victory. He had known what he was doing as much as it sickened him, and he had not even for a moment expected them to succeed.

And yet...

"I am, Sir," Arnold answered. As Squadron Leader Arnold Philby continued to watch the Koru leviathan turning in its death roll, the remaining UTC fleet began to emerge from behind it, attempting to gain a safe distance, and he knew in his heart that this day was still lost. "There are so many of them," he added, before realising that he had not closed the encrypted channel he had been using to speak with the Vice Admiral.

Internal explosions lit the Koru craft from within, flaring light through cracks in the exterior. It was beginning to come apart.

"Bring the remaining fighters around for one last defence," Vice Admiral Maxwell ordered, although Arnold could hear the knowledge of defeat in it. At the moment of hope, final defeat had become apparent. Their losses had been too heavy, and they were now vastly outnumbered by so many craft that—and this was the problem with rebellions—were so similar to their own.

"I... I'm not sure there's anyone left," he replied, then noticed a pulse on his readout above the squadron's comms channel. "One moment, Sir." He flicked across.

"Are you there, Squadron Leader?" came a familiar voice over the radio, "I'm on my way back to the RV."

Arnold gasped, momentarily grasping for something to say. "Mr Franklin," he finally managed, pointing to the stricken Koru ship that was still going through ever-more violent death throes, even though the pilot could not possibly have seen his gesture, "did you do that?"

ONE

Franklin walked along the bar, idly dragging a cleaning rag across the surface. The bar occupied one side of a good-sized lounge called the "SS Olympic Cocktail Lounge", appearing in fluorescent yellow letters above the door that recalled the signage of old Earth from a bygone age. The lounge's furniture walked a line between comfort and practicality, a combination of booths around the outside and round tables surrounded by simple, padded chairs in the middle.

After years of owning the place—not just a franchise or a rental, he literally held a leasehold on this little bit of the ship—Franklin still hadn't got around to changing the name, mostly because he didn't have a good one to put in its place. He was too modest to call it "Franklin's." Every other name he came up with had his ex-wife's name somewhere. That would not do at all. There had been a brief flirtation with "The Cockpit Bar," but the less said, the better. His friend, Gustav—or Gus for short—who was the fitness trainer, still smugly brought that one up every now and then.

The bar was—as the name suggested—on board the SS *Olympic*, a once-upon-a-time luxury liner that had seen better days. Now it ran a barely about profitable route that took in the McMurdo Rift—a stunning sight and a reasonable draw for tourists in an otherwise outlying area of space which, like the liner, had seen more glorious and profitable days. There had been a time, perhaps fifty years ago, when the *Olympic* had been packed with humanity's elite. They came as much to be seen on the journey as for the trip itself, when the sector had been full of mining colonies and all the infrastructure and traffic that brought with it.

The decline had been slow but steady over the course of decades as resources dried up or were no longer in demand. The McMurdo Rift was already a relative backwater by the time humanity was beginning to try and tear itself apart with civil war. The faded navy-blue fabric on the walls—like the sign above the door—needed replacing, yet there was little sense in making his bar the only well-presented part of the ship. That seemed, well... a little bit rude.

The bar was busier than usual this evening, which was odd. There was a group on board—Franklin could not and did not care to remember the name of this particular cult—who were on some pilgrimage, believing that the nebula of which the rift was a part had magical healing properties. They were, he had heard it mentioned, hoping that the *Olympic* would be the latest victim of the McMurdo Triangle, an area of the sector where an unusually high number of ships were known to have gone missing. They considered these disappearances, in essence, some sort of rapture event.

No, they were not his usual bar crowd and hadn't appeared evident among the punters tonight—unless they had shed the robes and put on wigs to cover the weird patterns they liked to shave across their heads. Who knew where all these people were coming from tonight, but Franklin was not complaining, even if he had struggled to keep up with the orders. Things finally seemed to be dying down a bit. He had found a few moments to wipe the bar and collect some glasses for the first time in hours.

The lull was only momentary, however, and when he looked up again, there were several customers waiting to be served. One of them was Koru which was unusual.

"Who's next?" he asked, looking at the Koru, who was closest. Her leathery, almost snake-like skin had a rust-red hue and Franklin remembered that Koru were known for having slow-acting, chameleon-like properties, slowly adapting over time to the predominant colours of their surroundings. That rust-red was nothing like the faded navy blue prominent on the walls around the *Olympic*—she probably hadn't been on the ship very long.

Having won the war for the UTC, the Koru had been uneasy allies in the decade since. Not so much isolationist as just plain aloof, they had even abandoned their embassy on Proxima some years back. Yet things remained peaceful and, judging by the craft they were capable of building, that could only be a good thing.

A swaggering drunkard to the left of the Koru jostled forward, even though there was enough room that he didn't have to. "I was firshtt," he growled, "you shouldn't be serving thish piece of shit in an Earth ship's bar anyway."

Franklin stared at the drunkard for a moment; the man was unshaven, his hair close-cropped with the hint of a fading tattoo along the hairline. This was not an "Earth ship"; everyone was happy fellow members of the United Terran Colonies nowadays, "Terran" an ironic nod, Franklin felt, to humanity's birthplace, which had been relegated to the status of a second-rate, half-destroyed regional capital.

After a beat, Franklin intentionally blanked the man and turned to serve the Koru. "What'll it be?"

"Mineral water, please," the Koru replied awkwardly. Like most Koru, she was short – they were, on average, around fifteen centimetres shorter than humans. Franklin noticed she did not have that slightly echoey voice that most of them spoke with, which gave a person the impression they were talking to a "collective," rather than just one individual.

Mineral water, *of course*. He had never met a single Koru who drank alcohol. Indeed, in the SS Olympic Cocktail Lounge, you hardly met a Koru at all, even though they had a colony on the other side of the nebula.

"That's bullshit," said the man on the other side of the Koru. Tall, with a chiselled chin and floppy hair, Franklin didn't know whether he was with the tattooed drunkard or not. He sounded less drunk, at least. "It's your bar, kick this lizard piece of shit the fuck out of it."

Franklin sighed and clenched his fist out of sight behind the bar. "You are right, Sir, it is my bar." His face darkened a little. "Do not tell me what to do in it."

The Koru seemed unfazed between the two men and patiently waited for her drink. Aside from the vast mothership, the Koru had shown themselves to have almost no military capability or aggressive tendencies. This one was keeping up the tradition.

"How can you do it, man?" the tattooed drunk said, stepping back and waving a dismissive hand at Franklin. "They killed so many of us."

Franklin turned and got a mineral water from the cooler. He had seen people he considered friends die at their hands and killed more than just a few of them himself.

The tall, handsome man glared at Franklin, a mixture of annoyance and disbelief creasing his attractive features. "Fuck you and your bar, man," he said sulkily, before turning his threatening gaze on the Koru and heading towards the door. The gaze was wasted on the opaque-eyed creature, who appeared not even to notice—reaching into the breast pocket of her beige jumpsuit—a variation on the bland clothing that almost all Koru seemed to prefer—to pull out her credit chit.

Franklin held out a hand to stop her. "On the house, for your trouble." Although, the Koru did not seem troubled in the slightest. "Just so that you know that every ex-Earther isn't still holding onto the war."

The Koru looked at him and blinked once. Without a visible pupil looking back at him, Franklin could not tell whether the alien being was confused or indifferent or something else entirely. "Thank you," she said flatly, then walked off to find a seat.

"Deftly handled, my boy." Franklin started a little, unaware that the captain of the SS *Olympic* had been watching him. Although, in the military, "captain" was a higher rank than "squadron leader"—as Arnold had been when Franklin had served under him—the title somehow seemed lesser here on a luxury cruise liner circling the outer reaches of an old empire and a newer... whatever the modern-day UTC was. Here, they were more like friends, although this didn't stop Arnold, as always, sounding like he was out of an old movie with his clipped British accent and twee way of saying things.

He had gracefully grown into his grey hair, even if he still insisted on dyeing the thin moustache. He was tall, pencil-thin, yet somehow dominating, with a narrow face and piercing blue eyes.

"War's long over," Franklin answered with a sigh.

Arnold sounded too jolly for Franklin's liking when he went on. "You would know, you ended it."

Franklin just gave Arnold a displeased look and continued wiping the bar and loading glasses into the vacuum wash. He had a feeling that Arnold liked embarrassing him, although it was more than the embarrassment he felt when the subject came up.

"You could make ten times the money this bar makes if you cashed in on the fact," Arnold went on. "Or, for instance, tell anyone what actually happened in there."

"I think you're the only one who still remembers or cares, Arnold," Franklin deflected, "it was a long time ago. Anyway, I said what happened. It's all in the report."

Arnold raised some neatly trimmed eyebrows. "Right, if you say so."

Geoff, Franklin's grey tabby cat, saved his owner by running out at that moment, looking for food and perhaps rum. He liked a good lick or two of rum. He jumped up onto the bar and Arnold began to fuss him. "I'm sure he's a health hazard, you know," Arnold said as he stroked the cat contentedly. "Against code or something."

"If it's the cat or the punters..." Franklin joked. Such was the world of the two war heroes, swapping jests as they drifted gently through the back-end of space. All of that, of course, was about to change.

About ten minutes later, Sarah walked into the bar. Franklin saw her the moment she came in, even though the place was still thronging with drinkers. Perhaps it was the ball gown she wore that first drew his eye. There was a classic style to the dress she had on, one that might have been more suited to the *Olympic* of fifty years ago than the one that now toured around the McMurdo Rift.

It was deep red, more burgundy than scarlet, complimenting long hair that was, itself, just as red as he remembered. Franklin watched as she crossed the room, either not seeing him or not caring to look as she weaved her way elegantly through the press of bodies. A matching clutch purse in her hand occasionally shimmered as it caught the light. As she drew nearer, he could see that time had taken away a little of her youth. Although it caused a small, sharp ache somewhere inside his chest, what had been left in youth's place was no less alluring.

Finally, reaching the small bit of open space in front of the bar, Sarah looked at Franklin. "Hello, Mark," she said, her voice not giving away even a hint of emotion—no warmth, but not the frostiness he feared either. Only Sarah had ever called him "Mark". She was making it sound more official than the surname everyone else used instead of his first name.

Franklin's mouth worked wordlessly for a moment, his brain still unable to believe it was her… here… in his bar. Then, out of the corner of his eye, he saw Arnold—who had been nursing a brandy at the far end of the bar for the last ten minutes—glance over and his eyes go wide, presumably with some sort of recognition.

"Don't you even have a 'hello' for me?" Sarah asked with mock offence.

Franklin hadn't realised that he still hadn't said anything. "Hey," he finally managed, forcing the word out through a mouth that didn't seem to want to work. Flying into certain death had been easier. And then—a stroke of genius. "What can I get you?"

Something flashed briefly in her eyes. Annoyance, perhaps, that he was speaking to her like any other customer?

"Wait," he said, memory flooding back with sudden, dizzying clarity. "Scotch, on the rocks."

She smiled at that and tilted her head. Her taste in drinks hadn't changed, at least. Franklin reached back, not even needing to fully turn around to pick up a tumbler and the best bottle of scotch on the shelf. "You look nice."

"Thank you."

"I would ask if you're going anywhere nice," Franklin said, "but you're in the nicest place on the ship and far too well dressed for it."

A little down the bar Arnold, who was eavesdropping, cleared his throat in a way that managed to sound quite offended. Sarah glanced over. "You're the captain, aren't you?" she asked him. "I saw your picture as I boarded. Captain Philby, isn't it?"

Arnold took his queue, slipping off the bar stool he was sitting on and sidling over, with a stiff gracefulness. "Yes, ma'am."

"And Mark's former commander?"

Arnold feigned surprise badly, thin eyebrows attempting to lift off from a long forehead atop an equally long face. "And you are Sarah, Frank... Mark's..." Arnold paused, perhaps realising he might be stumbling straight into a faux pas.

"Wife," Franklin automatically put in before his brain could engage itself. They had never officially divorced and, somehow, still being married to Sarah was like a ridiculous badge of honour he carried.

"No," Sarah corrected with another of those smiles that Franklin could not read, "we were never married. Thanks," she added as he pushed her scotch over. Franklin could feel the frown creasing his features.

Sarah pulled a credit chit from the clutch purse she carried, but Franklin held up a hand. "Your money's no good here."

Arnold sniffed. "Apparently, mine is."

"You were saying something about us not being married?" Franklin pressed on.

"Mars doesn't recognise marriages made under Earth jurisdiction," Sarah answered far too pleasantly for Franklin's liking, "before the peace."

"So, does that make us unmarried or never married at all?" It shouldn't matter, he thought to himself, even as he felt a desperate sort of anger beginning to bubble away under his skin. You let her go more than a decade ago.

"It makes me re-married," Sarah answered, and this time Franklin did catch more of an edge to her voice.

Next to Sarah, Arnold downed the rest of his brandy with a wince and started to back away. "Early night for the captain, I think." He nodded quickly to Franklin, then with a little more courtesy to Sarah. "Pleased to make your acquaintance."

Arnold stalked off, which was his version of "scurrying".

When Franklin turned back to Sarah, any hardness that had been there a moment before seemed to have melted away. She looked, if anything, concerned for him. He wasn't sure he wanted that either. "We need to speak," she said.

"Ahem," came a voice a little further down the bar. A large, middle-aged man was looking expectantly at him.

"Time at the bar," Franklin called and rang the brass bell he kept behind the bar, which filled the room with its bright, clear tone.

"What?" the man protested, once the ringing had stopped. Franklin was having none of it.

"We're closed," he added. "Drinking up time!" Then he turned back to Sarah. "You want to take a seat, give me twenty minutes?"

The bar was an ample space when all the people were emptied out of it. Sarah waited as patiently as she could manage at the furthest tables from the bar. At the same time, Mark—Franklin, she would try and think of him as that, even if using anything other than his first name still seemed strange—ushered the disgruntled patrons out of the door and into the tired, twisting corridors of the *Olympic*. She knew of the ship's illustrious history, as well, and how much it had fallen from its former glory. There was something deeply sad that he had ended up here, of all places.

Franklin came over, a pint of ale predictably in one hand—she remembered how, when he hadn't shaved in a few days, the head would always make a white moustache on his upper lip—and a second scotch for her. She took it gratefully and drank a big, steadying swig.

"This is all yours?" she asked as he sat down across from her.

"Yep," he answered, with a cheerful lightness that seemed forced. Once, this man had ended a war and saved Earth from total annihilation—instead of the semi-annihilation it had suffered anyway. Now he was some regular guy running a backwater bar in a backwater place.

"Of all the things I saw you doing..." she began, but faltered when she saw the immediate effect her words were having on his face that was trying so desperately hard to be cheerful. "I didn't mean... Well, it's a really lovely place."

"No, it's not," Franklin said with a grin. "But it is mine."

"And it's a few billion kilometres from anywhere else."

Franklin smiled self-consciously and took a sip of his ale. He was clean-shaven, so only a little foam stuck to his lip. "I'm sorry," he said, wiping it away.

"What for?" Sarah did not doubt that Franklin had things to be sorry for—or that he thought he might—but whatever his apology was about, she felt uncomfortable seeing him do it.

"For going to Earth that day."

"It's fine," she answered. It hadn't been, but it was now.

"We were perfect. You were perfect. I wouldn't have sacrificed us for the world."

Sarah gave a sad laugh. "Except that you did. It was your home, why wouldn't you go? And you saved a planet and so on. What kind of a human being would I be-"

"I went there to die with my planet," Franklin interrupted her, with shame in his voice. "And to leave you behind. But, instead, I lived."

There was a long silence at the table, broken only by the noise of the air recyclers kicking in and the clink of melting ice as Sarah picked up her scotch. She was looking at the wall on the other side of the bar and yet, at the same time, looking much further away than that.

"I tried to find you after the war," Franklin quietly told her at last.

"I didn't want to be found."

Franklin took a long, deep breath. "And you're married now?"

"His name is Vik," Sarah answered, "he's an activist."

Like you could never be. She hadn't added those words, yet it felt like she had, and Franklin's tight expression sure made it look like she had too.

"Suddenly 'bar owner' seems like a sound career choice."

As much as Sarah felt slapped by Franklin's snippy comment, she waited and watched his face, seeing—as she knew she would—the moment he inwardly punished himself for it.

"An activist," Franklin went on sulkily after a moment, "that's... vague."

"We campaign—well, we did campaign—to get the UTC to take the Koru threat more seriously."

"They don't already?"

"They won a war for us," Sarah said, almost singing the irony, "there would be no glorious UTC without them... Doubting their motives seems somehow... sacrilegious. Don't you think?"

"No, it seems sensible, but then I'm not a politician. Or a military commander. Or an *activist.*"

His sarcastic reply rankled Sarah. Even as lovers—as husband and wife, if you were counting their illegal union—they had never quite been on the same side, at least not of the polar disagreement that had eventually turned into war between Earth and much of the rest of the UTC. She enjoyed the arguments at first—Franklin's practical doubts about whether the UTC could ever work in reality—perhaps because it always seemed, however much they disagreed, that *they* were stronger, that their relationship was more important than any of it. Until it wasn't, and he left to go and die for Earth.

Earth, who had held itself like a colonial power, like the parent who never let the child just grow up and leave home—the stalker who did crazy, dangerous, cruel things because they could not overcome their own pride and admit it was over. Secession had been as inevitable as it had been for the empires of old, yet Earth's hubris had cost many lives in a war that lasted years and irreparably damaged the infrastructure of the network of worlds controlled by humanity.

In the end, the Koru had joined in and effortlessly turned Earth's imminent victory into a defeat, one that saw the origin of humanity—for no one had ever forgotten what Earth represented, even if it was no longer their home—reduced halfway to ashes. Franklin had left to try and prevent that, yet it never felt like anything less than a betrayal to her.

Sarah realised that she hadn't responded, and Franklin now just shrugged. "Have you ever found any evidence? I mean, ten years has passed, and the Koru have mostly just ignored us, as they did before. I was suspicious ten years ago. Who wasn't, especially if you were on the side getting pummelled by them. They never even wanted a part of the ruins they helped to create."

Sarah took a breath. She could hear the old bitterness in his voice. They could go in circles about the right and wrong of things all night. It wasn't why she had come, so it was time to lay out her hand, to take her gamble on this man she had once cared about, for the one she now loved. "Just over two weeks ago, Vik—my husband—went to Exonia V.

"The Koru colony here, past the rift?"

"Yes, the Koru refer to it as, 'Watch Nest', or that's the closest translation."

"Why would he go there? Worst holiday destination ever."

"He's missing, Mark," Sarah snapped at the flippant tone. "I got one communication the day he arrived, and I've heard nothing since."

Franklin sat forward, clearly engaged now. "And you've contacted the authorities there?"

"Apparently, they've no record of him ever turning up, which I know is bullshit."

Sarah saw the look in Franklin's eye and knew what he was thinking before he said it. "Is there any reason he would have lied about where he was?"

The look she gave him in return did the trick.

"Well, what did he go there for? What was he hoping to find?"

"I don't know what, exactly. Evidence that they were up to something that the UTC wouldn't like. Whatever it was, he didn't want to put it into the communication."

"Hmm, the McMurdo Rift being so strategically significant and all."

Sarah glared at Franklin again, although she knew he had a point. "Well, maybe they thought no one would look here," she tried. She could tell he wasn't convinced and, a little begrudgingly, decided to admit something. "Look, we hadn't been seeing eye-to-eye on the Koru thing recently. I remember how sceptical you were of their motivations when you joined the war. Well, he's been becoming more like that all the time I've known him. But I've been focused on just trying to make a living."

Franklin shrugged. "I was wrong. That, or the Koru have got a really shitty, really long-term master plan."

"I had come to think so, too," she admitted eventually.

"I stopped working with him," Sarah went on, feeling shame as she spoke, "started my own business and everything. It made things difficult between us because we had never turned up anything more concrete than hearsay and rumours, mostly from crackpot conspiracy theorists. But when he called me to say where he was going, he..." She took a breath. "I hadn't heard him that excited in years. Like I said, he wouldn't go into details, but I got the sense it was the breakthrough he was waiting for. The proof. He sent a check-in message when he got there, but nothing since."

Mark took a long swig of drink and rubbed his chin thoughtfully. As with so many men, age suited him well. Hints of grey were already beginning to show in that once jet-black hair and the stubble, which, she knew, was probably only a day's worth of growth. He had grown well into his body and seemed happier and healthier, except that there was tiredness around the eyes, which seemed to have dulled them slightly.

"So," he said, "you've come out looking for your husband?"

"No, I've come here to ask you to help me find him."

TWO

"So, what did you say?" Gus asked as he lunged at Franklin in one of the *Olympic's* versatile sports units. They were surrounded by beige-painted composite walls on three sides and a toughened glass side on the fourth, making them human goldfish bowls for anyone who wanted to spectate from the three tiers of stadium-style seating that lay just beyond the glass.

Gus' thick, heavy rapier made in the sixteenth-century style came in quickly at the bar owner's chest. Franklin got his own, nearly identical rapier up just in time to deflect Gus' blade slightly to his left. It wasn't going to be enough, so he instinctively twisted his torso. Still, the point of the blade scuffed the side of his rib cage.

He was wearing a padded gambeson, and Gus' steel composite replica sword was not kept sharp, yet Franklin still expected to have a bruise later. His sparring partner did not pull his blows much at all. Then again, neither did he; that was what made it fun. "Half-a-point," Franklin grumbled, and Gus nodded begrudgingly.

Gus, the *Olympic's* personal trainer, was the closest thing Franklin had to a best friend on the ship. Not too far from two metres tall, Gus had smooth, dark skin that he no doubt moisturised obsessively. Unlike Gus, whose whole life revolved around physical exertion and keeping fit, this was Franklin's main form of exercise. Around this point, after fifteen minutes or so of sparring, was usually when he started to tire—just as Gus was getting going. Gus removed his fencing mask to signal that he wanted to take a break. Of course, he didn't want or need to, but Franklin appreciated the gesture.

Underneath the helmet was perhaps the most ruggedly attractive person that Franklin had ever known. Although vain, stylish and perhaps the snappiest dresser Franklin had ever met, Gus hadn't gone for the reasonably cheap option of follicle therapy, so what little hair he had was kept shaved, his head smooth. Apparently, the ladies tended to prefer it. Lately, he was sporting a new goatee, which Franklin had to admit did suit him well. He wondered if that was for the daughter of the station commander on Regus, a mining facility that was a stop-off on the Olympic's regular route.

"I didn't say anything," Franklin said, finally answering Gus' earlier question.

"You just left your ex-wife hanging?" Gus asked. "Man, that's cold."

Franklin noted how Gus' tone was more impressed than horrified. "No, I just didn't really give her an answer."

They crossed over to the personal dehumidifier, which sometimes worked and sometimes managed to do the opposite, managing to make the user sweatier than when they had entered. "Welcome to the *Olympic*" was the refrain the two of them tended to use when anything like that happened. Thankfully, Franklin felt the sweat evaporate quickly from his forehead, cooling him further.

"Man," Gus went on, declining the offer of using the PDH next—he was barely perspiring, anyway—"she's asking a lot of you, if you think about it. 'Hey, I just engaged in a bit of polygamy. Would you mind risking your own life to go and rescue my other husband?'"

Franklin liked Gus' succinct way of seeing things. "She says it's not polygamy. Apparently, after the war, our marriage doesn't count."

"Fuck me, doesn't that conflict just keep on giving?"

Gus had never revealed what had led him to the life of a fitness instructor on the *Olympic* but, like most people working on the old ship, he got the sense his (sort of) buddy was running away from something. They were about the same age, and Franklin was prepared to bet that whatever had driven Gus out to the fringes of human-occupied space had its beginnings in the war.

"What did Arnold say?" Gus asked, putting his mask back on so that his voice took on a hollow resonance halfway through the sentence.

"The man's not my keeper," Franklin answered, sounding a little more defensive than he meant to.

Gus blinked,. "I'm just saying that he might have some... insight. He's known you a long time."

"No," Franklin admitted, "I haven't told him. He'll tell me to stay out of it, I know he will." He shook his head as he pushed his mask back on. "Dammit, I should stay out of it."

"But...?"

"But I never thought I would see her again. If I say no, then she's off the ship again before you know it, and... that's that."

Gus' blade came up again. "Man, that's..." his voice sounded full of sympathy, of concern for his friend's predicament, "possibly the lamest thing I've ever heard in my life."

"Fuck you!" Franklin roared. Angry, amused and humiliated all at once, he lunged recklessly, only to find that—surprise, surprise—Gus wasn't there when his blade arrived. He stumbled forward, feeling the flat of his friend's blade slap him on the ass.

"That," said Gus, "has got to be worth a double score."

The rest of that day was uncannily like the first few days after the end of the war—he saw Sarah everywhere in his minds eye. Except, this time, she actually was nearby.

While walking the old, labyrinthine hallways of the ship—which were like the corridors of a complex hotel—on his way to open up the bar, every person turning a corner ahead of him was her. Then, he and Geoff spent a quiet day with barely more than three customers in the bar at any given time, all of them Sarah for that moment as they walked into the bar, until they weren't. Knowing that she was somewhere within the labyrinth of the SS *Olympic* made each disappointment all the worse—except when it was the middle-aged security guy, Hultz, then it was just disturbing.

Yet Franklin dreaded actually seeing her, because he would have to tell her that he couldn't help. There were embassies for this sort of thing. It's just... he wasn't that guy anymore. If he ever really had been.

"Still here?" came the clipped, yet cheery voice of Arnold Philby. Franklin jumped—as did Hultz and the young, muscular, slick-looking Ensign Zhao, who was head of security. They were an unlikely pair of best friends, but they seemed to find common ground at the bottom of a glass every time they were both off shift. The captain had a habit of sneaking up on people, which was impressive, seeing that the man stood over one-point-nine metres tall.

"Always here," Franklin sighed. "Think it's going to be a long day, though. Maybe the evening will pick up."

"No." Arnold reached out to stroke Geoff, who had just appeared on the bar, "I mean, you're not off somewhere helping your ex-wife save her husband?"

Hultz and Zhao both raised their eyebrows, doing a good job of studying their drinks when Franklin glanced over.

"Oh, come on," Franklin complained. He wanted to swear, yet he rarely did around the genteel captain of the SS *Olympic*, even when things called for it. "It was Gus, wasn't it?"

"Among others," Arnold answered enigmatically.

"This ship is like a village full of gossips," Franklin moaned, knowing that Hultz and Zhao would soon be spreading the news like a virulent plague. That said, he liked the vague sense of community and camaraderie that ran between the crew members, staff and franchise owners of the *Olympic* as it drifted lazily between its stopping points in the sector. Franklin had come to the *Olympic* for a quieter life but—evidenced by his choice to run a bar—not to avoid all human contact.

"I like to think that I have my ways," Arnold grinned smugly, "above and beyond the *Olympic* rumour mill. A captain should know his ship."

Franklin made a show of glancing about the bar as if looking for bugs. "Do I need to send off for a nano detector?"

Arnold's answering smile was worryingly wistful. "I don't have the budget to bug every franchise on the *Olympic*."

"Every?"

"Well... any. But, if I did..."

"Old habits die hard, eh?" Franklin said with a chuckle. "Well, my wife's... or not-wife's visit would have been the first interesting thing you would have picked up in here if you had." Franklin began to pour himself half a pint of ale and nodded back towards the line of spirits with a meaningful look at Arnold.

"No thanks," Arnold answered, "this run hasn't driven me to drink on shift yet. Although I'm sure the time will come."

Franklin finished pouring and noticed that Arnold was giving him a thoughtful look. He was about to say something Franklin wouldn't like; the look was unmistakable. "What?" he demanded pre-emptively.

"Would it be so bad?"

"I'd say there's an ethical question with bugging the crew," Franklin replied, intentionally playing dumb.

"Your wife!" Arnold growled impatiently.

Franklin sighed and gave the man, who was sort of his boss, what he hoped was an annoyed look. It was hard, Arnold Philby could have emanated authority as "Chuckles the Party Clown".

"You're a young man still, Franklin," Arnold pressed, "and you've settled down to this dull life as a barman. Don't get me wrong, it's a solid business you have here, but... What's the harm in joining her for a few days, a week at most?"

Franklin narrowed his eyes. "Why do I feel like you're trying to get rid of me?"

"Because I am," Arnold answered straight-faced. "We've been tossing around the idea of building a spa on board for some time, but we didn't have anywhere to put it." He looked around the bar. "In fact, make it two weeks. I haven't decided where the sauna should go yet."

"Har-de-har."

"Seriously, at least go and talk to her about it one more time. She's on her ship in Bay Four. We can always find you cover for the bar," he added, "if you'll let anyone else behind it, that is."

Franklin had thought that Arnold would counsel the opposite, telling him to leave the past in the past. But, if even his wise old commander thought he should consider it, well... one more chat wouldn't hurt. He did want to see her again.

When Franklin walked into Bay Four, the *Olympic* was pulling into orbit above the planet of Enceladine, which lay as a marble of blue water, almost greyish land and white cloud below. It was one of eight large bays the ship had for storing smaller craft, although these days they rotated use of them, so that no more than four bays were in use at one time. This was partly because of their limited and predictable route. Many passengers simply transferred via shuttle, either from planets or other ships, which made the journey out from busier systems. Perhaps the biggest reason was that the bays—needing to be regularly open to space—were among the parts of the ship that were most vulnerable to catastrophic accidents. When things went wrong in a bay, people often died, so Arnold insisted on a regular maintenance cycle for the bays and all the aging parts within them.

Franklin had both laughed and felt a hollow thumping in his chest when Arnold told him the ship's name. Quickly scanning across the various-sized craft in the colossal bay—which was as long as a football field and almost as wide—he found her: *Mutt's Nuts*.

Now, looking up at the back of the bulky, rust-coloured little freighter as he crossed the bay floor, Franklin wondered why Sarah hadn't told him that she had bought his old ship, the one he had run a business with before leaving to defend Earth and changing everything.

"I knew you'd come," came a muffled, familiar voice from somewhere beyond an extended ramp near the back of the ship. A moment later, Sarah trotted down it, no longer in a flattering red dress but in a much more practical navy-blue flight suit that was gathered in slightly around her narrow waist and well-worn with various small rips, patches, and stains across it. Her vixen-red, hair was tied back in a high, out-of-the-way ponytail.

"You never told me..." he said with a laugh, his mouth falling open as he gaped at his old ship. She had seen better days, yet he had never expected to see her again, so it seemed that every inch of her was a miracle.

"I wanted to surprise you," Sarah said with a coy smile that set his insides aflame. "I stumbled across her when I was looking for a ship to start my courier business with. What were the chances, eh? Like it was meant to be."

A thought occurred to Franklin and, although it was maybe unwise, he couldn't help but air it. "Your husband knows that your ship used to belong to your ex-husband?"

"Just my ex," Sarah corrected. Although Franklin felt his jaw tighten, he guessed that he might have deserved that. "Come inside," she said, "I have someone for you to meet."

THREE

Sarah led Franklin up the secondary ramp on the rear of the port side and into the back of the ship. The cargo bay was small, yet big enough to get a fairly large vehicle in, like a planetary exploration rover or a small excavator of some kind. The main cargo ramp—which was shut—was designed to expose the whole rear end of the ship. The bay was designed to be environmentally sealed and opened on planets with little or no atmosphere—or even in space. He wondered if it was all still in working order as it had once been.

At the moment, the bay was empty, although various racks designed to secure smaller items of cargo lined two of the walls. Franklin could see two environment suits hanging next to them. He let out a breath he hadn't realised he was holding. The pain doubled, seeing her and his old ship at once—too many things he hadn't realised he wanted back. There was pleasure and sadness in reaching out and touching the almost reddish interior of the hold, which somehow seemed older and a little faded, even though it was undoubtedly being looked after by Sarah.

"How bad a state was she in when you found her?" Franklin asked.

Sarah turned and headed up a flight of steps to a gantry that hung over the forward quarter of the bay as she answered. "She's a work in progress. I could never have gotten her with my budget if she had been in perfect condition."

They passed through a sealed door and into the refectory. It was these areas—the main communal space for eating and socialising—that Franklin had always found to be the easiest clue to a ship's typical crew compliment, short of going around and counting the berths themselves. He knew that the *Mutt's Nuts* would run well on six crew, although there was likely room for eight or even ten. Yet he had only seen Sarah so far. Of course, it was part of the ship's beauty; that she could even be flown by one, although it was far from ideal when you spent a lot of time on the move. The crew compliment depended on what you were hauling. There was a dining table on the left side as he stood, with a long couch against the wall that reminded Franklin of the classic-era, American-themed diners. That was different to before.

Sarah looked around the space and gave an impatient huff. Then, turning back to Franklin, she tapped a wrist communicator and spoke into it. "Engee, you said you'd be back to the ship by now. You good?"

What Franklin had initially mistaken for frustration in Sarah's voice might, he thought, be something else, as there was a tenseness to the way she spoke. She worried about this "Engee", whoever the hell that was. Weird name, for sure.

"I am almost with you, Sarah," an odd, vaguely feminine-sounding voice replied after a moment. The channel was crackling, as Franklin knew that any system not going through the *Olympic's* own comms might if you were more than a couple of decks away. He narrowed his eyes and wondered. He was beginning to understand that Sarah was really scared and being extremely careful, even here on the *Olympic*. She had a missing husband, so it was understandable, but if the Koru had snatched him, they would not be coming after her on the *Olympic*, surely. "I am in the elevator," the voice on the comms added.

Itching to move through into the action part of the ship, Franklin nonetheless began to wander around the refectory—which, the more he looked, he realised felt more homely than it once had. He attributed that to Sarah's touch, although she had never been exactly the homemaking type. There were many personal effects. Beyond the kitchen, some pictures were secured to the wall on the opposite side of the dining table. One was the face of a distinguished-looking Indian gentleman who Franklin recognised straight away. Looking at the strong jawline, the hints of silver in the otherwise fabulous-looking, swept-back black hair, he couldn't believe that the penny hadn't dropped sooner. His eyes fell to another photo in which the man had his arm around Sarah, who in the picture was wearing the same red dress she had worn the previous evening.

"He's *that* Vikram," Franklin said, still facing the wall.

"I thought I said," Sarah answered. She hadn't, not really. She called him 'Vik,' which could have been with a 'c' and short for Victor. She had said that he was an activist, which again was sort of true. Although, Franklin now remembered, she hadn't even given him a surname. He turned back from the photos.

"Should I call you Mrs Shah?" he asked. In his head it had sounded a neutral, amusing thing to say, yet somehow it came out sounding bitter.

"That's me," she answered flatly. Then, more casually, "Although I've always been a bit free and easy about actually using his surname or not. Vik's never cared."

"He's been quite someone in the UTC since the war," Franklin smirked.

Sarah brushed Franklin's teasing aside. "I'm not sure he's really "someone" anymore. Always been an activist at heart, that tends to put you out of favour, no matter how many times you've been right."

Franklin remembered some of the news feeds that featured Vikram Shah. He was a civil servant who had been significant during the war of secession yet had some unpopular opinions about the Koru. He had called for the government to demand more transparency from their interstellar neighbours, although that was some time ago now.

In the distance, the sound of light footsteps ringing off the metal steps and gantry could be heard through the bulkhead. Sarah's head snapped around. Franklin could still see the worry creased across her features. A moment later, he found out why.

―――

"This is Engee," Sarah said after several silent moments. Franklin realised that his mouth was slightly open and he forced it shut.

"My original designation was NG-972," said the slight figure who had just come into the rear of the refectory, "but I am trying out 'Engee' since I have become separated from my whole. E-N-G-E-E," she spelled out helpfully.

Of course, he recognized the little Koru from nearly starting a fight in his bar the previous night. Well, that wasn't true, *she* had only wanted a glass of mineral water, but Franklin had felt a lot like punching the arrogant pricks who had tried telling him who he should and shouldn't serve in his own bar.

Franklin looked at Sarah, then back at Engee, feeling the confusion on his face. "You're Koru?" he asked, perhaps one of the dumbest questions he would ever ask.

"I am," Engee nodded, a helpful expression on her alien features. Franklin hadn't paid her much mind the previous night, but now, examining her more closely, he saw that she was young—barely out of adolescence by what he knew of their equivalent standards. She was slight and relatively short—even for a Koru, who were typically a little shorter than humans on average, her lizard-like skin turning browny-red here and there, especially around the opaque eyes—a colour that reminded Franklin a little of the exterior of the *Mutt's Nuts*. Something else was eerily different about her, too, but his mind could not quite place what.

Franklin turned to Sarah. "You didn't mention the person I was to meet was... Koru. That's unexpected," he said icily.

Sarah appeared unfazed by his tone. "Engee is... well, a 'fugitive' from her people, for want of a better word."

"I have become separated from my whole," Engee repeated, like this in itself was a complete explanation. However, as she spoke, something clicked in Franklin's brain.

"Your voice..." he said, remembering his slight discomfort with her at the bar the previous evening. That sense of hearing the voice of a multitude that Franklin had always found unsettling when speaking to a Koru was not present with Engee. Hers was a single voice with none of the added resonance. Ironically, he found that unsettling too.

"I can no longer feel the others," Engee said, understanding what Franklin was getting at.

"She has no memory," Sarah put in trying to hurry the conversation along. "I came across her only last week. But, considering what is happening, it seemed... fortuitous."

Franklin raised his eyebrows at that. Arnold—who liked to philosophise more than Franklin did—had said more than once that coincidence was merely unseen cause-and-effect." You sent her up to the bar to check me out first, didn't you?"

Sarah didn't answer him, instead turning to Engee. "You want to go up front and start prep?" Engee nodded sharply and made straight for the refectory's opposite door. "I'll contact bay control and make an opening request."

While more modern ships almost always had a host of smaller bays to house the individual craft that might want to come and go—and there were even prototype atmospheric fields in operation on the latest military ships, so he had heard—the *Olympic* was of an older design with much bigger bays. This meant that everyone and everything needed to be in a confirmed secure state when the outer doors were opened to the vacuum of space and getting off the ship at short notice was almost impossible.

"I don't want to sound like a Koru-sceptic," Franklin said once Engee had exited the room, "but are you sure you can trust her? Her people take your husband, and then she just happens to cross your path a week later?"

Sarah moved over to a larger comms panel on the wall to avoid looking at Franklin as she answered. "I've employed her. In fact, she's my only crew member right now."

Franklin glanced around the refectory, although his gesture encompassed the whole ship. "It's a lot of ship for two people," he said.

"Sometimes it's just me," Sarah answered matter-of-factly, then touched the panel. "Bay 4 control, this is *Mutt's Nuts* requesting permission to leave at first convenience."

"Stand by... *Mutt's Nuts*," the controller answered, "there are no current requests in Bay 4. We will start protocol now and return at commencement of countdown, be ready to leave."

Sarah turned back to Franklin. "Look, there are a few things that Engee knows. Our meeting isn't quite the coincidence you might think, and I'm just off to check some information that she's sort of given me down on the planet below." She made a slight movement, her shoulders seeming to turn one way, her hips another, her tied-back hair flicking outwards a little. Even in the oversized coveralls, Franklin found it an alluring pose. "If you're concerned about my safety, you could come with us?" she said, making the statement a question.

Despite Arnold's encouragement, Franklin had come to tell Sarah that he couldn't help. It was all too much, and he had a business to run. But a quick trip down to the Enceladine... well, he could manage that, he supposed. One little trip and he could be safely back in his bar. Plus, it would be nice to fly in the *Mutt's Nuts* just one more time.

The bay's clearance alarm sounded outside the ship—a klaxon-like whine interspersed with a colourless female voice declaring: "Exterior door opening in ten minutes. All personnel and passengers must clear the bay or be secured in vacuum-proof conditions. Doors will be locked in five minutes and counting."

Franklin sighed. "I'll come down to the planet with you, follow this lead, but-"

"-Arnold says you have to be back by tea?" Sarah teased.

"Yeah, something like that."

"I know who you are," Engee said as the approaching planet began to fill the front viewport. They were coming in towards the northern hemisphere, a significant amount of which was covered in glacier. Franklin stood a little behind Engee in the fairly cramped confines of the ship's cockpit, which had two front seats and an observer's seat that could be used as a navigation station. The front viewport curved away above the front seats and came almost to a point a little further down the nose. Two-handed control columns came out of a wide instrument panel, and Franklin had been eyeing the young Koru working smoothly at the ship's controls in the co-pilot's seat, trying not to feel envious. He was almost salivating at the idea of laying his hand on the controls of this—let's face it, hardly agile—ship again. He always sat in the back of shuttles and never really went onto the bridge of the *Olympic*. Maybe he had been intentionally avoiding these places.

"Who am I?" Franklin replied, unable to keep a note of challenge from his voice.

"The human who is death," she answered matter-of-factly. She caught a horrified look from Sarah and corrected herself. "I am sorry, that is not appropriate. I am not getting your human need to lie to spare feelings."

Sarah put her head in her hands.

"That's what they call me, your people?"

"It is one name."

"That man is gone. I'm a different person."

"And yet," Sarah put in, "I still think the war thing will be on your obituary. Now, sit down and buckle up." Franklin did as he was told and found a handy headset to connect to the ship's comms, while Sarah spoke to Engee. "Good job," she said kindly, "you're coming along nicely. Now, I have control."

Engee took her hands off the control column and replied, "You have control."

"I have control," Sarah said again, finishing the switch over just seconds before they hit the turbulence and resistance upon entering the planet's atmosphere.

The ship shook as its shielded front section heated up and pushed its way through the quickly thickening layer of gases that surrounded the planet and allowed life to live there. The sound of the ship's complaints was disconcerting yet strangely comforting to Franklin. As impressive as it was for Sarah to own the *Mutt's Nuts*, it was still a "bucket of bolts" against almost everything else he had flown in, including the *Olympic*... Only a pilot listened to a ship the way he was listening to it right now. And, perhaps, a very nervous flyer. He might have had a little bit of both going on.

"Still just as good at landing, are we?" Franklin asked through gritted teeth as Sarah adjusted the angle and he felt an unexpected pull.

"About the same," Sarah answered wryly. With an effort, Engee turned to look at Franklin and, for the first time since he had met her, Franklin thought he saw an expression in those opaque eyes. It said, "Prepare yourself for a bumpy landing".

Sarah stared worryingly myopically at a readout in front of her. "This is a bloody backward place, Franklin," she grumbled. "It's a tiny little settlement and yet their crappy little spaceport still gets lost in it, and they've got this terrible ILS that's worse than what we would have had two-hundred years ago."

It all sounded like a line of prepared excuses to Franklin, but he kept that thought to himself and nodded agreeably.

When the moment of breaking came, it felt more like an emergency stop. The craft tilted backward at an even more alarming angle, so Franklin found himself staring past Sarah and Engee at Enceladine's sky for a moment, before the nose dived forward again and found the ground with a thud, giving Franklin the feeling that he should be checking the landing gear over when he got out. He let go of a breath he hadn't realised he was holding.

They disembarked and made their way past the customs post—a smiling and seemingly inoffensive native woman at a small table outside of a wooden shack who could have been selling homemade lemonade. Like all of the Enceladines, she resembled a human being much more closely than a Koru did, except for being a good seventy centimetres taller and with skin the colour of a deeply blue sky. Franklin thought they all seemed to wear a drunken expression and stood like they were permanently leaning against an invisible wall, which had earned them the moniker the "Cool Locals" when first encountered more than sixty years ago. Although they mixed happily with alien species, allowing them to come and go as they pleased, not one Enceladine had been known to leave their own planet. They took on technology shared with them by the other species only very reluctantly, and after much persuasion.

They were almost all polite to a fault and the customs lady seemed extremely apologetic for keeping them the thirty seconds that she did.

Franklin moved through first—he had been on the planet more than half a dozen times before and had a port card that guaranteed him a quick entry. Apparently, it wasn't worth much, as Sarah and Engee took no more time to pass through than he did.

"Always nice when a young Koru lady bothers to come and see me," the customs official said in overly jaunty English as Engee moved on. Franklin was always impressed by how, for a backward planet on the edge of things, many of its inhabitants spoke two or three Earth languages with a soft fluency. Of course, he had to remember that this sector had once been more critical to the UTC than it was now. English, spoken by an Enceladine, sounded a little like a Welsh accent to him. Yet somehow even more lyrical.

"What did she mean by that?" Sarah wondered as they walked away from the customs post, then shrugged and turned to Franklin. "There's someone on the other side of town I want to meet with. She's sort of my eye in the McMurdo Rift. Which isn't much of an eye down here on a planet full of people who aren't bothered about space travel themselves, but a contact is a contact."

They moved through run-down streets that nonetheless had a much friendlier feel than similarly run-down towns and cities in other places. No buildings were above two storeys—which was a little higher than the human standard due to the height of the local population. Almost all were a dull grey that made it feel like the settlement was covered in a layer of volcanic ash. The whole place felt like a giant market, with colour added by the wares hanging from every available spot. This was a place where no corporations or franchises penetrated, so it seemed possible that you might find just about anything, if you were lucky. So, Franklin was a little surprised when they found the little shop that was their destination.

Perched at the top of a small hill was a single-storey building—they were almost all single storey this far from the centre, although that single storey was, of course, adjusted to the height of the locals—with tables displaying its wares out the front.

"You brought me to a shop selling tourist crap," Franklin complained as they approached the front.

The shop's wares—if not the whole tumbledown shop itself—could almost have appeared at any popular holiday destination on Earth, as it had once been, or on any of the other planets the UTC had settled on. There were mountains in snow globes and cheap, printed clothing, even a hat that said, "Born to be Cool!" This presumably referencing the old moniker that the locals were, supposedly, not all that keen on. Franklin's previous opinions of the planets' inhabitants were taking a slight nose dive. There was also a lot of "nebula" paraphernalia and a guitar with the words "McMurdo Riffed" on it. Geez.

A young female Enceladine came out from inside the shop as they got close. She was almost waifishly thin and subtly pretty, which came out as a sweet "girl next door" look mixed with how her heritage shaped her face and expression.

Sarah shared a quick hug with the alien woman, a little like a child hugging an adult, then turned to Franklin and Engee. "This is Emma," she said.

"Emmakanchooka-evangeklide-hik," the Enceladine woman said as she offered a long, thin-fingered hand.

"That is all your name?" Engee asked as she took the hand, but Franklin, with his local knowledge, was already wise to the joke being played.

"No," Sarah interjected, waving a reprimanding finger at Emma, "she's being an ass."

"It really is just Emma," the Enceladine said as she let go of Engee's hand again, "the horrible humans have colonised us and destroyed our culture, and now we all want to be like them."

Sarah shook her head. "Still being an ass."

Emma grinned wolfishly at Sarah, showing long teeth like those of a carnivore. "You only put up with me 'cos I give you all the good shit every time you pass by. Want to come inside?"

The homes and other inside spaces of the Enceladines were generally quite spacious, yet Emma's shop seemed to be the exception. Instead, it was more like a storage area that aspired to display some goods, with piles of boxes looming left and right and the odd selection of actual saleable wares poking through on a table or a shelf here and there. Franklin, trying to find somewhere to stand, came close to knocking over a stack of boxes that was nearly twice his height.

"You said you had something for me?" Sarah prompted eagerly. Like the street outside this oddly remote tourist store, the shop was devoid of people, local or otherwise.

"Yep," Emma said, picking up a long, dark-coloured glass pipe and sucking on it. As she did so, some liquid bubbled in the bottom. "You know my cabin I go to, up near Dead Lake?"

"Where you store your 'special' gear?"

"Yep," Franklin was acutely aware of the barely-veiled subtext to their conversation, that whatever Emma was storing at this place she called "Dead Lake" was probably not entirely legal. He was more fascinated by Emma's fluency with the English language. It was better than the customs official and without the accent that usually gave it such a lyrical sound. She could have grown up on the same streets that he did for the way she spoke to them, although he knew that had to be impossible, as it was with all her people. "There were a whole bunch of these guys out there," Emma went on, pointing at Engee.

"And I'm guessing that's not usual?" Franklin asked. He had been to the planet several times during his time on the *Olympic* and guessed that Koru were at least as rare here as they were in his bar, but he wanted to hear Emma say it.

"We have the occasional visitor from the *Olympic*," Emma replied, "even one or two have found my shop. But I've never seen more than two together at a time, not all my life." Emma made herself sound old with those last four words, although she did not look that old. Still,

Franklin had to admit that he did not know how for sure how Enceladines aged or how long they lived.

"Any idea what they were doing out there?" Sarah asked. "I know where you said it was before, northeast of town, but is there anything important out there?"

"Small mountains, lots of scrublands, and a very salty lake with nothing much living in it," Emma said. "Eventually, you get to another settlement, but it's much further than Dead Lake. What is it, you humans say...? *Yes*, perhaps they were looking for some cheap real estate."

Sarah and Franklin both looked to the Koru in the room. "What is 'real estate'?" Engee asked.

They thanked Emma and walked back out of the shop. "Are you up for taking a look?" Sarah asked Franklin as they came back out onto the street.

"How far?" He was already feeling a little itchy and sweaty from being away from his bar for so long.

"Probably less than an hour. Emma's given me pretty good directions."

Engee, who had been taking a great interest in all the... well, *rubbish* in the shop, was trailing behind. Franklin noticed a couple of similarly cloaked and hooded figures standing on one side of the wide street. They were too short for locals, and Franklin briefly wondered if they were from one of the many odd religious sects that seemed to flock to the McMurdo Rift—also making up an increasingly uncomfortable number of passengers on the *Olympic*—especially as they weren't given to spending money in his bar, apart from the purchasing the odd ceremonial bottle of wine.

It was odd; whoever they were, they were out on the edge of the town. At least Emma might have a few customers for her, um... souvenirs, he guessed. There was the sound of a scuffle behind them, and Franklin spun around to see two hooded figures—dressed the same as the two figures he had seen across the street—wrestling with Engee, one of them having grabbed her from behind.

"Hey, what the hell are you doing?" Franklin bellowed at them and was about to run to Engee's aid when he caught a blow to the back of the head and tumbled to the dusty, grey gravel that covered the streets throughout all but the most central parts of the settlement, the world momentarily spinning for him. He looked over to see that Sarah had seen her assailant coming and that they were now wrestling, although a headbutt from the hooded and caped figure also put Sarah on the deck.

Franklin managed to get to his knees, pushing back a wave of nausea because his head still appeared to prefer the prone option. Not having owned or even touched a gun since leaving the military, Franklin was now regretting having become such a pacifist. Well... perhaps "pacifist" was a strong (or weak?) word because he was definitely not above thumping someone, but something shooty would have suited the situation best.

The two figures that had stood on the side of the street and attacked Franklin and Sarah as soon as their backs were turned, now moved to help their two colleagues, who were attempting to subdue Engee. The diminutive and slight Koru was not so much fighting back as doing an excellent job of wriggling and repeatedly slipping from their grasp. However, with the arrival of the other two, they finally held her still. Franklin saw a small, thin tube pressed against her neck, which instantly caused Engee to fall limp.

Finally, Franklin's legs agreed to work again as he stumbled to his feet, continuing with the unsteady forward motion to barrel into the four men at speed. Reaching out with flailing arms as he did so, Franklin pulled back the hood of one of the assailants to reveal an eerie, almost skull-like mask underneath, which was made of a rubbery substance and covered the entire head. Although there were eyeholes, he could see no eyes within them, only blackness.

In a reaction that was more fearful than anything else, he punched the figure in the face, which seemed to harm his wrist and knuckles more than the masked assailant's face, while two of the figures quickly carried Engee back behind Emma's shop. He saw Emma's blue head poke out of the doorway, then quickly vanish again. It seemed a slight betrayal, even though he had only just met her and knew that she was only a "business" acquaintance of Sarah's.

There was a sudden bright flash close to Franklin, and he staggered away from it, turning to see that the fourth member of the attacking group was on the floor, his cloak smoking and slightly aflame at the shoulder. Glancing back towards Sarah, he saw that she was on her feet with a smear of blood across part of her temple and the bridge of her nose. She had a compact black object that he recognised as a small, concealable CEW pistol in her hand. On the side of it, in faint, silvery writing, was "B-17 Black Arrow".

The wounded assailant sprung to its feet and fled. Franklin tried to dive out of the way to let Sarah get in a shot at the remaining attacker—the one whose hood he had pulled down—but his foe was perhaps wise to the tactic, as the masked figure grappled him in what seemed to be an attempt to use Franklin as a shield.

Seemingly undeterred by this tactic, Sarah aimed the weapon at Franklin and the attacker, who was a little smaller than Franklin but seemed solid and strong. She closed one eye and stuck her tongue out of the side of her mouth as she concentrated on aiming, none of which gave Franklin any confidence. "No... what the... Sarah, don't bloody shoot!" he cried, fearing for his life.

In the end, Sarah shrugged and threw the weapon to him. Perhaps it was the pilot's reflexes, still there after so many years but Franklin caught the weapon, even with his arm mostly pinned. Bringing his other elbow up into the mask, he made enough room to turn and fire the gun at point-blank range. He meant to go for the leg or somewhere else that would usually not be lethal, but his foe grabbed at the weapon at the last moment. The weapon went off half a second later than planned, and straight into the assailant's chest.

Franklin tried to let go of the trigger as soon as he saw where the red beam of the CEW was going, but the attacker also had a hand around the gun and clenched it tightly for a moment when struck. As a result, the little weapon—meant for personal defence and concealment and probably one of the least-lethal compressed energy weapons a person could own, only stopped firing when it overheated after another couple of seconds, by which time there was a gaping black crevice in the chest of the masked and cloaked figure.

At last, its hand let go of the weapon, his now-dead foe toppling to the floor. "Fu-u-ck," Franklin whispered unsteadily. Then, loud enough for Sarah to hear, his eyes bulging and his throat suddenly dry and raw, "That's one more person than I was ever supposed to kill again."

As Sarah strode up to Franklin, he glanced about, seeing no sign of the other three attackers or Engee. Emma emerged from the door of her shop, holding a literal hand cannon that said "Encela-die!" on it in shimmering script. All three ran past the shop and around the corner, but there was no clear evidence of where they might have gone and an eerie lack of witnesses to ask about it.

Returning to the street, a couple of locals had come out of their dwellings and were stood looking down cautiously at the corpse. Emma tried to hide her hand cannon behind her back, pointing at Franklin when the gathered locals looked over at them.

"Where did they go?" Sarah asked, a note of breathless panic in her voice. "I was responsible for her, damn it!"

"You... er, didn't happen to put a tracker on her," Franklin asked, "or anything else useful like that?"

Sarah's blue eyes gleamed like angry sapphires as she glared back at him. "Of course I fucking didn't, Mark. What do you think? That I made her promise me her firstborn too?" Her fury suddenly ceased, and Sarah glanced down at her wrist communicator, working to tap at the tiny screen for a few moments, mumbling, "Got the next best thing, though." Franklin didn't release his next breath until she spoke again.

"Ah, no good! Either they broke it, or they have a signal dampener. Not stupid then, unfortunately."

The three of them looked at the dead figure in the street. Four locals now stood over the body, although none had touched it. A part of Franklin didn't want to go over there, did not want to see the being he had just killed, even if he had come to kidnap Sarah's first mate. Yet, any answers might be on that corpse. When they got there, Sarah pulled off the mask, which seemed to cling tightly to the face it covered, now a death mask trying desperately to hold onto its secrets.

"A Koru," Emma breathed as they all peered down at the face.

Sarah shrugged. "Well, that fucking figures."

FOUR

The *Olympic* coasted on its final approach to match orbit around the largest settlement in Enceladine's northern hemisphere, which would make it easy for the many small craft visiting the surface to make the trip down and back without incident. The ship's own shuttles knew their way and kept all their navigational equipment up to scratch. However, the multitude of private vessels found in the *Olympic's* vast bays were not always so well maintained and all too often crewed by idiots. The *Olympic* left when it was due to leave. They waited for no one. Any non-interstellar craft left behind would have to wait three weeks until the *Olympic's* closed route brought it this way again.

It was almost time for the night shift to come on as Captain Arnold Philby climbed the steps up to the viewport at the front of the bridge and looked at the approaching planet. In all these years travelling through the blackness of space—too black even here with the strange brightness of the nebula so close by—Arnold had never failed to be lifted by the sight of an approaching planet. Its light, its life—all of it serving as a minuscule beacon in the vast darkness.

Even when the ship was made, the Olympic's viewport had been unnecessary, and you would never find one on an interstellar passenger ship nowadays. Still, Arnold was always glad to see an approaching planet with his own eyes—well, through at least ten centimetres of transparent polymer—and not on a screen or projection, views that were always only interpreted digitally by a camera.

Those were available on the *Olympic's* bridge, too, of course, with just about every view conceivable laid out along a set of screens just below where he now stood. While so many modern ships worked with 3D projections and virtual spaces created by an instant composite of all the available images, the *Olympic*, in its inimitably old-fashioned way, just had lots and lots of screens, and Arnold was kind of okay with that too.

Descending back to the main floor, Arnold handed over his command authorisation to Lieutenant-Commander Yelland, who had just arrived to take over from him. The bridge commander was always the first position to change over. Yelland had been foisted upon Arnold by the owners of the *Olympic*. He was oily, simpering and Arnold had a sense that, if the SS *Olympic* were Ancient Rome, the shift commander would stab him in the back for even a remote shot at the top job. *Not surprised it's you, Brutus.* Even within the short thirty-second exchange as Arnold handed over to him,

Yelland managed to irritate the captain, and Arnold found himself needing a drink.

His plan for a sneaky after-work drink was scuppered when he found the SS *Olympic* Cocktail Lounge closed. It was odd as it was coming up to the busiest part of the day for Franklin, whose heart and soul went into running his bar. The ex-pilot's refusal to employ anyone else to work in the bar meant that on the odd occasion when there was something he absolutely had to do, it might be found briefly closed during mid-afternoon or when the ship was exceptionally quiet, Franklin might even close an hour or two early. But Arnold could never remember it being closed at this time, right at the start of the evening.

Turning instead towards the mess hall, he got out his slate—which had coded access to much of the vessel's logistics, as a captain's work was never truly done—and did a quick search for Franklin's name to see if he flagged up as being seriously ill in the med bay, or something, as this was the only likely reason the bar would be closed. No fancy DNA sweeps to locate his position on the ship, of course, this was the *Olympic* after all.

Franklin's name did flag up, although not where expected, instead registering as having been among three individuals that had gone down to the surface of Enceladine earlier in the day. Oh, of course, the ex-wife.

Arnold shrugged and headed to the mess hall. He had a "Captain's Table"—a private dining room where he could turn up and instantly distract the waiting staff, then eat alone at a table that would seat up to twelve. Years in the military had made the novelty wear off well before he came to the *Olympic*, so now he only used it when courtesy—or the bosses—made it necessary to host a passenger or passengers of importance.

"Good evening, Captain," came a slightly nasal voice, catching Arnold by surprise as he wondered again about Franklin and his friend's trip down to the planet. The voice sounded like the owner was about to try and sell him something. When he turned to see the person speaking—a Caucasian man, likely somewhere in his thirties—Arnold quickly decided he was, indeed, about to try and sell him something.

"Hello?" Arnold replied, trying to sound patient and helpful and pleased to be accosted in the hallway of his ship by a stranger. But, of course, he was still in his uniform, so this might just be an over-enthusiastic passenger. To some of the starship spotters, the type who sit out by the New Titan docks noting down registry numbers, the captain of the SS *Olympic* was virtually a celebrity. He now wished he had gone straight to his cabin and had his dinner brought to him. Some of the privileges of rank had not yet grown completely tiresome.

"I'd like to introduce myself," the man simpered, reminding him a little of Yelland. In fact, as he looked, he noticed how the man had similar slicked blonde hair to Yelland, and the same slightly disingenuous smile. Although he was in a light-grey suit, even that had the feel of a uniform. "My name is Bennett."

"A pleasure, I am sure," Arnold wondered if the man had another name to go with "Bennet". It was one of those ambiguous names that just might be a first name. How formal or informal was he being?

"I wonder if we can speak for a moment," Bennett interjected quickly as Arnold made to keep moving. Dinner was out there somewhere. "My card." He held out a business card, which seemed rather quaint to Arnold, but then he wasn't averse to a little bit of quaint. He noted that the logo was reminiscent of—extremely close to, in fact—the old United Nations logo. Having such a logo seemed almost as old-fashioned as the whole idea of carrying a business card. Indeed, if one considered a little more, it seemed vaguely heretical, as no business that wanted to do its business anywhere outside of Earth—or, in many cases, on Earth itself—would use Earth-based iconography in their logo. The past was still undergoing the long process of being swept under the carpet. Earth had lost the war and was busy being suitably contrite about it.

Still, the card—if not the man who had handed it to him—had Arnold intrigued. Of course, he was ever-more easily diverted these days.

"Shall we sit?" Arnold suggested, indicating a nearby seat in a shallow alcove, many of which dotted the wider corridors and thoroughfares on the ship.

"Ah, I knew you were a patriot," Bennett said enthusiastically, as if something meaningful had already been decided.

Once they were seated, Arnold looked at the man expectantly, becoming worried that he was about to be sold something. Which, in a sense, he was.

"My organisation comprises people who feel that Earth has got a bad deal out of a war it should have won," Bennett began. "We feel," he waggled the business card between the index and middle finger of his left hand, "that Earthers have already spent too long being ashamed of our history, of our achievements. We are sick of being contrite for the benefit of the UTC."

"And you think I feel the same way?" Arnold's voice remained neutral as he eyed those passing by—this was not a conversation he should be caught in by the wrong person, not if he valued his job. Thankfully, Yelland was safely on the bridge.

"You were quick to take a backseat and… extract yourself from your military role when the opportunity presented itself," Bennett pointed out.

"The UTC absorbed Earth's military," Arnold said, "dismantled us."

"But you could have stayed."

Arnold didn't answer, narrowing his eyes slightly. Dismantling Earth's independent military capability made perfect sense, and absorbing its officers—particularly the more high-profile ones—gave the action a respectable face. The UTC and Earth were now "one single entity". That, of course, had always been the aim for both sides. The war had been about who, within that "one single entity," would end up on top. Who wrote the history books, controlled the narrative, and lived as first among equals. Arnold had accepted defeat but hadn't been keen to help with what came after.

However, he did not want to admit that to this stranger who now looked at him with a kind of nauseous confidence, like he was so certain that he knew who Arnold Philby was inside.

"I also assume that you do not have much love for the Koru," Bennett said, changing tack.

"It was the Koru who defeated Earth," Arnold answered, his teeth grinding slightly as he spoke, "not the UTC. It's been conveniently forgotten how much of a damned good thrashing we were giving them. The Koru changed that."

It wasn't exactly an answer but Bennett was seemingly satisfied. "Quite right." As the man's skin occasionally caught the glow coming from the corridor's lighting strips, Arnold noticed it seemed covered in a sheen of sweat. Although the *Olympic's* environmental sensors were not always the fastest at reacting to rises and dips in temperature across the ship, Arnold himself had become well attuned to the ship's climate and felt quite comfortable. Nevertheless, he found himself staring at the slick shininess across the man's forehead—it was as if a fleet of snails had been marching back and forth across it. "You get them on this ship, don't you?"

"Huh?" Arnold asked distractedly.

"Koru."

Arnold tore his eyes from Bennett's clammy skin and met the man's eyes, which now fixed him with a laser-focused intensity. "On occasion. We pass close to some of their territory—one planet in particular—so the odd one or two come through. I don't…" It seemed hard to find the words that he wanted for a moment. "I mean, they are just passengers, like hundreds and thousands of others."

"What about the bartender?" Bennett went on, the intense look falling away as the subject quickly shifted again. Although Arnold got the feeling they were still having the same conversation.

"Franklin?" Arnold asked, playing dumb just a little.

"The one who took down the Koru mothership."

"He's a friend," Arnold answered neutrally.

Bennett seemed to scoff a little, although the man had barely half an upturned lip. "That's very magnanimous of you."

"How so?"

"The man may have taken out the Koru ship that day, but you were in command, Captain; you gave the orders. He did it under your instruction."

Arnold had no idea what Franklin had done that day; no one did.

"It seems to me that you never got your share of the credit," Bennett went on.

"It never…" Arnold began but stopped himself. Had it really never crossed his mind? Back on that day, even in the days that followed, he had only been relieved to be alive, for Earth to have been spared and nothing more. It was true that he had never been given his due, the recognition for his part, because the UTC had taken over and no one had been interested in the heroics and actions of Earth generals, only in the extraordinary and mysterious exploits of one man. "Being in the military is about being a part of the team," Arnold mumbled, unsure about the point he was trying to make and whether he agreed or disagreed with Bennett.

"Of course," Bennett said, nodding sagely as if he knew what Arnold was thinking. He proffered his card again. "Keep hold of this. Maybe you wouldn't mind letting me know of any comings and goings that might be of interest to a group of... old-style patriots?"

Arnold was unsure whether this was something that he wanted to do, but this Bennett seemed to encourage rebelliousness in his own lips. "I could do that," he said, sounding almost enthusiastic.

"Soon, I'll head back to Earth," Bennett said, rising from his seat in the alcove, "and I'll send you a little more info about us once I'm there." He pulled up two fingers in a familiar offhand salute. "Be seeing you," he said, heading off along the corridor, seeming to slip seamlessly in with the other passengers and almost vanish from plain sight.

As the seconds ticked away since the man's departure, the whole event took on a surreal, no... unreal sort of feel for Arnold. If he hadn't been looking down at the card between his fingers, he might have been tempted to believe that the man called Bennett had never been there at all and that he should stop having conversations with himself, because talking to Bennett had been far too much like talking to those parts of him that he kept hidden, parts of him that he denied and would wish away if he could. Because what use were such thoughts to the Captain of the SS *Olympic*?

FIVE

"Are you able to run the bar for me?" Franklin asked Gus from the comms station in the corner of the refectory aboard the *Mutt's Nuts*, which—and perhaps it was his occupation colouring his view here—was above a piece of furniture that looked like a home bar. It was almost a quarter circle in shape, with a gap at one end that had him wanting to slip behind it to serve shots, perhaps put together a Manhattan. "Even if it's just a few hours to catch the evening trade, I'd appreciate it. Arnold might chew me out a little less when I get back. He'll pass on all the necessary authorisations, I'm sure."

"For how long?" Gus asked.

Franklin had opted for an audio-only transmission, so he couldn't see the panic in Gus' face—but then he didn't need to, because it was evident in the slight shrillness that had entered his voice. The lack of a video signal wasn't entirely a technical thing, they could have got a grainy, low-res picture going with the *Mutt's Nuts'* comms no problem, but Franklin had somehow picked up a bruise just below his eye during the scuffle—as well as the egg-sized lump on the back of his head—so he didn't want Gus worrying more than he already was. Or, for that matter, passing these details onto Arnold, whom Franklin was very deliberately not going to call. It was cowardly, but he didn't care.

"Until we get back," Franklin answered far too vaguely, hoping that the note of apology he heard in his voice was coming through on the transmission. "Hopefully only a day or two, maybe even less." He genuinely had no idea and was still wondering how he had ended up in the position he had, feeling the responsibility to Sarah that he now felt again—something that should have been history, like the idea of Old Earth—and also to Engee, a Koru he had only met earlier in the day.

"Okay." He could hear the grumbling note in Gus' voice. " You'll take care of Geoff too?"

"Sure." He sounded much more pleased about looking after the cat. Franklin could hear the unspoken questions in his friend's voice: *What the hell is going on? Why do you need to stay longer?* But, to his credit, Gus didn't ask.

Franklin came off comms and turned to Sarah. "Are you sure we don't just want to fly the *Nuts* around until we find the salt lake and Emma's hut?"

Their Enceladine contact's hut was their best to track what might have happened to Engee, as it was close to the hut that the Koru had consistently been seen.

Sarah shook her head. "The presence of Koru agents here in town scares the shit out of me. If the Koru have eyes on us, then the *Mutt's Nuts* within a planet's atmosphere is like a great big fucking beacon for them. Once I start the engines up, there's no way that they don't know where we are."

Franklin knew this, but he had been hoping for the answer of least resistance. "So, what do we do instead, find a vehicle?"

"Let's get on public transport," Sarah suggested. "However much the Koru have going on here, they're less likely to keep tabs on us if we're travelling with the rest of the population. If we use cash. I got some local currency as they exchange it on the *Olympic*." Sarah put on a large wall screen with an overhead view of the region of Enceladine where they were. She pointed out the town—Eir, the largest settlement in the northern hemisphere, which wasn't saying much. "There's a maglev line, one of the few bits of technology they've accepted from the UTC."

"Only because we convinced them it would be good for the tourists," Franklin said.

"Yeah," Sarah managed a brief, wry smile. "It runs from Eir up to Dagda, where the tours up to the glacier go out from," she traced a line above the screen with her finger, stopping at a settlement about half the size of Eir, then made a perfect quarter-circle curve down to the right. "From what Emma's said, the Koru are coming down to where her hut is from the north. So maybe we hire a vehicle once we're there and come down from the other direction."

The station was only a short walk from the ship's dock and—true to form on Enceladine and completely suiting Franklin and Sarah—they could buy tickets for the train without any fuss or need for identification. If you had money, the Enceladines were more than happy to accommodate you. Never leaving their planet, Franklin sometimes wondered what they did with all the cash.

When the train pulled into the station, Franklin noted how the Enceladines had managed to make one of the UTC's more low-tech terrestrial travel options look even more basic. The engine section was somehow reminiscent of the more sleek-looking trains from Earth's steam era, and he kept expecting to hear the thing give off a loud hiss.

Getting into the carriages felt like even more of a let-down than the engine had been, with most of the seating being simple bench seating. Still, it was a short journey up to Dagda—only about an hour—so his backside would only be in minor agony when he got there. Franklin was amused to see that the one bit of vaguely modern technology the locals had opted to go with inside the train carriages were screens suspended in the middle and the end of each carriage. The screens played endless advertisements, which was most definitely like the Enceladines, never missing an opportunity to sell someone something.

When the train pulled away from the station, Franklin found the ride was smooth, and they soon gathered good speed. The rocky landscape they passed through was dreary, with only a smattering of trees and a seemingly endless expanse with few people and virtually no fauna on it. He thought his unwillingness to go beyond Eir on his infrequent visits to the planet had been a failure on his part... apparently, it had been wise.

"You ever been up to Dagda?" Sarah asked, breaking a silence that persisted between them since leaving the station. Franklin was unsure how long that had been, as the bleak, uninteresting landscape seemed to have hypnotised him, his thoughts spiralling away to his bar, to where Engee might be and to anything else that took his mind off being in the company of his ex-wife. He felt nervous. It was the first pause since he had stepped aboard her craft back on the *Olympic*, and it almost felt like a childish victory that she had been the one who felt the need to make chit-chat.

"No."

"Apparently the glacier's quite something," Sarah said with what felt like a forced cheerfulness.

"Don't you get tired?" Franklin asked, his mouth moving before checking with his brain whether it was a good idea.

"What do you mean?" There was only the slightest edge in Sarah's voice, only the hint of defensiveness, yet the years had not dimmed Franklin's ability to pick up on these things with Sarah.

"Of... trying," he pushed on. Sarah was younger than him, but he had been tired of getting involved—of fighting or trying to make a difference—years ago. He had been tired of all that even before he got into a fighter above Berlin, the day the war ended. "Of fighting. The universe will always have another fight to win, Sarah. It doesn't matter how old you get."

"My husband's out there somewhere, Mark," Sarah snapped, almost spitting his name at him. The anger faltered almost immediately, and she drew in a shuddering breath, half-gasping, half-sobbing the next words that she spoke. " Now I've gone and got Engee taken too."

Franklin made half an attempt at reaching out a hand towards her, but she either didn't see it or didn't want to take it. "Engee's not your fault."

"Are you kidding?" Sarah seemed to force back a sob. "I brought her right back to them, to people she was trying to get away from."

She had a point. Franklin looked idly up at the nearest advertising screen, speaking again after a few moments' silence. "But there is one good thing," he mused. Sarah looked sharply at him, daring him to bloody-well find the positive in their situation. "They came for Engee, not you."

Sarah's brow furrowed further. Half confusion, half anger still.

"If the Koru have taken Vik," Franklin explained, "then surely, if they knew who you were or were worried about you investigating his disappearance, they would have tried to grab you too."

Sarah inclined her head, her face relaxing a little. "So, what you're saying is that we're slightly less fucked than we were an hour or two ago."

Franklin was about to agree with her, then he saw something on the advertising screen that changed his mind.

"I wouldn't say that," Franklin squeaked. He cleared his throat and spoke again, unable to pull his eyes away from what he saw on the video screen. "Don't look-"

His warning was too late. Sarah followed Franklin's gaze up to the video screen, which was filled with a picture of Franklin's face. It was a recent shot, an ID picture from only a year or two ago. Below it, written in big yellow letters that would look comical if it wasn't his face up there, were the words "WANTED: Mark Franklin. Considered dangerous."

"You're considered dangerous," Sarah whispered. Franklin shushed her.

"This is bad," he hissed. "This is really fucking bad. I thought we had the neutrality and couldn't-give-a-shit attitude of the Enceladines on our side. Now they're fucking hunting us."

Suddenly, their hiding place amongst the tourists and anonymous populace on the train felt like a trap, like a small box—even if a tall, Enceladine-sized box—that was closing around them—a compactor of some kind with a hundred arms ready to reach out and stop their escape. Franklin tried looking at other passengers without looking like he was doing so. He attempted to discern if any were looking at him, drawing a connection between the face on the screen—if they had even been looking—and the man sat on the bench seat.

Rather stupidly, Franklin was trying to convince himself that he didn't look so much like the "him" of about two years ago.

"Behind you," Sarah said urgently. Franklin glanced back to see that one of the passengers was talking to a train guard and pointing up the carriage towards them. Yep, that was pretty much the worst-case scenario that Franklin had pictured in his head.

"Let's move," Franklin said as they both got up and moved towards the opposite end of the train.

"Do we have a plan?" They moved at a brisk walk along the aisle, abandoning any slim hope that it was not the two of them that the passenger had been identifying.

"We need to stop the train if we're getting off; it's going too fast for us to jump." Over three hundred kilometres per hour, if he was any judge.

As they reached the end of the carriage, Franklin glanced back and saw that two bigger-looking guards had joined the first guard. Unlike most lanky-looking Enceladines, these two were more anatomically proportionate to humans but still as tall as the other guard they had joined.

"There's three of them now," Franklin said, and they burst into the next carriage halfway into a run, which earned them the eyes of most of the passengers in their half of it. "There must be an emergency escape button, something for passengers to hit to stop the train?" he asked Sarah.

"We'll look at the next carriage connection," Sarah called back, sounding as uncertain as Franklin had. He wondered if she still carried the concealed compressed energy pistol she had used when Engee was taken. He believed Sarah to be mindful enough to bring it but should have checked. Calling out: "Do you have a gun?" to her right now, well... that might not be the best idea.

He did not want to be caught by the train guards, but he did not want to shoot them when the fight had nothing to do with them. Franklin wondered, not for the first time in the last minute, how the Koru had arranged to have the Enceladine authorities put out a warrant for his arrest. However this went, shore leave on Enceladine would be a bit more complicated from now on.

"Stop!" came a call from a carriage length back as they reached the doors at the far end. Another glance over his shoulder told Franklin that the guards were gaining on them. They needed to find a way to stop the train right away, or they would run out of carriages.

"Where is it, where is it?" he demanded, bursting into the carriage connection area a few moments behind Sarah.

"Um...?" Sarah said uncertainly, pointing at an important-looking panel with some red on it. Franklin reached out to grab and pull a grey-tinted cover that protected it. When that didn't work, he stepped back and brought his heel down hard on it, half-falling to the floor and grabbing his painful knee a moment later.

"Fucking hell!" Sarah exclaimed, pushing Franklin to the side as she drew her pistol. After less than half a second, the cover burst into flame and Sarah's little beam continued burning into the panel beneath.

Pulling himself along the wall as he tested his now-painful leg, Franklin looked back down the carriage and saw that their pursuers were only seconds behind. Then, as if reacting to a desperate plea on his part, the panel suddenly burst into a shower of sparks, throwing Franklin forward so that he barrelled into Sarah and landed on top of her as the train began to brake.

"Mark!" Sarah protested as they fought to get to their feet again under the weight of the heavily braking train. He reached out and grabbed the gun, which had been knocked from her grasp. They charged into the next carriage as one of the heavyset guards came forward too fast, slamming into the door at the end of the previous carriage, before the sensor caught up a moment later and slid open as he staggered back, clutching his face.

As they moved into the next carriage, Franklin pulled some heavy luggage from a rack just inside the door as an obstacle for their pursuers. The passengers in this carriage looked around in panic as the train continued its heavy braking. Those who did look their way—or had noticed Franklin's act of luggage vandalism—quickly looked away again when they saw the pistol he now carried in his right hand.

Franklin and Sarah had almost a whole carriage length on their pursuers again; the train now close to stopping. Franklin was hopeful that they could just open the doors and get off the train then. They would be on foot in the middle of nowhere and still hunted by the Koru, but the immediate danger would have passed at least.

"Shit!" Sarah exclaimed ahead of him. "Fuck, shit, bollocks!" A moment later, he saw the problem... They had passed through the last passenger carriage, and only the very secure door into the engine and—presumably, on Enceladine—driver's section lay beyond the next connector.

Franklin spun back around and pointed the pistol at their pursuers, who were now about half a carriage away, and several screams and gasps went up as he did so. "Stay the fuck back," he snarled, knowing full well that he wouldn't—couldn't—shoot the gun at Enceladine men who were just doing their job.

They came to a stuttering stop. Hands went into the air, although the second biggest guard let his hand drop towards his belt.

Franklin's heart hammered, trying to see what the man was going for. He did not expect Enceladine public transport security men to carry guns, but who knew? "Put those damn hands up, I said!" he bellowed, taking a couple of steps towards them, hoping to buy Sarah the time she needed to get the door open. Which might, of course, require the gun he was holding.

"Come quietly now," the smaller guard said in that wonderfully lyrical accent, which lost little of its music, even with the tension in the man's voice. He had the look of being the supervisor, Franklin supposed, and he could not help but be impressed that he was trying to talk the gun-wielding maniac down. "Where are you going to go?"

For the first time since before they had started to flee, Franklin glanced out of the window. He noticed how the previously uninteresting landscape had been made slightly more interesting by a light dusting of snow that iced the top of rocks and made a speckled tableau of the more open bits of the terrain.

"You're in the middle of nowhere," the guard said, "and the weather is closing in. You do not want to be walking in that."

"Just let us go," Franklin replied, backing towards the door. He glanced back and saw that Sarah had another panel open that was larger than the previous one and full of little red and green lights. "We get off the train. You all get to carry on to Dagda and finish your journey alive." In his head, Franklin's threats sounded kind of pathetic. He glanced around at the people seated nearby, wondering whether grabbing a hostage might help. They all looked too much like pleasant people to be put through that, though.

The second big guard's hand was slowly going lower again, and Franklin could see something on his belt—a dark, cuboid shape that was perhaps some non-lethal weapon.

"I won't be opening that door," the smaller guard said, although he didn't sound entirely sure about that. The train finally came to a halt with a slight jolt.

Suddenly, making a satisfying hydraulic hiss, the exterior did open, and Franklin smiled back at the guards. "Never mind," he said, turning to dash after Sarah. Something flew past his shoulders as he turned left in the connecting area, splattering with a loud, wet noise against the door through to the engine.

Franklin did not look, instead he jumped from the train and out into the snow, which was starting to come down heavily.

Sitting on a rock, of which there were many lying around like so much litter across the flood plain close to where they had exited the train, Franklin was beginning to feel like a part of the landscape. The snow was steadily getting heavier since they had made their dramatic exit from the Eir to Dagda maglev service thirty minutes before and was starting to lay on Franklin in the same way it was settling on the rocks, just starting to move the uniform appearance of their surroundings from volcanic grey to something a little whiter.

He had initially been worried about the guards continuing to chase them after they left the train and was confused when they just shut the doors and took off again. Of course, now he was starting to realise, as the first little shiver made his body shudder, that the guards had probably been thinking something along the lines of, "Idiots, they're going to freeze to death out there." If the pay for a maglev train guard on Enceladine was comparable with the UTC's public transport workers, they were probably not paid enough to risk their lives chasing fugitives once they had left the jurisdiction of their train.

There was a quality to these rocks around them—a smooth, consistent, medium greyness not dissimilar to the colour of your average stone statue. Which, coincidentally, was how he was starting to feel as the cold seeped into him while he sat still and waited for Sarah to finish doing whatever it was that she was trying to do.

"Any luck?" he asked as Sarah continued to mess with her handset, trying unsuccessfully not to let the impatience in his voice show. "I could..."

"I've got it," she growled, seeming to jab at her handset even harder. "I can program my ship's systems, so I can damn-well... Ah!"

Apparently, she damn-well could.

"What magic have you made?" Franklin asked as he got to his feet, warily casting his eyes around the landscape, although it was as devoid of movement and any signs of life as it had been for the whole time he had been sitting there. Given that they were in a place that made pursuit far too easy for the pursuer, he was pleased that the train staff had assumed their job ended when Franklin and Sarah left the train. Of course, the gun he was wielding might have had something to do with that too. All the same, the two of them had done some serious running for a couple of minutes, as it had seemed like the thing to do.

Also, more pertinently, if there was communication going on between the Enceladine authorities and the Koru—they didn't know this, but they had to assume so—it wouldn't do just to sit around where the train had stopped, waiting to get caught. At least, he now thought with an inward roll of his eyes, do that a good kilometre or so away.

Sarah gave the handset one more uncertain look before answering. "I'm bouncing a signal off the ship and onto the *Olympic's* guest service. We've got something that passes for satellite navigation." She looked about at the quietly falling snow. "Well, provided this snow doesn't get too much heavier."

"Do you think it's wise to be running a signal with the Koru and the Enceladine authorities after us?" Franklin asked. "Especially on something as open as the *Olympic's* guest service?"

Sarah's face darkened immediately. "No, I think it's better to get lost out here and freeze to death."

There was something almost familiar in the way that Franklin felt himself respond to Sarah's snippy reply, even though it had been more than a decade since he had done so. "I just asked," he complained, feeling his blood rise in a way that felt equally attractive and shameful, "you're the one who said we should take the train. If we'd taken the ship, we'd be there by now."

"Or captured," Sarah shot back. "Look, the Enceladines have no satellites of their own, so unless the Koru have a proper operational unit up on the *Olympic* or their own ship very close by, they won't be tracking the signal. Even if they do, they'll be tracking it to the *Mutt's Nuts* first and have to either board the ship or decrypt the signal to get to us."

Sarah glared at Franklin, and he found himself glaring back, although his own glare felt more on the sulky side to him. He thought that she might leave it there, but a parting shot could not be resisted, just as it had once been between them, even when things were at their best. "I haven't been sitting around making drinks for people all these years, you know."

It worked. "I was just fucking fine be-"

Franklin stopped mid-sentence, and Sarah cocked her head as she looked back at him, eagerly awaiting her chance to snipe back. "What?"

Franklin was looking just beyond her, but Sarah evidently couldn't tell, and she started feeling her face. "Have I got something... Look, if you're just being a dick."

"Shut up," Franklin hissed quietly.

"Don't you-"

"No, shu-u-ut u-u-up." Finally, Sarah caught onto the fact that he was looking behind her. She slowly turned around with the hunched shoulders of someone expecting to be attacked before they did so.

Franklin had spotted movement nearby as they argued, something which, in the slightly dimmer afternoon light that existed beneath the puffy snow clouds that now hung overhead, stood out only very slightly from the smooth, statue-grey rocks that lay all around them. It was pretty much dumb luck that he had been looking in the right direction as it snuck between two of the larger—almost boulder-sized—rocks. With a little humility, Franklin was already rethinking his assessment of the amount of cover available in the landscape.

The creature—part-big cat, part-warthog, part-armadillo... perhaps—realising it had been made less than twenty metres away from them, poked its head up slightly, then sidled out from behind the rock and just stood there, as if sizing them up.

"Is it... dangerous, do you think?" Sarah asked, turning to face the creature fully.

Franklin coughed out a laugh that was equal parts sardonic and terrified. "Look at it. It's a threat to life and limb; that's what it is." Then, as if to illustrate the point, the creature opened its mouth in what looked like a sneer, revealing fangs and needle-like teeth.

"Ah, look," Sarah said, "it yawned."

Franklin glanced at her incredulously, then remembered her tendency to just "go on" when she was nervous. In this instance, it was not a good survival mechanism.

"What's it doing?" she asked.

"I think it's deciding whether it can take us without the surprise attack," Franklin answered, slowly bringing out the little pistol he had kept hold of.

Suddenly, the creature darted forward, and Sarah turned to run with a shriek—a somewhat fruitless endeavour in a landscape almost devoid of cover—while Franklin brought up the pistol and fired. The thin, red beam seemed dazzling in the muted afternoon light, instantly connecting the weapon's muzzle and the creature's right side in a pretty impressive shot by Franklin, scouring a path along its flank. Although it skipped to the side to avoid the beam, the shot barely slowed it down. It didn't even cry out, its armadillo-like scales having provided a good degree of protection.

Sarah ran diagonally away from her pursuer, zig-zagging between small rocks that the large predator—probably slightly bigger than a lion—would be able to leap over. It now seemed fixed on her, perhaps because Franklin was the one with the weapon, or maybe because she had chosen to flee. Franklin was surprised by his own calm—although it was always a little easier when you were not the one that the terrifying creature had fixed upon.

He aimed again when it got closer, this time more able to target its unarmoured head, but the creature's speed and agility made it hard and he worried about the chance of only a glancing blow from the lightweight weapon being effective.

"Mark!" Sarah cried out as it was almost upon her. He didn't see whether she tripped or made a perfectly timed roll, but suddenly Sarah was tumbling head-over-heels at just the right moment, and the creature's killing leap overshot. It scrambled for purchase and was able to stop and turn alarmingly quickly. Sarah had ended up on all fours and, a little incredibly, Franklin saw his ex-wife set herself almost like a sprinter on running blocks.

He didn't know whether she planned to suicidally spring at the Encedinian predator hunting her, maybe meeting it in mid-air, or whether she hoped to dart to one side when it came. However, the creature was now facing Franklin and was momentarily almost still, so he took his shot. The beam caught it squarely in the forehead and scored downwards across its left eye. The creature howled—an unexpectedly high-pitched sound that seemed to echo for a fraction of a second, even though the terrain was flat.

It faltered, falling for a second on its side, and Franklin glanced down at the heat-meter on the Black Arrow pistol, which was at seventy percent. He aimed a second shot at the head, but the creature had regained its feet and was running away from them, moving in a way that suggested it was disoriented and likely in pain. Hopefully, the big fucker wouldn't be back. He was also beginning to realise that the train guards might not have given chase because they thought, "Idiots, they're going to get eaten out there." Sarah was on her feet by the time Franklin reached her, doing a good job of trying to hide her terror, although she was looking even paler than usual, her red lips and flame-like hair stark against her face and the ever-whiter scenery around them

"Let's get moving," she said, holding up the hand with the T-Slate in and shivering, despite her recent exertion. There was a crack on the screen that must have happened during her dramatic roll, but it looked to still be working. "If we head straight back across the maglev track and keep going, I think we'll be heading towards the cabin and the lake."

SIX

Arnold paced around his cabin—the Captain's Cabin. Although not the largest or the most ornate aboard the SS *Olympic*—that honour went to the Kings Suite on G-deck—it was still larger and more luxurious than anything he had known while in the military. Should the captain need to entertain in his quarters on the Olympic, the surroundings had to impress at least a little. There were hints of gold, amber and cream, although, as with everything else on his increasingly underfunded ship, the decor had seen better days, so now it was something more like 'flaking gold paint, dirty yellow and beige'.

He had hosted Dame Hatherleigh on the first night of this tour, a former Earth politician who had been a big part in soothing over the political transition to Proxima—hence the "Dame" bit. She was evidently politically very shrewd, yet Arnold had found her entirely too full of her own importance for his liking, especially as she had been retired for some seven years. Yelland, his second-in-command, had got on with her well. He even seemed to be something of a fan and had practically invited himself along to the dinner. The man was a shameless social climber, but Arnold was glad of his presence on this occasion.

Now, as he paced, Arnold twiddled the business card that Bennett had given him around in his right hand, occasionally pausing to absentmindedly roll it between his long fingers, like a gambler with a chip at a blackjack table. In another life, perhaps. Arnold hadn't much taken to Bennett at all—he had possessed the manner of a salesman selling "knock off" merchandise. Nevertheless, the man's words had touched something within Arnold and highlighted a sort of itch that he hadn't been able to scratch in many years.

With a determined set coming across his long, almost aristocratic jaw, Arnold made a decision. He went over to sit on the white, Proximan-leather couch that occupied the centre of the room and, like almost everything else, was well-worn with an intricate spider's web of cracks across its aging surface. He switched on an oft-repaired holographic communication terminal and looked at the card one last time before dialling the code that was printed in a small font beneath Bennett's name and the logo. He pressed the blue "Send" button suspended in front of him and almost immediately changed his mind, reaching out to cancel the call; however, he was a moment too late.

"Good, Mr Philby," an older man's voice said from the image projected a metre or so in front of the sofa. It sounded like Arnold's call was exactly what the man had expected. Arnold could not see his face very well, as it seemed mostly in shadow, and the image was grainy and flickered in a way that kept distorting it. The slight dimness of the holo projection—even under the relatively dim light in his cabin—was probably not helping either. There was something about the mysterious way the figure presented himself that reminded Arnold of Bennett's theatrics earlier in the day.

"Good evening," Arnold answered, trying to keep his composure as, the moment he had pressed on the connection request, he had been filled with a strong sense that he was making a mistake. Unfortunately, what he now saw on the screen in front of him wasn't making him feel much better in that regard. "Your associate, er... Mr Bennett, he gave me a card and suggested that I contact him. Or you... perhaps."

"Yes, Captain," the shadowy figure replied, "it is a delight to hear from you." He spoke as if from some already written script, as if Arnold hadn't just rambled at him. "I won't beat about the bush, as it were," the mysterious figure went on, still not having introduced himself. "I represent a group of people who feel that Earth should once again come first."

"I wouldn't disagree with that," Arnold answered cautiously but honestly. It would be a strange tactic to approach a man commanding a ship at the old, almost-forgotten edge of an empire to test his loyalty, but something about all of this almost screamed "TRAP!" to

Arnold. Like the UTC command was testing him, even though he was no longer part of their military.

"I sense you are somewhat hesitant, captain," said the mysterious man, "and I can't say I blame you. So, many of those who are now staunch members of our little... *club* were apprehensive at first."

"I'm not sure what I can bring to your table, that is all." Arnold was, perhaps, being a little too modest. His hackles were still raised, an itching, crawling sensation around the top of his shoulders and the back of his neck. He wanted a way to override the enormous curiosity he was feeling and something else that the man's opening pitch had set off inside him, a kind of yearning that felt attractive in the way that nostalgia often can.

"You're the captain of the biggest UTC-related ship moving around the McMurdo Rift, Mr Philby," the man said with a touch of awe in his voice, although the awe—like everything else about this man—felt a little staged... just a touch overdone. "You don't need to do much at all, except keep an eye on what is happening around you and occasionally reporting back to us."

It sounded almost disappointing bland. Or bullshit, one or the other. "Is there anything in particular that you would like me to look out for?"

"I am so glad that you asked." The way the words were spoken reinforced Arnold's sense that the whole conversation was progressing along a predetermined path. "We have been hearing reports of Koru activity in the McMurdo Rift."

"Out here? Really? The occasional few Koru travel aboard the *Olympic*, but I haven't noticed any increase in their numbers."

"Nonetheless, they are being spotted on the UTC and the neutral planets and stations in the sector with increasing frequency. We even have reports of Koru ships. Nothing military, at least not yet. If it were almost anywhere else in the UTC, then someone would probably check their reasons for transit."

That's because this is the McMurdo Rift, Arnold thought, although he kept it to himself. There was nothing worth being concerned about. You had to go several decades back, at least, before finding much in their region of space that any potential enemy might have prized. Rare minerals that had once been important in FTL propulsion had made the area a boom town about fifty years ago. Still, technology had moved on, and the minerals mined in the sector served an ever-dwindling market.

"They have several colony worlds along the rift," Arnold mused. "If they were planning an invasion of UTC space, it could be somewhere to gather forces with less risk of getting too much attention."

The figure on the display was silent, and he leaned forward fractionally for a brief moment, revealing a pronounced brow covered with bushy, almost-white eyebrows. For the first time, Arnold sensed that they were getting off-script. "We feel that... something subtler is happening. So if you find out about any concentration of

Koru, anywhere their civilian ships might be heading... that would be very helpful."

"I will do my best," Arnold replied as the figure leaned back again, those thick, white eyebrows vanishing into shadow.

"It's going to be a pleasure working with you, Captain," the man said, then the screen flicked off.

SEVEN

The snow kept falling, so thick that they could never see all that far in it, leaving the pair of them trudging through an almost silent, featureless landscape—ever-more-so uniform underfoot as the snow laid itself down thickly to make a world of white, punctuated by occasional bumps that became less distinguishable from everything else with every few minutes that passed.

Both of them were cold—Franklin could see it in Sarah, as much because of rather than despite the level of sheer determination she put into hiding it. He was only thankful for a complete absence of wind, or else he was sure the two of them would have frozen to death within an hour of starting their walk. Even then, they were afraid to stop, as the heat and energy generated by walking felt essential, as if stopping for more than a few seconds might mean seizing up like a piece of machinery. Moreover, if another predator-thing tried to ambush them, Franklin rather fancied its chances of getting its meal, as they would not see it coming and would probably be far too tired and numb to fight it off.

Although it struggled to operate as the snow got heavier, Sarah's improvised navigation device kept them going in the right direction—they hoped—and after a couple of hours of walking, small trees with bark that was almost black began to appear, and the little rocks of the flood plain vanished. Half-an-hour after that, as the heavy snowfall finally abated, Sarah pointed to a line of trees growing on the horizon.

"The l-lake and Emma's c-cabin should be somewhere just beyond th-those trees," Sarah told him. Franklin realised that it was the first either of them had spoken in a long time.

The effort of speaking caused Sarah to start to shake violently. It seemed that once she had started, she could not stop. For his part, Franklin was just feeling numb. It was a sort of painful numbness, but bearable. Although the lack of feeling might ultimately be covering worse things that were happening to his body, he found himself vaguely thankful for it.

The possible promise of their destination just beyond the line of trees enabled them to find a new reserve of energy and pick up the pace. However, Franklin feared that if the cabin was not as close as they hoped, they might be using up their last energy reserves. Seeing Sarah shake uncontrollably, and the effort she needed to put into each step, pulled at something within him. He had never stopped loving her—had never allowed himself to go through any sort of mental separation—but time had brought its own sort of distance. Now the ability to feel for Sarah, to be concerned about her, was hitting him like a freight train.

Franklin touched one of the trees when they reached them, which had a smooth, almost plastic feel that was so unlike bark. In fact, it was almost as if someone had made all these trees, printing them and placing them here in the middle of the planet to give it features it might not otherwise have. There were no leaves on the trees, and the branches and twigs jutted at odd angles that were almost too random to feel natural.

The crunch of their feet through the snow was less in the woods. The eerie silence present when the snow was falling heavily returned. Franklin began to feel a sense of dread, like they would either emerge from the trees to a vast, flat, featureless landscape with no cabin. Or, perhaps instead these trees would just go on forever.

When the trees did clear, it was so sudden that Franklin was almost caught out. The blackness of the trees and the whiteness of just about everything else played a visual trick on his mind. Suddenly all the straight black lines were gone, replaced by only whiteness that was broken only by a single grey rectangle and a large dark shape roughly that of a peanut in its shell.

Franklin put a foot forward and found air, having suddenly reached a steep hill. He tumbled head over heels and must have dropped some way before he came to a stop on his back. The first thing he realised was that he no longer felt numb, because suddenly he was hurting about his hands and face and feeling slightly winded.

"What the hell?" Sarah cried as she ran down after him. "Mark, are you okay?"

Still lying on his back, managing to feel a little humiliated, it occurred to Franklin that Sarah was worried that he'd collapsed or something—that Franklin had done what he feared Sarah would do for the last fifteen minutes or more.

He subconsciously licked his lips and then spat in response, finding whatever was on them was disgustingly salty. "What the hell?" he said, kind of echoing Sarah from a few moments before.

Franklin picked up a small handful of what he was lying in and, examining it closely, realised it was large flakes of crystalised salt rather than snow as he had thought. Lifting his head a little and looking at the landscape that lay slightly below and around them, he could see that it was just about as white as the snow they had trudged through. But, at some point while they were in the woods, it had changed from snow to salt instead.

He looked up at Sarah, holding up a handful of salt for her to see. "Emma wasn't kidding when she called this the 'salt lake'."

Sarah held out a hand and helped him up, and the two of them surveyed the landscape for a few more seconds. It was primarily white, presumably all salt and not snow, which would have probably melted on contact with it. As she had first thought, the lake and the rectangle that had to be Emma's cabin were the only things visible.

"No other cabins?" Franklin observed.

"Only Emma's."

It was, of course, a dead landscape, as even on relatively barren Enceladine, nothing could live in such an extremely salty environment. Emma's cabin might stand out, but who else was likely to come out here anyway? Well, unless they needed some salt.

They had to make their way around the edge of the small lake. Franklin and Sarah approached cautiously, even though the landscape offered almost no cover for anyone trying to ambush them, there was the cabin itself. Approaching the front of the cabin, which was made of grey wood, they could see that the door was slightly ajar. Franklin pulled out the Black Arrow pistol, which, since he'd grabbed it from the floor of the train, seemed to have become his without any specific mention or agreement of the fact. He wasn't really sure that he was the most qualified to carry the weapon but didn't feel compelled to give it back to Sarah either. It was a manliness issue. Perhaps he needed to work through it.

The cabin had a low porch that ran the entire length of the front side, and it creaked as he stepped on it. Franklin cringed, and Sarah gave him an annoyed look, which tickled that manliness issue. He went ahead and kicked the door in dramatically, pointing the little pistol into the semi-darkness beyond.

No one was in the cabin, which had only the most basic furniture and, as Emma had said was the case, was used for storage. It had, however, been ransacked. There was a long desk along one side, its draws were pulled out and emptied onto the floor.

"You think this was the Koru?" Sarah asked him as she surveyed the mess.

"Could be, although just about anybody who wanted could have broken into the cabin."

"And not taken any of Emma's stock?" Sarah pointed out.

Franklin shrugged and wandered back out of the front of the cabin, uneasily scanning the line of the trees that lay beyond the lake and atop the small hill that he had managed to tumble down a few minutes before. "Well, whoever it was, doesn't seem to be here now." The way he said the words sounded far too hopeful and not exactly convincing to his own ears. He felt watched, although he was fine admitting that it was more likely paranoia than instinct.

He paced idly towards the lake, the edge of which was perhaps a good fifty metres from the cabin, although the ground in between showed signs that the lake might have shrunk and been a little larger at some point.

Sarah followed him. "I hoped we'd find signs of the Koru, some idea where they might have taken Engee." Franklin could hear the despair in her voice.

"Well," he said, "the ransacked cabin could be a sign of the Koru. But no one is here right now."

Suddenly, with Franklin's back to the lake, Sarah's eyes went wide. "Shit, shit, shit! Mark, get the hell away from the lake."

Franklin nearly jumped out of his skin as he leapt away from the water's edge .He turned around to see some black, oozing mass emerging from the water. The mass, however, was not much bigger than the size of his foot.

"Yeugh," Franklin said, "what the hell is that?"

"Guess this lake isn't as dead as we thought," Sarah said.

The oozing mass looked like it was feeling about on the ground just beyond the water, as if sensing that there was recently something there, then retreated back into it, sliding along like a snail, slug or a worm, until it was far enough in to swim away.

Looking further along the water, refocusing his eyes, Franklin thought he could see quite a few of the things moving just below the surface. "You know what," he said, "I think I'm really getting to hate this planet."

EIGHT

As the two of them headed back up to Emma's hut, Sarah began to tap away excitedly on her hand-held unit's screen, so Franklin tried his best to wait patiently as she fiddled with it. The ever-present cold had only improved a little since they had come out of the snowstorm, digging its cold, invisible fingers further and further inside of him.

"I've got it," Sarah said triumphantly.

"The meaning of life?"

"No," she answered distractedly, continuing to fiddle.

"Well, tell me it's Engee's location, at least?"

"Not quite. I've been using the passenger feed on the *Olympic* for our location, and it's just turned up overhead again. So, it's going to be right above us, at least for a little while, and I've managed to get a good resolution live feed of the area."

They moved into the shade at the front of the hut to get the best look at the screen. "Look," Sarah said, pressing a finger to the screen, "there's several figures moving about just beyond the trees to the north.

Franklin leaned forward, seeing the hazy, greyish spots moving around on the landscape. The image on the small screen made them look extraordinarily close to the hut. He looked up to where the strangely dark trees they had emerged from a little earlier curved around the north of the salt lake. Squinting, Franklin thought he could see something like a path between them, although he could not tell if it was natural, random or man-made, as it were.

"That's close," he observed. "We should go up there, see if we can see who they are."

Sarah's nervous look tempered his reckless enthusiasm. Franklin squeezed his hand lightly around the little pistol that was currently in his pocket. She nodded bravely, though, and he felt a small wave of affection towards her.

With caution, they headed up into the trees. The sound of their feet crunching across the salty ground now seeming much louder than it had moments before. They could not hear any tell-tale noises coming from beyond the trees at first, not until they got onto the vague path among the trees, and then distant, muffled sound of work, bustle and machinery began to float over to them.

"It would be nice if your little up-link device could tell us exactly how many of them there are, who they are and what they're up to," Franklin said.

"I'm about to lose the signal," Sarah answered.

The trees quickly began to thin out again, the land falling away into a much smaller clearing than the one that held the salt lake. The two of them crouched down as they neared the point where the land dropped away again, struggling to take cover with no underbrush to speak of with the trees becoming sparse again.

The satellite image hadn't seen the depressions in the land, including an overhang on the opposite side, where several tunnels were dug. So even though only three individuals had been seen on the live feed, milling about in the middle of the depression, perhaps a dozen more were around the entrance to the tunnels, which were at least two or three times the height of a person.

All of the individuals in front of them were Koru—a mining operation of some sort, it appeared, with what might have been a cart system of some sort visible around one of the tunnel entrances. Over to one side of the overhang was a bulky-looking shuttle with an open rear cargo door.

"I would say this is our smoking gun," Franklin whispered to Sarah, even though it would have been almost impossible for any of the Koru down below to hear them.

"I wonder if this was what Vik was onto," Sarah mused quietly. "If they're holding Engee on Enceladine, this has to be a good bet where they are keeping her."

"Can't see any Enceladine people down there," Franklin said.

"Best way to keep it quiet."

Franklin nodded. "From my experience, the locals here are not the best at keeping secrets."

"And maybe they wouldn't like it. Whatever this is," Sarah said, "I can't believe it's being done with UTC knowledge either."

Franklin shrugged. "Technically, this isn't UTC territory."

She frowned, like that wasn't the point. "But if they are keeping this a secret, there's got to be a reason for that."

Suddenly, something slammed into the tree trunk only about twenty centimetres above Sarah's head, showering several wooden splinters down on her. "Get down," Franklin gasped, "someone's shooting at us!"

"Incoming transmission, captain," the acting comms officer on the bridge of the *Olympic* said to Arnold. "Marked as 'Captains Eyes Only'." The captain or duty officer stood on a slightly raised platform above all the various ops stations, towards the front. Arnold rarely sat in the throne-like chair that dominated the centre of it.

He raised his eyebrows, letting a thin grin onto his face below the equally thin moustache. "Well, that's exciting," he joked, "I wonder if it's from an eligible young woman."

"It doesn't say who it's from," the comms officer remarked, perhaps missing Arnold's attempt at humour.

During his years on the *Olympic*, he hadn't had one Captain's Eyes Only message, which hadn't even occurred to him until this moment. Only friends and family—his niece, Zoe, on Proxima—ever sent him anything that could be considered private, and that was through the regular personal methods. The last time he had received such a transmission was probably when he had been in the Earth military.

"Okay," he said, "send it through to the office." He walked off the bridge into the office he barely ever used when he was on duty. It wasn't even really "his" office, but rather a separate room available for the duty officer, if needed. The transmission came through, much sooner than expected, and the shadowed figure he had spoken to hours before appeared on the screen.

"Ah, Mr Philby," the figure said in an overly jolly tone, "thank you for accepting my call again so soon."

"You came through on the official channel?" Arnold said, making his statement sound like a question.

"Yes," the man replied, "the best way to keep things confidential, as it turns out." The half-shadowed face turned up a little at the corner of the mouth, which caught a little of the light source. "Ironic, I suppose."

"How can I help you?" Arnold said, feeling a slight fluttering in his stomach and wanting this done with quickly. He hadn't expected to hear from this man again so soon. This man whose name he had not been given and, equally, still found himself unwilling to ask about.

"We've had some more information since we last spoke," the man said.

"Oh?"

"We have reason to believe a ship will be in your vicinity in the next five to twelve hours. It's a small cargo transport, taking off from Enceladine."

"I see," Arnold replied, even though he didn't see at all. "We have not long left and are still within easy reach of the planet," he went on, somehow thinking that the shadowed man on the office screen already knew this.

"We require you to intercept this vessel and to seize its cargo." Where before the man's voice had a humorous edge, like they were always sharing some private joke, it was now hard-edged and official. Arnold felt like he was being given an order, and, with that feeling, came a small sense of familiarity. For the first time, he thought he recognised the voice.

"The *Olympic* is not equipped for such things," Arnold protested. What he was saying was true, although he knew that his answer was born out of an inner reluctance as well.

"I understand," the man replied, although the hard edge was still there, and it sounded a little like the man didn't understand at all. "You are, however, given certain prerogatives in the articles of operation that allows you to enforce UTC laws in the absence of a local United Territories government and law enforcement or any military presence. Seeing as neither are present in your location, you certainly have the authority."

"Technically... Yes."

"Well, let's just say that this is a matter of national security, shall we?"

Is it? Arnold thought to himself.

"That you intercept the ship and seize its cargo is of the highest importance," the man went on like he had read Arnold's thoughts, "I cannot stress this enough. You may even be able to prevent a war."

The last words hit Arnold like a body blow. He was already used to the theatrics of this group he had become involved with, but there was a lack of the usual irony in the way the shadowed man now spoke. *You may even be able to prevent a war.* As far as Arnold was concerned, one of the highest duties for anyone in the military was the preservation of life, the keeping of the peace.

"Very well," Arnold said with the manner of a soldier accepting an order," I will see it done."

"Good." The man now leaned forward enough that Arnold could finally see his face. The breath caught in his chest.

"Admi-"

The transmission clipped off, leaving the captain of the *Olympic* in quiet shock for long moments. Finally, Arnold turned off the screen and walked out of the office and back onto the bridge, feeling like he was back in the Earth Navy and doing something important after so many years of irrelevance, because the shadowed man was Admiral Maxwell, one of the highest-ranked officers in the UTC Navy.

NINE

The needle felt like ice as it went in, sending a jet of coldness spreading through her arm. It billowed outwards like ink poured into water, flowing into her torso and legs, sending a shiver up through her neck and into her head. The last thing she saw was Mark Franklin running towards her along the outlying street in the Enceladine capital... Then everything went black.

When Engee awoke, she was in a small room made of bare concrete blocks, save for a metal door with a small slat that opened from the other side—despite Engee's efforts to pry it open with her fingers. There were no windows in the room, just a bench—or, perhaps, what was supposed to be a bed, as she had woken up on it—made of the same concrete blocks as the walls.

The roof and the floor, however, were cut from rock, and Engee found it interesting that the slat in the door was just about at her own head height. Not made by the tall Enceladines, but on the short side even for humans. So, unless someone had made this cell specifically for her, which seemed unlikely, then it was Engee's own people who had captured her. The thought came with a flash of fear and a sad, dreadful inevitability. Had she really expected to escape the clutches of her people for long? Resistance and dissent among the Koru were just not done. The last time they had wiped her memory, what would they do to her now?

Engee had not seen the faces of her attackers, but she, Sarah and Mr Franklin had been on Enceladine looking for more Koru, so maybe those Koru had found them first. Or, perhaps, just her? At least they had grabbed Engee before the others, although she wondered about the fate of Sarah and Mr Franklin, hoping that they had survived whatever fight was erupting as she had slipped into unconsciousness; and that, if the attackers had been after them as well, they had escaped and were not similarly imprisoned.

She listened at the door for a while and heard occasional shuffling, although it seemed that the door must be quite thick, as everything sounded terribly distant. Eventually, she caught a snatch of conversation that was undoubtedly Koru, although she could not make out enough of it to get any real content.

Engee went back to sit on the cold concrete blocks of the bed, only then realising that she had not felt the presence of any of her kind as she sat in the cell, or even as she listened at the door.

She was still dealing with that revelation when she heard the door open, and a Koru male entered, larger than her and almost the colour of the rock that was under their feet. He had been here a while, then, wherever "here" was.

"Identify!" He demanded of her.

"NG-972," she replied instinctively before—too late—another thought came to her that she might have kept quiet, noticing at the same time that she had jumped to her feet as she replied. Refusal, she thought with a dizzying rush of adrenaline, is an option.

"NG-972, why are you on this planet?"

Engee drew herself up to her full height, which still left her quite a bit shorter than the other Koru she was facing and perhaps only half as wide. "We are not in Koru space," she stated with all the force that she could muster, amazed at how even she was keeping her voice, "I do not recognise your authority to interrogate me, this is an independent world under human jurisdiction."

"Negative, NG-972," the larger Koru stated, "all Koru are under central authority, wherever they are. His opaque eyes narrowed slightly, as he took a step back from her, looking her up and down. You have acquired an interesting dermal tint," he observed, taking in her reddy-brown skin, with various shades of mud and rust that occasionally faded out almost to cream. "Where have you been these multiple tens of planetary revolutions, NG-972? We know who you are and have run your biological ident."

Engee tried to school her features, to mask her surprise. They knew more than she did, then. "I will not tell you a thing until I have had my phone call," Engee bluffed through gritted teeth.

This stumped her erstwhile interrogator, who blinked in surprise. "Phone call?"

"It is a human custom," Engee told him. "I have seen it on their entertainment screens. You must allow me communication with an individual who will represent my interests."

The other Koru continued to look back at her, perplexed. After a moment he sighed, his manner seeming to change a little—perhaps more that of a teacher dealing with an imbecilic student, rather than just a superior to an unruly subordinate. "You have been spending these past revolutions with humans. They are affecting you with their lack of discipline. These are the humans you were with when we found you?"

Something in Engee's pupil-less eyes must have given her thoughts away, and a small smile of satisfaction briefly broke the stern line of her interrogator's mouth. "Yes, you were attached to those humans."

"Were?" Engee asked, feeling a sharp tightness across her chest.

"What are you doing on this planet?" The interrogator repeated, ignoring her question, his gaze bearing down upon Engee. Suddenly her legs began to feel weak, and she wanted to back up and sit down on the concrete block bed. But, at the same time, Engee found herself not wanting to give the other Koru the satisfaction.

"I do not recall," she answered quietly.

"You do not recall what you are doing on this planet?" Engee's interrogator asked her doubtfully. "You do not know where you have been since leaving Home Nest?"

"I do not recall," Engee insisted with more vigour.

"And how you came to be with these humans? Who are they?"

Engee brightened at that, coming back to herself slightly. "You do not have them, do you?" It was the way he had asked the question, she realised. Hanging around humans—who seemed to hide at least a little something in almost every conversation they had—was helping her to spot these things, even among her own people.

Her interrogator bristled, letting Engee know straight away that she was right. Interrogation, to be fair, was not much of a skill with the Koru. Their society was mostly based around the assumption that they were honest with each other.

"That is who I would use for my phone call," Engee told him. "I would contact my friends, and they would come to find me."

"Friends?" the interrogator scoffed. "A humanism. You are Koru." He went quiet for a moment and looked her slowly up and down. Finally, Engee did back up and sit down on the bed, resting her shaking legs.

"You do not know," he said, breaking a growing silence in the room in a tone that made the statement sound more like a decision. He reached up and rubbed a strong, square jaw. "But you will need to be returned to Home Nest to finish reconditioning, so I will place you with the other prisoner until transport can be arranged for you both."

He called in two guards and Engee let herself be taken. Each guard gripped one of her arms with vice-like strength and hauled her up and out of the cell. To them and the interrogator, she may have looked overwhelmed or defeated, but Engee was in fact being hit by shards of memory, each returning piece stunning her a little, yet nothing adding up to anything solid. One of the words that the interrogator had said was running over and over in her mind, each time dislodging another confusing snapshot. "Reconditioning."

The corridor was hewn out of the rock in a way that was familiar—large, smooth, slightly curved sections. Engee found herself able to imagine the small vehicle used in such a process, yet the meaning of 'reconditioning' was coming back more slowly, and she could barely even picture the world that the interrogator had called 'Home Nest', even though she knew it was her own point of origin.

Engee realised after some time that she should have been paying attention, trying to hold within her mind some semblance of the layout of the place, but it had been a maze and now they came to another cell, the door opening to reveal a larger space than the last one, with proper furniture in it and another occupant—a man with light brown skin and disorderly black hair. He looked up as they pushed her in, his brown eyes interested but hard to read. He then moved to the door and listened as the guards retreated.

Engee watched him, moved to a seat on the other side of the room, wondering whether to sit down. Eventually, the man turned back to her, his eyes wide—wild, even. A small stab of fear hit Engee and she checked to see if she could pick up the chair, ready to hit him with it. But then he spoke.

"NG-972?" the man asked in heavily accented English. "What the hell are you doing here?"

TEN

While he and Sarah lay face down on the cold, dirty ground, it became apparent that there were more animals in the undergrowth around them, and in the trees above them, than Franklin had realised. The woods seemed to come alive as several more violet-coloured beams streaked overhead, searing through foliage or thumping into the dark tree trunks with a resulting shower of sparks. Little creatures scuttled, bounded or took flight. So, Enceladine was not as dead as it seemed, but its fauna did hide well.

For a moment, Franklin found himself falling down the tunnels of time, tumbling backwards over a decade. Then, another violet beam struck the tree just behind them with an audible thud, the Koru's strange guns carrying a weight, an "impact" that no other compressed energy weapon he had come across did. He remembered that unexpected weight as if the battle for Earth had been only a few days ago, clearly visualising the larger beam that had wrought such destruction on Berlin. Again, he had a sudden sense of facing an old enemy, one that destiny seemed determined to put in his way, no matter how much he tried to avoid them. Perhaps this time he would die, and perhaps the Koru race would finally have their revenge on Mark Franklin.

"When was the last time someone shot at you?" Sarah hissed as the firing from below ceased for a moment.

"It was in a ship," Franklin answered tightly, as he had been holding his breath while the woods had exploded around them, "in the war."

"It shows," Sarah said with the manner of someone who had been shot at a lot more recently. Franklin wasn't offended; it would be a stupid thing to be offended about.

"Touchy about visitors, this lot," he quipped grimly.

"Don't forget that pistol you've got in your hand there, cowboy," Sarah said more patiently than the situation deserved.

Franklin glanced over at her and brought the weapon up. "You want it?" He had already killed one more Koru since leaving the *Olympic* than he had ever planned to kill again.

"Keep it," Sarah said, crawling sideways on her belly to find some partial cover behind one of the tree trunks. When she spoke again, it was with an affected Oklahoman accent. "I want me one of them guns." As if to illustrate the point, another beam strafed overhead, either vaporising or immolating everything it touched.

Franklin scooted after her, hoping that Sarah would feel like sharing her meagre cover with him. The shooting seemed to have stopped again, and, the smoke clearing a little, they could see three armed Koru moving around to the right, heading for a ramp that led out of the depression.

"Shit," Sarah said as she looked about them. The area had possessed little undergrowth even before half of it had been set on fire by the Koru weapons. "They'll be here any moment. Maybe we should just run."

Franklin took in a sharp breath and stood up, remaining a little bent over as he moved away from Sarah, finding another tree trunk—which was barely half his width—to take cover behind. Sarah hissed after him, asking him what the hell he was doing, but Franklin barely heard her. Instead, he found himself remembering the drill sergeant from his basic training with Earth Force—the same training that had to be undertaken whether you were planning to be an infantry soldier or a pilot—whose mantra about combat was "overwhelming but controlled aggression".

The Koru were now cresting the top of the ramp, had fired upon them without question or warning and did not have the look of those who wanted to take prisoners. It was too late to run, so Franklin took aim and stepped out from behind the tree.

The human who Engee had been put into a cell with, who had just spoken to her as if they should know each other, had the hint of a familiar accent, which went with his equally familiar light brown skin. "South Asian" came to mind unbidden—Engee had been having quite a few unbidden thoughts over the last few weeks.

What the hell are you doing here? the man had asked her, as if it was the last place in the galaxy he expected her to be. "I am not sure I exactly know where 'here' is," she answered him, finally deciding to sit down on the chair, which was next to a small desk. This room was larger and a little better furnished than the one she had previously been held in. Instead of concrete blocks, the walls were—like the floor and ceiling—carved from the slightly reddish rock. The man had an intense look about him. His eyes wide, he did not seem about to attack her and, even if he did so, Engee did not much fancy her chances of defending herself, even if she used the chair.

"You are kidding, right?" he asked in a strongly accented form of the English language. "It is you who told me about this place." He glanced sharply back at the door, as if to check whether the guards were listening. They weren't, but Engee was sure that her people could secretly bug the room if they wanted to.

"I... did?"

The man nodded slowly and came back into the middle of the room, his excited features relaxing just a little. There was something handsome about him, something distinguished, almost regal. Pieces were starting to fall into place in Engee's muddled brain, although they were not memories, only logical facts, pieces of a puzzle and, she was pretty sure she just happened to have the few pieces that gave enough of a clue to the whole picture. "I last saw you a little over three weeks ago," he said, "on Home Nest. You sought me out, do you not remember?"

"I do not," Engee admitted, "but I believe I know who you are."

The man frowned, confused and perhaps caught off guard by Engee's unlikely statement of the obvious.

"You are Mr Vikram Shah, husband to a woman named Sarah."

The thin, red CEW beam missed the Koru furthest on Franklin's right by no more than an inch, and he had time to sweep it across, dragging the searing beam across his opponent's eyes before his enemy had even a chance to react. The Koru dropped his weapon and clutched his face.

The other two were not slouches. They brought their weapons to bear. Franklin jumped to the right, just as the middle—now right-hand—Koru fired his thick, violet beam where Franklin had been only a moment before. He ducked down and performed a barely-controlled roll—because he lost his balance—as his attacker swept the beam across as Franklin had done. Unfortunately, the beam cut off more quickly than Franklin's little pistol would have done, even though it was a much larger, two-handed, rifle-like weapon, so Franklin's little roll did not save his life, after all. In fact, it made him look like he was in a comedy vid.

Coming up, he sent a second strafe in the general direction of his two remaining adversaries. It was a much clumsier shot than his first attempt, but Franklin got lucky and swept the beam—albeit far too quickly—across the shins of the same Koru guard who had just fired at him. They were only wearing light-reflective cloth. It was not going to be permanently damaging, but it was enough to make the guard cry out in pain and fall onto his knees.

The guard kept hold of his weapon, however, and Franklin would have, at best, just a few seconds before he recovered enough to shoot. There was also, of course, the matter of the third guard, who had been taking a bit more time about aiming and now had his weapon pointed quite squarely at Franklin.

Fuck it! Franklin thought, before realising that he had bellowed the words at the top of his voice as he rushed towards his adversaries. At least he had the little pistol up, although all his thoughts were about throwing his body at them. Which was stupid, so he was probably about to get shot.

The blast came and, with seemed like precognition, Franklin twisted slightly at the same time, turning what could have been a significant melting of his ribcage into a glancing blow. Nonetheless, it was perhaps the most painful thing he had ever felt in his life. All the Koru had to do was twitch to the left while the weapon was still firing, and Franklin would be out of this fight… and, quite possibly, out of existence.

A dark blur flashed out from the periphery of Franklin's vision as he tackled the Koru to the ground with an audible crunch. It was Sarah, who, although far from tall for a human, still had a height and weight advantage over your average Koru. Not that Franklin would ever have reminded her of that.

Despite the wound, momentum carried him forward, just as the kneeling Koru he had shot in the shins straightened enough to receive a right-footed punt in the head. Franklin watched with fascination as his ex-wife drove the Koru guard's head into the ground several times until he was either unconscious or dead. Couriers needed a varied skillset, so it seemed.

He staggered for a moment, remembering the blinding pain in his side, but the first Koru that he had shot in the face was making doing so difficult, as he was shrieking incessantly, so Franklin shot him again, a strange numbness coming over him. Unlike during the fight outside of Emma's shop, he made a completely conscious decision to end a Koru life.

Sarah stood up, a short-nosed Koru rifle in her hands, and she finished off the other two with a cold, emotionless look on her face.

"Couldn't leave them alive," Franklin muttered as they turned to each other. Sarah nodded, but something in her eyes made him think that she hadn't been through any such thought process herself.

"Might not matter if a hundred more coming running out of there in a minute," Sarah said, looking back down towards the depression. The almost a dozen workers they had seen milling around the entrance to the tunnels earlier were now nowhere in sight. Franklin could not decide if that was a good thing or a bad thing.

"What now?" he asked, looking down again at the dead koru that was his responsibility.

Sarah glanced down at her own feet, where two more lay dead. "I'd say we've come too far, wouldn't you?"

"It's too far to go back for help," he agreed reluctantly, "that's true."

"And if Engee is still on this planet, then this is our best bet." She used the Koru rifle to point towards the tunnel openings.

Franklin picked up his fallen adversary's rifle, the one who hadn't even gotten off a shot, tucking the Black Arrow pistol that had seen him good so far away. "Okay, let's do this."

Arnold could feel Lieutenant-Commander Yelland staring at him again. He didn't need to see his second-in-command to know he was stood with his arms folded across his broad chest. The man had one of those absurdly shaped bodies that looked like someone had tied a cord too tightly around his waist, making it far too slim, and everything from around the midriff had been pushed upwards into an overly-wide chest that looked like it might just pop with the proper application of something pointy. As Arnold understood, it was a body shape considered quite attractive to the opposite sex. Which was fortunate, he supposed, because the rest of Yelland had the appearance of an oily turd.

It was Yelland's shift, yet Arnold had stayed on well beyond the end of his shift to oversee a course change back towards Enceladine. Yelland was put out, to say the least, especially as his captain was keeping him in the dark about the reasons for this highly unusual change of plans. He was likely hoping that Arnold was doing something that he shouldn't be, and Yelland did not want to miss the opportunity to snitch on the person he considered to be the only thing between him and "the top job."

Of course, Arnold *was* doing something wrong. There were schedules to be kept to, the *Olympic* was not his own personal runabout. He had received coordinates in a simple text communication, destroyed them once committed to memory—as instructed. It all felt very clandestine and... well, dodgy. Now he was stood above the sensor station operator, a junior officer called Stanley, looking desperately for any sign of the ship that he had been instructed to intercept. A Koru ship, so the message had told him.

"Can I help you, Captain?" Stanley asked. The young officer had been looking increasingly nervous over the time that Arnold had been stood above him.

Arnold squinted a little myopically at the huge sensor display and waved a finger at it. "Any way to increase the capacity on this thing?"

"I ran the diagnostic only last week, sir," Stanley insisted hurriedly, "and I can assure you-"

"I do not doubt its effectiveness, Petty Officer. Just... please indulge me. As our resident expert."

"Are you looking for range or sensitivity, Captain?" Stanley asked, the encouraging words seeming to help him regain a little of his composure.

Arnold thought for a moment. The *Olympic's* sensors were already attuned to pick up very small bits of space debris as they approached the ship. Nothing had been mentioned about stealth technology on this Koru ship but, like so many things, stealth on a spacecraft was a matter of degrees. The shape of a smaller vessel, the coating on its hull, subtle jamming technology... all of this could help to keep a ship off another craft's sensors, or at least reduce the range at which it would be picked up. "Sensitivity, I suppose. But at a longer range than the collision sweeps."

"It would help to know if you're looking for anything in particular," Stanley pressed. "What sort of size are we talking about?"

"Just see what you can do, Petty officer," Arnold grumbled a little shortly and stepped back.

Yelland appeared behind him. "Looking for something on the sensors, Captain?" his second-in-command asked in that solicitous tone of his.

"Hmm," Arnold grunted non-committally.

Yelland leaned forward and pointed at the representation of the planet that they were heading back towards, Enceladine. "There's a planet there, you'll see." Somewhere behind the two of them, Arnold thought he could hear one of the other bridge staff snigger.

"A good job they cover the basics at the academy," Arnold replied, trying to inject at least the tiniest note of humour into his voice, which was hard between his gritted teeth. *Arrogant whelp.* Yelland was less than five years out of the academy on Proxima. In most cases, being second-in-command of a ship so soon—even one like the *Olympic* on its backwater run—would have indicated the brightest of talents. Arnold, however, had already come to understand that Yelland's talents revolved around his ability to place his lips on the correct boot.

"Focus on the planet," Arnold whispered to Stanley as Yelland withdrew again. His onerous second did have a point. The Koru craft was most likely going to be coming from Enceladine. There was nothing else anywhere nearby. He couldn't ever remember seeing a Koru craft come or go from the planet. It was an event to see one flying through the sector at all, as most Koru that did travel through UTC space did so on UTC public transport, like the *Olympic*.

"We're looking for ship traffic, Captain?" Stanley guessed.

"We are, indeed, Mr Stanley. But... like I said, any signatures that catch our eyes. Anything out of the ordinary, or too ordinary, or..." Stanley raised his eyebrows. "You get the picture," Arnold finished uneasily.

What the hell was he doing here? Pulling the *Olympic* off-course on the say-so of people who hadn't even given him their names. Did he not want to have a career anymore? And yet, Arnold had always harboured a nagging doubt about the Koru, whose forces had so easily overrun the Earth's own—and the victor, the Proxima-led rebellion that had become the heart of the new UTC, had ships and military technology that was similar to that of Earth's. Maybe, just maybe, this Koru ship would have an answer for him, some proof that the Koru were not the benevolent, vaguely disinterested neighbours that everyone assumed.

ELEVEN

"Sarah was using you to try and find me?" Vik asked Engee.

"This is correct," Engee confirmed with a small inclination of her head.

Vikram Shah was still showing an expression that Engee was becoming familiar with as one of confusion. "I was not aware she knew that we had met."

"She was not," Engee informed him. "Nor was I."

He was still on his feet, pacing slightly, as if the revelations Engee had provided had filled him with too much energy, so he needed to work some off before he could be still. Vikram Shah wore an extremely grubby, white suit, which gave him the appearance of someone who might have been hanging out in a casino or perhaps the lobby of an expensive hotel—before he ended up in his jail cell, that was. He poured some water into a cup and offered it to Engee, who accepted. "A lucky guess then?" he asked, sounding understandably doubtful.

"She picked me up in an orbital maintenance pod beyond the Lagrange Point of Home Nest," Engee explained. "I could not remember how I got there and was almost out of air. She rescued me."

Having poured himself some water, Vik finally sat down on one of the beds—presumably the one he had been sleeping on, as it had a half-made look to it. "The last time I saw you, you did not have any memory problems." He gave her another searching look, incredulity played across his features, obvious even to Engee's untrained eye. "You really don't know who you are?"

"I am NG-972," Engee answered simply. "I am administration-type."

Vik shook his head, leaning forward on the bed, the cup clasped between his hands. "You are so much more than that," he told her. "You, NG-972, are a revolutionary leader."

Engee blinked, an unpleasant and unfamiliar feeling beginning to burn somewhere inside her chest, sinking down into her stomach. A dozen questions raced into her mind at once, but she did not get to ask any of them, because that was when they heard the shooting.

Franklin and Sarah had come down into the depression via the same walkway where the three Koru guards had earlier left from. It was an open route but was also the only one. Reaching the bottom, they saw a craft—a little smaller than the *Mutt's Nuts*—tucked into another overhang on the opposite side of the clearing from the tunnels. Its back was open and there were crates visible inside. The reddish-coloured rock and earth were at odds with the landscape they had seen and travelled through so far on Enceladine.

The approach towards the tunnel entrances felt terribly exposed, with nothing of any size to hide behind as they crept along, below what had become a sunny sky on Enceladine, now the snow had passed. However, the tending-towards-orange ball of the system's star was beginning to fall low in the sky behind the tunnel entrances, making them appear even darker than they might have. At any moment, Franklin was expecting violet beams to lance out from the inside, to feel an instant of agony, and to be no more. But it didn't happen. The eerie silence and emptiness of the broad, crater-like depression should have been a good thing, yet it was fraying his nerves as much as weapons' fire and chaos would have. Well... almost.

"Maybe they were the only guards," Sarah hissed across as the entrances loomed less than twenty-five metres away. "An operation like this, they must be working to a minimum to try and keep attention away."

The gall that the Koru had to just turn up and dig holes in someone else's planet made it seem to Franklin that the chameleon-like alien race may not give a damn. But yes, Sarah might have a point, one that became more plausible the longer that no one else shot at them. Then again, perhaps there was a whole detachment of Koru soldiers somewhere below their feet.

They could sneak over to the ship and steal it. That could be a plan. Whatever was in those crates could well have an answer for them about what the hell the Koru were up to on Enceladine. Maybe people needed to know. Despite his desire to rescue Engee, Franklin's recent brush with deadly combat was helping to remind him that they were only assuming that Engee was in there. His "Let's do this" bravado from a minute or so before had quickly faded, along with the adrenaline. "She could be in the shi-" he began, but Sarah held up a hand for him to be quiet.

Okay, I just want to be sure that the two of us assaulting the Koru facility all on our lonesome was still plan number one.

They neared the left-most tunnel and Franklin could see that the way it was carved out of the rock was quite specific—in large, curving cuts, the rock almost shiny beneath it. There were lights dimly visible now, a little way into the tunnel, although they were not bright enough to let Franklin see any more detail from where he was.

A sudden whirring noise came from a little way down the tunnel, and they both levelled their weapons at the sound. A dot of red light hovered there, less than a metre off the ground, then, a moment later, a similarly hovering mine cart resolved out of the darkness around it, coming towards them from down in the mine. The cart held what appeared to Franklin to be nothing more than rubble—a mixture of limestone grey and sandstone brown. Some sort of guidance system or proximity sensor on the cart "saw" him as he stood there—still hunkered down in a firing position, his weapon pointed straight at the cart like it might find some little hands to raise in the air—and the little autonomous vehicle manoeuvred around him, leaving the tunnel and quickly turning to disappear into the next one over.

Franklin shrugged at Sarah and began to move forward again, but she stopped him. She touched a finger to her lip, as if she were thinking, then pointed it into the tunnel. "Mine," she murmured, then flicked the finger towards the next tunnel, the one that the cart had gone back down into. "Refinery." Finally, she stretched the arm out a little to point at the furthest tunnel, over to their right. "Ops." She looked up at Franklin. "They'll be holding her in Ops."

The two of them turned to head across but were stopped by a violet blast appearing across the front of the tunnel they were exiting, coming from near the entrance to the third tunnel, which Sarah had supposed was "Ops". It slammed into the rock just beyond where they stood, sending out a shower of sparks and slivers of stone. The two of them ducked back again before the beam could find them. Franklin crouched down, risking a quick look around the corner. There were three Koru over near the third tunnel entrance. One was in half-cover by the entrance. The other two stood brazenly out in the open—and one of those was dressed differently and was large for a Koru. The two standing in the open saw Franklin and pointed their weapons towards him. He darted back into cover, feeling and hearing a weapon discharge hit the rock somewhere just behind him.

"Three that I can see," he told Sarah, looking around to find that she wasn't there. Looking further, he could see she had moved a little way into the wide tunnel; she looked like she was searching along the edges. "What the fuck are you doing?"

"Just keep them busy," she called back, making it sound simple, like perhaps he should just break out some juggling balls and impress them with a few tricks.

Not knowing how long he needed to keep them busy for, Franklin moved back to the corner and, holding the small Koru rifle in one hand, put his arm around the corner and pressed the trigger, waving it back and forth. The weapon was powerful, but its burst time was short, perhaps not even a second-and-a-half. Three distinct shots followed as he pulled back his arm and watched a small power bar on the side of the rifle creep back up.

The colour changed after about the same amount of time that he had fired it for—around a second-and-a-half—when the bar was only about a third full, then again when the bar was full. Franklin guessed that the first marker was when the rifle was ready to fire again. Compared to the Black Arrow pistol, this—admittedly—more powerful weapon had a much shorter firing time and at least as long a recovery. If he wasn't careful, he would give his adversary a chance to flank and hit him while he sat waiting for the thing to recharge. Small bursts were the way, although he fished out the pistol as a possible backup.

As if in confirmation that they knew better what they were doing, short bursts of fire began to streak across the tunnel entrance every second or so... perhaps covering fire while another tried to sneak closer?

"How long?" he called back, taking a small step backwards, waiting for an arm to appear around the corner and start strafing.

"You don't want to rush this shit," Sarah replied, "especially when it's alien technology."

Franklin couldn't resist it—what the hell was she doing? He risked a quick glance, but she was still too far back in the darkness to be sure. However, he could make out that she was crouched down and working with something on her lap.

Franklin took a deep breath and stepped out past the cover, keeping his head low and loosing off a few quick shots. He would have been pleased to see that none of the three Koru had tried advancing yet, if that hadn't been tempered by three more shots coming his way, one searing through his right sleeve and causing a small jet of pain to lance along his arm. He jumped quickly back, resolving not to try that again.

Looking down, Franklin found a red gash across his skin, seared black at the edges. Thankfully it was only about an inch and a half long, although that hurt like hell.

"I think I've got it," Sarah cried out from behind him. Franklin risked another look around to see her emerging from the dimness with a roughly rectangular package in her hands that had a small black and red cylinder sticking out of it.

"Watch out!" Franklin called, noticing that two more Koru were coming up behind Sarah, using another mine cart for cover. He aimed a couple of quick shots their way, missing in his haste, and they both ran back down into the darkness, neither of them carrying weapons.

Sarah proudly held out the package she was carrying to him, and it suddenly dawned on Franklin what she was doing.

"You're fucking nuts," Franklin told her.

"Desperate times." Sarah grinned at him as the mine cart came level with them and turned to head towards the middle tunnel and what was presumably the processing centre. "I have no idea if this is even going to work."

She ran out, using the mine cart for cover, and Franklin followed her, shooting a quick strafe to keep their opponents' heads down. Then Sarah threw the thing that was in her hands, which was basically a brick-sized block of explosive.

On the bridge of the *Olympic*, Arnold had wandered back over to stand behind Stanley again, knowing that he was loitering impatiently over the poor scanning officer but unable to help himself as time was passing and the ship he was expecting had yet to show up. At least Yelland had finally agreed to take a break after much encouragement from Arnold, because he was fed up with feeling his second-in-command's eyes upon him. But, of course, sending Yelland away had only made Arnold seem even more like he was doing something untoward. He was also, rather disconcertingly, becoming aware of the fact that there were factions on his bridge. Yelland may have gone but there were still suspicious eyes upon him when he looked around at one or two of the other officers.

"Did you see that, Captain?" Stanley asked, pointing at the display in front of him.

Arnold had seen it—a sudden flare on the wide view that Stanley had quickly and expertly zoomed in on to show what now appeared to be a small cloud of smoke some kilometres to the north of the main settlement. Small was, of course, a relative term when you were looking from hundreds of thousands of kilometres away. "An explosion?" Arnold asked, even before the junior officer had a chance to move a replay of the event across to a different part of his display.

"Looks that way, sir."

"How big?" Arnold asked as he watched the replay begin and saw a bright, flaming flare appear briefly on the landscape.

Stanley shrugged a little. "There's not an awful lot out there to compare it with, Sir." The nearby trees are the best marker, so guessing that they are average-sized trees as I would think of them, I would say it was big enough to level a small apartment building. Or at least put a damned big hole in it, sir."

"No buildings out there to blow up, though," Arnold mused.

"One over by the lake, perhaps," Stanley said, pointing to a small rectangular point on the grainy image.

"Is this our maximum magnification?" Arnold asked. The picture was already grainy and, although the sensors had some ability to look through light cloud, they were lucky that the earlier heavy weather had cleared up, so they could see what was going on.

"That's as good as it gets, unless we move closer to the planet."

Arnold rubbed his chin, then let his forefinger move up to smooth his moustache. "Not yet, Petty Officer. Let's just see what happens."

TWELVE

For a time, it had seemed like the explosive wasn't going to go off. Long seconds had passed as Franklin and Sarah had continued to follow the hovering mine cart as it moved serenely forward and began to turn towards the second tunnel. There was no shooting coming back their way, which could be considered a bonus.

Franklin imagined the Koru scrambling for cover, or perhaps just staring at the explosive, frozen with horror. He thought about peering back around the mine cart and seeing if the opportunity to dispatch one or two of his enemies might be presenting itself while they were distracted. Funny—but not funny at all—how quickly combat gets one used to the idea of killing again.

Before he did that, however, a second thought came, one where the explosive went off and he was facing it with no cover at all. In fact, a third thought quickly followed, where they were hiding behind a mine cart that was more likely to flatten them than protect them if that explosive was any more powerful than a small antipersonnel grenade. Which it sure looked like it was.

He had glanced across Sarah, who was already looking back at him, an expression on her face that suggested she might be having some of the same thoughts that he was having—and perhaps reconsidering a few recent choices. Franklin was fairly sure that the cylinder Sarah had pushed into it was some sort of timed detonator, which she could have placed incorrectly, or perhaps set the timer for two hours by mistake. Who knew?

Instinct took over in the end, and they both ran from behind the mine cart, waiting for the searing pain of a violet beam to hit them in the back. Instead, a heartbeat later, everything went white.

"What the...?" Franklin now managed to ask. He couldn't see anything, but then again it was possible that he didn't have his eyes open. Somehow, he couldn't feel a thing, and yet, at the same time, it seemed that he hurt all over.

"That was... bigger than I thought," Sarah groaned from somewhere close to him. A wave of relief hit Franklin as he heard Sarah's voice, a wave that he might have found shockingly big had he been in any state to think about it.

Franklin was lying on his back, even though he had been running away from the blast when it went off. He tried again to open his eyes and pushed himself up a little, although only his neck seemed to want to move at first, and his eyesight was still mostly filled with white. "You okay?" he asked. It was the question to ask, although, at the same time, it seemed a wholly inadequate two words in the face of what had just happened behind them.

"Ask me again in ten minutes," Sarah said with another groan. He could feel her moving close to him, perhaps getting to her feet. With a herculean effort, he managed to get himself halfway up towards a sitting position and continued blinking his eyes, his vision now at least giving him the occasional impression of a lot of collapsed rock somewhere in front of them.

Franklin continued to blink away the afterimage of the explosion, searching to see if there were still any Koru with weapons stood close to where they had been by the entrance. He became suddenly aware of a large shape just behind him and looked back to see the half-wrecked mine cart on its side. A memory from moments before suddenly came back him, of a dark presence in all the whiteness arching briefly overhead.

"Are they dead?" Sarah asked as she found her salvaged Koru rifle and waved the end of it back and forth across where the enemies had so recently been, as if daring any of them to emerge and start shooting again. Some of the overhang had collapsed down and at least half of the third tunnel entrance—the one that Sarah had supposed to be Ops—was now concealed. It seemed most likely to Franklin—his eyesight now mostly coming back—that their erstwhile opponents were somewhere under all that rubble.

"I didn't mean to..." Sarah began almost apologetically.

"Let's get in there," Franklin said grimly, finally getting to his feet. If he had felt doubts up to this point, it somehow now seemed that they had gone too far to turn back, had done too much not to take this too its full conclusion. They had to fully search the mine and find out if the Koru had Engee in there somewhere. He hoped they wouldn't have to kill anyone else trying, but they were set on this path.

Franklin looked about for his rifle and found it in a sorry-looking state a couple of metres behind him. The hardy Black Arrow pistol was close to it and still looked to be in working order, so he picked it up, slightly reassured by the feel of it over the more powerful rifle.

The pile of rubble was still shifting as they moved around and over it. There was a moment when Franklin thought that the top of it might collapse down on them as they crossed towards the third tunnel entrance. He glanced back when several Koru from the first tunnel—the ones who had tried to creep up on Sarah as she prepared the explosive—came out and began shouting at them. None made a move to get too close, though, perhaps because Sarah waved her rifle back towards them threateningly.

Inside the third tunnel there were more lights than there had been in the other two, although one wasn't working and the rest were flickering on and off. Dust seemed to fill the tunnel, making it even harder to see far, and every now and then a few shards of something rock-like dislodged itself from the ceiling, bringing with it the constant fear of being brained by the stuff, which was becoming more reddish—almost orange—as they moved further in.

After about fifteen metres, they came to a right-hand turn and, just after it, was a door that looked very much like a cell door to Franklin. It was shorter, in the Koru fashion—thank goodness the tunnels were just about tall enough that he didn't have to crouch—and Franklin cautiously leaned forward and pulled back a sliding section in the middle of it to allow him to look inside. The room beyond was dark, and he couldn't make out much.

"Anyone in there?" he tried quietly. No answer.

"Fuck this," Sarah said, taking a step back and then shooting the door with a powerful Koru CEW. Franklin found himself dancing back as sparks erupted from the door.

"For crying out loud," Franklin exclaimed, "we don't want to kill her if she's in there!"

Sarah stepped forward and gave the door an experimental kick with the underside of her boot. "Didn't work, anyway."

There was the "slap-slap" sound of someone running along the corridor towards them and Franklin spun around, his weapon ready, as a Koru apparated out of the dust and darkness. The Koru—a small female, no bigger than Engee but, unfortunately, not Engee—stopped when she saw him, her opaque eyes going wider and hands coming up in what appeared to be a universal gesture of "Don't shoot me!"

"Where are the prisoners?" Franklin shouted at her.

The Koru appeared to look back quizzically at him, head tilting to one side in another gesture that made her seem more human than anything else.

"Prisoners!" Franklin growled, as if his aggression was going to aid understanding.

The Koru cowered slightly and pointed back down the corridor in the direction she had come from, all the while trying to edge round Franklin and Sarah. Perhaps shouting louder had worked, or else just terrified her into pointing the way she wasn't going just to get rid of them.

They carried on in the direction indicated—the only alternative to heading back out—soon finding that less of the lights were working and less of the time, so that there were moments of almost complete darkness, punctuated by flickers of a murky dimness. Finally, they came across two more rooms, both looking like operations rooms or offices, maybe doubling up as accommodation. There were low-slung style beds in both of them, the type almost universally used by Koru as Franklin understood it. The corner came to a crossroads, and Franklin and Sarah looked at each other.

"Any ideas?" Sarah asked wryly.

Somewhere behind them, there came the sounds of activity, of footsteps and quiet chattering. Perhaps reinforcements coming from the processing tunnel, or those from the mine having finally worked up the courage to face them—likely after procuring some weapons.

"Let's just keep going," Franklin said, glancing back in the direction of the noise. He crossed the intersection, moving off into almost complete darkness.

"Engee?" Sarah called out. "Engee, are you here?"

Franklin was incensed. "For crying out loud, do you want to bring every Koru down on us?"

"No, friend Sarah," came a voice from further on down the corridor, "I am not there, but I am here. In the prison cell!"

Franklin tried not to look at Sarah for fear of seeing the smug expression that would be there on her face. He was not going to hear the end of this.

....

"Engee?" came the voice from somewhere outside of the cell. "Engee, are you here?"

Vik, the man she had been sharing the cell with for the last half a day or so—Sarah's missing husband—snapped his head around, his eyes briefly catching the amber light from the desk lamp, as the main lights had been flickering and, about a minute ago, cut out. That had been just after Engee's interrogator, the tall Koru who loomed over her and first grilled her in the other cell, had run into their cell carrying a weapon and hurriedly locked the door behind himself. Which, in turn, had been a few minutes after the sound and vibrations of a large explosion that had followed what might have been the distant report of weapon's fire.

"Everything okay?" Vikram had asked their visitor. A reasonable question, although Engee noted the inflection Vikram had used when he asked the question. She thought it similar to something that Sarah had once called "sarcasm."

"Quiet!" the interrogator had commanded in a quiet but insistent voice, waving his gun and retreating into the corner of the room, looking nervously at the door.

Now, having heard Sarah's call, Engee felt brave enough to defy the interrogator and his waving weapon. "I am not there, but I am here. In the prison cell!" she called back, then turned to the interrogator, who was—as Sarah would say—glaring daggers at her. He had not yet, however, shot her. "See," she said. "I told you I had friends."

Franklin burst into the cell and found Engee, a South Asian man and a Koru male—the last of them with his hands in the air, a weapon dangling loosely in one of them.

"Do not shoot me," the Koru male said. Duty was a strong concept for the Koru, especially those performing any sort of military role. Despite their tendency towards what sometimes seemed like a hive mind, he knew that your average Koru still had a strong sense of self-preservation when it came to matters of life or death, yet Franklin couldn't help but wonder how well this particular level of cowardice might go down with the "higher-ups." He was in the cell with Vik and Engee, possessing a weapon, he could have made life a lot more difficult for them than he had. In fact, the more Franklin thought about it, the more this potential hostage now seemed like a gift.

"This is my interrogator," Engee said, introducing the other Koru like she was presenting her fiancé to them. Franklin almost found himself saying, "Pleased to meet you."

Sarah let out a gasp and ran across to Vik. In fact, it was more than a gasp, it was instead like an ecstatic groan, as if weeks of tension were being let go of at once... which they probably were. The sound set off a strange feeling in the pit of Franklin's stomach, which grew stranger still as he saw Sarah throw her arms around her husband, all trace of the explosive-wielding, hardened ship's captain gone for the time being.

Husband and wife drew apart, and Vik seemed to spot Franklin for the first time. Even as a prisoner, with a patchy beard and in clothes that were in dire need of a wash—albeit a white lounge suit that looked pretty damn good on him—the other man still managed to exude an air somewhere between dignified and dashing.

Vik's eyes flicked back to Sarah, something like an amused grin playing about at the corner of his mouth. "And you brought your ex-husband to rescue me."

Franklin was sure that he was supposed to feel offended, was searching for a comeback of some sort, when Vik stepped across to him, a hand out to shake his.

"Vikram Shah," he said. "Big fan."

"Fan?" Franklin parroted dumbly, caught a little off-guard as he limply took the offered hand.

"Yes, of the way you single-handedly blew up the biggest largest ship ever encountered by humanity, saved Earth from total annihilation and all that."

"Oh... yeah... I was on the other side in the war. You know that?"

"Heroism is heroism," Vik told him, "whoever does it." He glanced across at the Koru interrogator, who seemed confused by the whole scene. Engee chose that moment to move over and relieve the larger Koru of his weapon. "We should respect our enemies first and foremost, no?" Vik went on, slapping his free hand onto Franklin's shoulder. "Not that we are enemies anymore, of course."

Not even if we've both loved the same woman? Franklin wondered. But damn, there was something about this man that was darn hard not to like. *And* he had referred to Franklin as being Sarah's *ex*-husband, which was more than she would allow him.

"Are you planning any sort of escape?" the Koru interrogator inquired, almost as if he was reminding them of the traditional next step in a rescue of this kind.

Engee looked towards the door. "They are coming," she confirmed. "It sounds like all the workers have come from the other tunnels. There will be many to get past."

"Oh yes," Franklin told the Koru interrogator with a grin as he walked over and behind him, lightly placing the end of the little pistol to the base of the Koru's skull. "That is where you come in."

THIRTEEN

"Captain!" Petty Officer Stanley called across the bridge.

Arnold Philby had been on the brink of giving up. As the hours had passed, he had been feeling more and more like a fool while the space around Enceladine stayed eerily empty. It reminded him what a minor backwater planet it was—a backwards place whose population shunned space travel for themselves. What of any importance could be taking place here?

How long could he keep the ship where it was—behind schedule, many of its passengers with destinations to be at? The bridge had already received several official complaints from passengers, all of which would need an official response and also need to be logged and reported to his superiors at the end of this circuit. He was going to lose his damn job helping these mysterious people.

The *Olympic* usually rolled around the sector at a sedate pace. Of course, it could speed up and, eventually, make up the lost time, but even then there would be an increased fuel cost in doing so which, again, someone would have to answer for.

As he hurried over to the sensor station, Arnold eyed Yelland, who had returned to the bridge less than thirty minutes before, wondering if the man would be making his own report to their superiors at the end of this particular tour.

"A ship launched off the planet," Stanley told Arnold when he reached the sensor station. "It has some company just behind it," the petty officer went on, "and it looks like they are shooting at it... Yes, definitely an energy discharge."

"Can you ID the ship being chased from here?" Arnold asked.

"I'm not getting a transponder, hold on." He zoomed in on the screen, struggling to sharpen the picture, which was difficult as the ships were mere distorted blobs racing along in the planet's shadow. Stanley hit a button and froze the image, zoomed in a little more on the larger, leading ship and started a database search.

"Thought so," Stanley finally said in triumph as a name came up. The *Olympic* had a comprehensive database of every ship it came into contact with and, for no reason Arnold had ever understood, astonishingly sophisticated recognition software. "That ship was on board until yesterday, Captain. It's the er..."

Stanley paused, thrown by the name. "*Mutt's Nuts*," Arnold finished for him, had somehow known before the name even appeared on the screen.

"Yes, sir," Stanley said, blushing slightly.

"And what ships are those ones firing at it?" Arnold knew that the Enceladines had no ships of their own. Moreover, the kind of ships that carried weapons on them would be exceptionally rare in the spaceport that the indigenous race ran for visitors.

"No transponders, either," Stanley told him. All three ships were heading in their direction and the sensor station operator caught another still image, only slightly less blurry than the one of the *Mutt's Nuts*. "They're smaller; I'll give them a run through the database again."

"Don't bother," Arnold told him. He knew that shape, it hadn't changed in the last decade as far as he could see. "Those are Koru short-range fighters."

"Koru?" Stanley looked back incredulously at his commanding officer, his expression caught between wanting to be respectful and deferential towards his boss and, Arnold understood, the extremely unlikely scenario he was proposing. "The UTC hasn't registered a Koru military ship outside their territory since the war."

"Bastards," Arnold hissed under his breath. What the hell were the Koru doing putting military ships down on a neutral planet that was, technically, suspended in UTC space. "How far around the planet does Enceladine space extend?"

Stanley shrugged. "I'm not sure anyone's ever really cared before," the sensor station operator answered, then smiled wryly, "not even the Enceladines."

It was a fair point, but there would be a number recorded somewhere, a place where Enceladine space ended and where this little part of the vast UTC empire—which wholly surrounded the planet—began. While those fighters were still in Enceladine space—no matter how they got there in the first place—Arnold had a harder time justifying getting involved. That said, the facts did not much change when they entered UTC space. He was on a civilian ship with no weapons and many lives under his protection. While he was considering the facts of the situation, the fighters were gaining on the *Mutt's Nuts*. He watched the main sensor station screen as the latest shot looked like it might have glanced the starboard side of the ship.

"What's going on?" came a voice at Arnold's shoulder. Yelland had noticed that something interesting was happening. Somehow, the presence of the man who was most likely to make this whole situation come out even worse for Arnold only made him feel even more decisive.

"Helm!" he called out, turning and ignoring Yelland. "Move us towards the planet, please. Quick as you can.

"Comms, hail *Mutt's Nuts* and tell her she has permission to dock. Also, set the clock for emergency opening of Bay 4."

The flight controls vibrated in Franklin's hands, as did the whole ship around it for a brief moment.

"What the hell was that?" Sarah barked, glancing nervously all about her. There were four seats in the cockpit of the *Mutt's Nuts*, two in front, two behind. While Engee and Vik occupied the rear two, Franklin had taken the controls at Vik's suggestion after they had dumped their stolen Koru vehicle and hostage near the spaceport. Sarah, of course, had insisted on at least occupying the co-pilot's seat.

Vik's suggestion that the ex-fighter pilot fly based on a feeling, he had told them, that the Koru had ships capable of pursuit in the area, and he had been proved right. Which made the decision not to swipe the little freighter full of whatever they had been digging out of the ground the right one. It had been tempting to relieve the Koru of their prize, to hopefully deliver whatever the ore was back to somewhere that it could be analysed. But it would also have been a more difficult ship to fly and quite possibly easier for the Koru to track. Who knew, perhaps the Koru even had the means to order a self-destruct at range? That would have sucked.

So, they had stolen a hovering personnel transport vehicle that seemed to be a variant design on the little mine carts—the Koru were ever economic in adapting one concept into many different uses—and crammed the five of them into it, remembering to swipe a sample of the ore on the way, and then risked the journey back to the spaceport. On the way south to Eir, the planet's largest settlement where the *Mutt's Nuts* was docked, they expected to be pursued by land or by air, or perhaps to be suddenly evaporated by a large energy weapon fired from too far away to be seen. But it didn't happen.

Franklin suspected their good fortune might have been due to a combination of their captive's apparent importance—or seniority, at least—and his cowardice, as Engee's interrogator had been keen to stress to all his subordinates that they had passed on the way out of the operations tunnel, and the quarry-like bowl beyond it, that no one should attack them. All militaries tended to be defined in part by their command structure and the expectation of subordinates to follow orders. This concept, however, permeated all of Koru society, so that even the lowly miners felt they were a part of the chain of command.

"That," Franklin now answered Sarah's nervous question about the vibration, "was a weapon striking the ship."

Sarah glanced sharply over at Franklin, as if that were somehow his fault. "Can you make it not do that?"

"I'm trying!" Franklin wrenched on the controls, pushing the ship into a twisting dive to port that it probably wasn't meant to undergo. He half-closed his eyes, waiting for a different vibration or noise that meant the *Mutt's Nuts* was starting to come apart. "Er... hang on everyone," he said belatedly, glancing around to see that the other three being thrown about in their seats like rag dolls. Engee, in particular, was looking rather ill, her cheeks puffed out like something was about to come out of them.

A comms speaker on the panel in front crackled to life. "*Mutt's Nuts*, this is the *Olympic*."

Franklin, levelling the ship out again, glanced out of the front viewport as if expecting the big liner to be filling the front of it. It wasn't, of course. It was supposed to be many millions of kilometres away by now, but the voice on the comms speaker was, like some beautiful miracle, trying to disagree with him. Franklin remembered the ship's little sensor display, something generic, low-powered and civilian, but on which the *Olympic* should be pretty obvious. There it was, a fuzzy dot right at the edge of sensor's range.

"This is the *Mutt's Nuts*," Sarah wheezed, as Franklin pulled the ship up and to starboard. He was mostly guessing about where the pursuing ships were, as the little courier's freighter was not well-equipped for avoiding the pursuit of military-grade ships from behind. They had some rear manoeuvring cameras but, if the pursuing ships started appearing in those, it really was all over.

"We're coming to you," the *Olympic* comms operator went on. "Clearance to land in Bay 4. Three minutes, fifty-six seconds and counting."

"Understood, *Olympic*," Sarah replied. "Thank you."

Sarah sounded relieved and Franklin was grateful for the unexpected lifeline, but he didn't know if they even had the thirty-four seconds, let alone the other four minutes. Sooner rather than later, one of the pursuing Koru ships would score a meaningful hit. The comm crackled to life again, a different, more familiar voice sounding over it.

"I would recognise that flying anywhere, Mr Franklin," came Arnold's clipped, British voice. "Stunning stuff. Now, let's see if we can encourage them off your tail."

Buoyed though he was by his old commander's words, Franklin did not know what else the *Olympic* could do. It was a weapon-less cruise liner with the comparative manoeuvrability of a snail. Franklin felt the controls vibrate as another beam from the pursuing fighters hit them. That one felt more significant, and Franklin was now worried that Sarah might have a hole in the back of her ship. Dammit, they should have kept hold of their prisoner. He pulled right again, spiralling in of corkscrew motion. At least the thrusters were still working.

"To the Koru fighter craft currently pursuing the small freighter above Enceladine," came Arnold's voice again on the comms speakers. Presumably, he was broadcasting on a wide range of bands, something that the Koru would be likely to pick up. "This is the Captain of the SS *Olympic*, currently approaching the planet. We ask you to cease and desist your attack on what is a UTC registered vessel."

"You think they care?" Vik put in from the back.

Franklin glanced across at Sarah, who cast a hand towards the controls he was fighting with. "Keep doing your thing," she told him. He half-rolled and then dove into what would become about a half-loop, hearing a cry of something like shock from Engee in the back.

Threats were all Arnold had, Franklin guessed, and he wondered how much a race that had almost run through all of Earth's defences with one—admittedly very big—ship would care about causing a diplomatic incident if secrecy about that mine and the ore were important to them. Still, they might be flying for their lives but, *oh my fucking God*, how alive did Franklin feel right now? Maybe he did not want to admit it, but he had missed flying like this so very much.

"We would also like to inform you that we have all sensors recording and broadcasting, and you are... around ten seconds from entering UTC registered space.

He rolled back out of the half-loop and continued to speed towards the *Olympic*, bracing as he straightened out, waiting for the next hit. It was amazing he had kept them off him as long as he had in a ship that was massively outperformed by them, but all this darting this way and that was not helping them get closer to the lumbering *Olympic*.

Suddenly, the two ships—which had been too close to register on the limited sensor screen—appeared again behind them. It worked, Franklin thought, they're dropping back.

A couple of final shots petulantly streaked past, both well wide of the mark, then the pursuit was over.

FOURTEEN

A war hero, an ex-spy, an activist and an alien walked into a bar. Gus, tending the war hero's bar on the *Olympic*, looked like he might be searching for a punch line.

Franklin, still dealing with their recent brush with death and the implications of the last day, just pointed towards the taproom-cum-storeroom, the door to which was beside the far end of the bar, and the four new arrivals hurried towards it.

"You're welcome for me looking after your business and keeping your bar running," Gus grumbled sulkily.

"A bottle of the 18-year-old special reserve," Franklin said, indicating a top-shelf scotch whisky that only ever came out for very special occasions, "and four... *five* glasses. I think you've earned a few shots of the good stuff."

Gus, mid-pour for one of the customers, raised a mollified eyebrow. "I'll bring it through in a moment."

Franklin paused in the doorway to the taproom, glancing back and around the bar. It seemed that a lot of eyes were on him—some obvious, some more surreptitiously. It shouldn't be surprising; the *Olympic* was some way off its normal route and they had arrived back at the ship with fighters hot on their tail. That little bit of knowledge will not have stayed on the bridge, or with the docking bay operators—perhaps it had never even been restricted to the ship's crew in the first place. Then the four of them had walked into the bar looking like they had just come from a warzone—dirty, beaten and bloodied.

He looked over at Gus again. "Put up the 'back in five minutes' sign when you bring the drinks through. Then, I'll... er, bring you up to speed." He owed the man an explanation, he realised, although perhaps Gus would rather not know.

Geoff the cat appeared from across the bar, his lithe body weaving between chair and table legs with the rhythmic precision of a slalom skier and dashed for the taproom door to make his way through it just as Franklin was closing it behind himself. The cat made straight for Sarah and wound his body and tail around her legs affectionately.

Looking at the other three in the room, Franklin thought they looked shell-shocked—even Vik, whom he had imagined, from the times he had seen him on newscasts and other media platforms, to be supremely confident and unflappable. There was not a lot of spare space between the crates and boxes he stored next to the post-mix and the real-ale casks that he brought on at some expense, whereas that *other bar* on the ship used post-mix beer to maximise profit.

"So, what do we know?" he asked, hoping the question would bring everyone around a bit, loosen them up—at least until the whisky arrived to finish the job. "What the hell is happening down on Enceladine?"

"The Koru are conducting an illegal mining operation down there," Vik said, his strong jaw set and his teeth grinding a little as he said the words.

Franklin rooted around in his pocket, pulling out the piece of ore that they had taken on their way out of the mine. "For this," he said, holding it up to the room.

Franklin had visited a transport museum as a child—the same visit that had first made him want to fly ships, although this was many years before he made the decision to join the military—and had seen a rebuilt steam locomotive, complete with a pile of coal that helped to power the thing. The ore reminded him a little of the coal, although its colour was more a dark grey than the deeper, richer black that he remembered the coal had been.

He remembered feeling an odd sense of wonder that these dirty, black rocks could be instrumental in powering such a vast machine like the steam train. His father had told him as he marvelled, that those little black rocks had once powered much of planet Earth.

Franklin now turned the piece of ore from Enceladine in the weak light of the taproom and it caught little orange flecks on the surface of the ore. These orange flecks were reminiscent of the rust-red rock and earth that had been most prevalent in the mine and there were hundreds of them that almost caused the surface of the little rock in his hand to shimmer as he turned it.

"What does it do?" Engee wondered out loud.

"It can be used to power an energy field," answered Vik. *There* was the confident, all-knowing guy that Franklin had been expecting, although he ruined things a bit by adding, "...somehow."

"How do you know that?" Engee asked. Although she didn't seem to be questioning the truth of what Vik was saying, as such, there was, nonetheless, a little incredulity in the way she asked the question. She could not, however, have been expecting the answer.

"You told me."

Just then, Gus burst into the taproom. He had a tray with the requested whisky and glasses on it. Everyone turned to look at him. "What did I miss?" he asked.

"The Koru have shield technology," answered Engee, the only Koru in the room.

Then she turned back to Vik, her usually smooth, alien face creased into a particularly human frown. "Did I hear you correctly?" she asked him, "You said that I told you."

"That's right. It's like I said back in the cell at the mine."

"That I am some sort of activist?" Engee asked.

"You are more than just an activist, NG-972. You are the leader of The Unbound, a rebel group looking to disseminate information more freely throughout Koru society."

Franklin watched Engee's face as she tried to absorb information and felt a deep pang of sympathy for her. She looked overwhelmed by the idea. From what he had seen of her so far, and her rather unassuming personality, he could see that the responsibility of being some sort of leader did not sit well.

"That is what you got when you hacked the core on Home Nest," Vik told her, "lots of juicy things, but the most important was the information on this secret shield technology that few outside of the upper echelons of the Koru military know about." He indicated the little bit of rock in Franklin's hand. "This has *got* to be something to do with it."

While Franklin was thinking that Vik was making a rather big assumption, Engee's brows creased even further. "Hacked?"

"You accessed the deeper levels of the Central Knowledge System remotely, without clearance." As Vik went on, Engee looked impressed with herself. "And that's why you contacted me and I came to Home Nest—you didn't know what to do with what you had because, as far as I've ever heard, no Koru has ever managed such a breach. You needed to make sure that someone could get the information out."

"So what happened?" Engee asked him, a little like a child eager to hear the conclusion to a story about someone else.

"I'm guessing they were on to you," Vik answered, "before we met. I was grabbed just after our meeting, and I wouldn't be surprised if it was the same for you too.

"They flew me off Home Nest. I may be a bit of an outcast these days, but maybe I was still too high-profile to be kept on Home Nest. It's your one planet, above all others, that is frequented by other races, especially the humans of the UTC. Too many eyes and ears if my government was looking for me. As for you... well, if you can't remember anything, then I can only imagine what they did to you."

The room was silent as everyone seemed to take in the implications of what could have happened to Engee, even the Koru herself.

"An artificial shield?" Sarah said, breaking the silence with a breathy, wonder-filled exclamation. "Considering what the Koru mothership was able to do to the Earth military last time around, I'm not sure that them having shield technology sounds like a good thing."

"We do not have another of those big ships," Engee said. Then she added, tapping the side of her head, "Well, as far as I know. Not sure what I know and what I do not know."

"And yet," Franklin noted, "you led Sarah to Enceladine, where the Koru are mining for the very stuff needed for that shield." He gave her a reassuring grin. "I think you might know more than you realise."

Franklin held up the piece of ore again. "So, what should we do with this?"

"We should give it to the UTC," Vik said without hesitation.

Franklin, despite thinking that he had a lack of prejudice where the UTC were concerned, failed to stop grimacing at Vik's comment.

Vik saw it. "It might wake them up to the potential threat the Koru pose. And, either way, they might find a way to refine it and get the shield too. I don't like arms races," he admitted, "but then this is more of a defence race, really."

"Is there a way for us to look into it ourselves?" Franklin suggested, feeling that he wanted to understand more about this supposedly remarkable ore before handing it over to the mighty and highly secretive UTC military.

"What about Regus?" Gus suggested, mentioning a mining planet that was the nearest human-inhabited world to Enceladine. "It's in the same direction that the *Olympic* is headed anyway."

"But it's a UTC facility," Franklin complained.

"Barely," Vik argued. "And former Earth, if you're that worried about it." Franklin could tell that his own aversion to trusting the UTC authorities was slightly ruffling Sarah's husband. Although everything that once belonged to Earth technically belonged to the UTC now, the reality was that UTC high command had only taken much notice of the interesting bits, and everything else hung in a sort of no-man's land that left them—for all intents and purposes—independent, with all the lack of central support that implied.

"And do we have any better alternatives out here in the McMurdo rift?" Sarah put in, likely playing peacemaker between the two men and their differing viewpoints.

"I kind of know station commander," Gus said helpfully, seeming keen to be involved. "Although I know his daughter even better. Just... don't mention that."

FIFTEEN

"I thought you were dead."

Sarah had booked herself and Vik into a cabin on one of the *Olympic's* passenger decks. Even by the standards of the aging liner, it was not the most luxurious accommodation available, although it was still a definite upgrade on the cramped crew quarters of the *Mutt's Nuts*. The flaking, gold-plated furnishings somehow made it feel homely, and the mattress on the bed was thick, the crisp, white linen genuine cotton, or so the tag said.

Sarah was worried about Engee and had almost enquired into a larger cabin. However, the diminutive Koru had insisted that she would be fine to return to the Mutt's Nuts if she needed to rest. Sarah had come to care for the strange alien in the last few weeks and wondered about the effect that her kidnap and brief incarceration would have had on her. Perhaps it would have been worse if she could have remembered the last time she had been captured, Sarah mused. Who knows what had been done to her then? And, if Engee could have remembered, perhaps it would have made being in the clutches of her government again at the mine all the worse.

Vik was clearly exhausted, as was Sarah. Not that she had anything physical in mind right now, as much as ripping his clothes off would have been a fantastic way to release a lot of fear and tension. But no, she had a conversation to finish.

"Must we do this now?" Vik complained as he sat on the bed, his jacket discarded over the back of one of the chairs and his shirt open to most of the way down his wonderfully hairy chest. *Dammit*, he was trying to distract with all that... manliness.

"Yes, we fucking-well must," she shot back at him, giving her passionate feelings a different form. She wasn't going to let her relief in having him safe stop her from doing this; it was a conversation that had been coming for much too long.

Vik had looked like he was about to say something, to argue possibly, because he was very good at arguing, he had made a career out of it. Instead, he closed his mouth again and looked suitably abashed.

"This has to stop," Sarah hissed quietly between gritted teeth.

"But I was right," Vik whined, sounding like a ten-year-old child.

"But that's not the point. I knew what you were up to before with that secret agent friend of yours and I said nothing. Out there taking risks you never told me about. I can't do this anymore."

Vik shifted his position on the bed forward a little, reaching an arm out towards his wife, who currently had the physical advantage and the high ground, as she stood over him, glowering down. The gesture was at once an olive branch and just a little bit of subtle manipulation. "Sweetheart," he said, imploring and smooth, "I had to go. The Koru are planning something, I know it. They are going to move against the UTC. So now, not only do we have something that looks like proof but, at the same time, a chance we might defend ourselves against it."

His fingers had lightly brushed hers, which were dangling at her side; then, just as she felt herself melt a little at his touch, his fingers withdrew and he stood and began to pace the cabin they were staying in.

"I'm not arguing with the benefits of the end result," Sarah's voice was calmer and quieter again. "But there's only so many times I can survive this Vik. The worry, the not knowing if I'll ever see you again or have to live with never knowing what happened to you. It's too much.

"Time is getting on, you're not a young man anymore and I'm not as young as I'd like to be. Courier work is not exactly the most stable, staying-in-one-place job, but I'm trying and I want a future with you that doesn't involve infiltrating alien governments and trying to get your damn self killed. I want..." She stopped, the word "children" somehow catching itself on the end of her tongue.

Vik turned back to her, his face now a picture of regret and, if it could be called such, submission. "You're right," he said with a twist of the mouth that she knew so well. "I've been a terrible husband."

She had heard this one before, it was Vik's equivalent of pulling the escape cord, or the handle on the ejection seat, his safe, agreeable exit from the argument. Yet, she found herself playing along. "The worst," she agreed.

He moved towards her and took her hands in his. "I don't know why you put up with me."

"Neither do I," Sarah pouted.

As it turned out, the extra space on the bed in the *Olympic's* mid-class cabin was going to come in useful after all. Yet, even as she lay down with her husband, Sarah did thought that she would give him an ultimatum once they brought this episode with the ore to its conclusion. Vikram Shah was going to settle down and become a responsible husband.

Engee had intended to go back to the *Mutt's Nuts*, largely because the inside of the ship felt safe to her—especially the tiny confines of her cabin, which was only a little bigger than the infant pods at the nurseries on Home Nest, where almost all the planet's children spent large portions of their day as their parents did their duty, getting back to work almost straight after birth for the good of the nest. She felt cocooned within her little cabin onboard Sarah's courier ship, feeling a little less like her people might, at any moment, grab her again; and remove this identity, as they had the last. She could remember how it felt to be a child but almost nothing of the adult she had become.

That fear had crept into her as she had sat for what had amounted to only a very brief time in the cell with Vikram Shah. The idea of a future of endless mind-wipes and new identities, of never again really knowing who she was, terrified her.

Engee had not returned to the ship, however, and now she found herself sat at the bar with Gus the other side of it. It was late and the place was almost empty—so different to when it had been packed with guests on her previous visit. It was a strange space when it was this empty, with all those chairs and tables that had no purpose. In a nest, there was little that did not perform its function all the time.

It was true that being with the muscular fitness instructor-come-barman—two jobs that were both unfamiliar to Engee—felt even safer than staying in her cabin would have done. Despite Mark Franklin's return to the ship and to his bar, Gus had insisted that his friend get rest, offering to keep running the bar for one more night at least. A good friend, Engee thought.

Gus had been persuasive—the biggest reason she was now sat where she was—and had talked Engee into trying some drinks at the bar that he called "spirits." It was a word that Engee thought related to death and the afterlife, as humans saw it. Looking at the first glass tumbler he had handed her, full of a clear liquid that Gus had called "gin," she had privately hoped she was not about to drink the essence of a dead person. The harsh, burning sensation that followed her first sip did nothing to reassure her that she hadn't.

"Come on," Gus had encouraged her, "drink the whole thing. It's only a single." She did as he asked, against her better judgement. Perhaps it was his bald head and strange facial hair that somehow made him so persuasive. More humans should try this, she felt.

The next drink that Gus poured her—a liquid just a shade darker than amber that seemed to capture much of the room's low light—was called "whisky." Gus watched her intently with his dark, intense eyes as she tried some of it, finding it was harsh, like the gin, but also finding that she liked the taste a little better. She held the glass out in front of her again for a moment, quickly swallowing the rest.

"Woah," said Gus, "you might want to slow down there."

"But you said...?" Engee began, confused. She slightly slurred the last word, her tongue feeling loose and floppy in her mouth.

"I know what I said, but I'm an idiot. You told me that you don't have any alcohol where you're from. Maybe you should take it a little easy." Gus looked at her curiously. "So, how is it making you feel?"

"A little peculiar," Engee admitted. "I feel like my cognitive function is being impaired."

"Yep. That's called 'being drunk'."

"Why is it happening?"

"Well..." Gus began, shrugging slightly, "technically, what you're drinking is poison."

Engee dropped the glass onto the bar, making a loud noise that caused everyone else in the bar to look at them. At least the glass didn't break. "You are poisoning me? Why would you do that?"

Gus looked around uncomfortably. "Everyone in the bar is poisoning themselves. That's what alcohol is."

Engee narrowed her eyes at him. "You humans are strange," she said, then considered the warm, pleasant feeling that was rising within her. "But I like it. And," she added, pointing at Gus and moving her finger in a circular motion, "I like you very much." She wasn't quite sure why she was telling Gus this, except it seemed like a sensible thing to do right then.

Gus smiled, his eyes seeming to slide over her. "I like you too, but tell me that one again when you're sober."

"Sober?"

"In the morning, maybe, when you wake up. If you are not hungover."

"We Koru do not need to regenerate in the same way that you humans do," Engee informed him.

"You don't sleep?" Gus asked her.

"Sometimes we temporarily reduce our consciousness."

"Sounds like sleep to me," Gus observed. "What do you do when you reduce your consciousness?"

"I like to solve problems."

"Oh... Do you ever dream?"

"Ah," Engee answered brightly. "Sarah told me of dreams. No, we do not. Sometimes there is just... nothing."

"Shame," Gus said, "you're missing out."

"I do not see why. What is the point in a dream if it does not happen?"

Gus poured himself a shot of whisky and lifted it to his lips, looking at it for a moment and then back to Engee. "You've got a point there," he said, swigging the drink. "What's that missing time in your memory like? Is it blank, like when you reduce consciousness?"

"No," Engee said, her slender fingers reaching out and relieving Gus of the glass as he was about to put it to his lips again. "Well, it was at first. Just nothing. But now, it is more like shadows. Dark shapes that I cannot see. But they are there."

"It must be hard, missing a whole part of you. How do you know who you really are?"

Engee raised the drink and stopped just an inch from her lips. "But it is also freeing, starting again. Sometimes, there is a part of me that does not want to remember."

SIXTEEN

Arnold's quarters were cold as he paced up and down the same stretch of carpet, even the warm beige and tan of the walls and furnishings seemingly tending towards blue at this cold, early hour. Then again, maybe that was just his ambient light setting. It was usually how he liked his quarters, especially first thing, as he found that being just a little cold kept him sharp, much more so than the mind-fogging comfort of warmth. Yet this morning, the chill seeping through his clothes, then his skin and into his bones, was too uncomfortable, almost to the point of distraction.

He knew that he should have gone and checked in with the passengers and the one crew member who had come off the *Mutt's Nuts* the previous evening. He should have seen if his friend was okay; or at least found Gus—who had been looking after Franklin's bar for the last couple of days—to get news. He was aware that they had a new passenger, an important figure; and again, given the circumstances, he should have presented himself, asked the pertinent questions and so on. Or, at the very least, sent a suitable subordinate in his place.

But he hadn't. He had, in fact, been avoiding doing so, because perhaps he wasn't sure he wanted to know what they had been up to. He also knew what certain people—those who had sent him back to Enceladine after years of never deviating from the *Olympic's* route—would be expecting of him. Being a casual member of a potentially treasonous club had been easier when he hadn't felt that much was likely to be required from him, that he would be far from any real action.

The incoming message tone sounded; the noise knocked Arnold from his thoughts, making him jump slightly. He looked up and noted that he did not recognise the ID on the call, which conversely meant that he was sure he knew where it would be coming from.

"Good evening, Captain," came Bennett's oily voice a moment before the image came through. He had been expecting the other man, Admiral Maxwell. Arnold noted that, familiar though Bennett's voice was, some of the solicitousness it had held before seemed to be missing now. Exactly as with his previous contact, Arnold could not make out Bennett's features on the call, as the light source in the room was dim and set at an angle, so that only a part of his face could be made out. It was like a weird organisation trademark, and it somehow—in his perfectly well-lit quarters—made Arnold feel a little exposed. He briefly eyed his old-fashioned desk lamp that had been a gift from his mother many years before and wondered how he might set it up to similar effect. Perhaps Bennett and Co. would think he was making fun of them if he did.

"Ah, Mr Bennett," Arnold answered, modulating his voice to contain an insane little wave of nervous amusement that his thoughts had caused to wash over him, "what can I do for you?"

Bennett didn't beat around the bush. "I understand there have been significant events this last day in your region of McMurdo Rift."

"Yes," Arnold agreed, "things have certainly been happening here." He was, of course, not naive enough to think that he would be the organisation's only source of information in the sector. Perhaps even on the ship.

"Is there any truth to the reports of an explosion on Enceladine?"

"Yes, that's right," Arnold answered equally casually. "It appears that there has been some destruction to a previously unidentified Koru facility on the planet."

"And do you know who carried out this attack?"

Although perhaps an attack was the most obvious assumption to make, Arnold nonetheless noted that there was no thought by Bennett that what had happened could have been an accident or, perhaps, something environmental. "Well... I have my suspicions."

When Bennett spoke again there was a slightly more dangerous edge in his voice, almost a growl. "The reason I ask, Captain Philby, is because it has been reported to me that there was a member of the *Olympic's* crew involved."

"Now wait just a minute!" Arnold answered, adopting an authoritative tone that on occasion his crew would have been familiar with, and wondering why Bennett and the other mysterious figure even needed him at all.

"I thought we had an agreement, captain," Bennett interrupted, his voice losing some of its edge and yet the menace from his words somehow increasing. "This is exactly the sort of thing I require you to let me know about *immediately*, so that we can work towards our mutual goals."

"Er... I..." Frustratingly, Arnold found himself stuttering. "I was, of course, going to debrief the crewmember involved," he finally answered, feeling very much like a subordinate having to explain himself.

"Good," Bennett said, although he did not sound mollified at all, "because I am certainly interested in what the Koru were doing on the planet, and I'm assuming this crewmember will have some insight."

"Right, "Arnold agreed.

"If it was, indeed, some sort of mining operation, then we need to know just what the Koru have been after down there, and if they have already got very much of whatever it was off the planet.

"I know you can't divert the *Olympic* back there again right now," Bennett added, for the first time perhaps showing some appreciation of the limits of what Arnold was able to achieve, "and we will be doing our best to get eyes on the ground, but you may just have the best answers right there on your ship."

"I will see what I can find out."

"Please do," Bennett confirmed, "these details may prove crucial to our ultimate effort." He then signed off without waiting to see if Arnold had anything more to add. Almost every call that Arnold ever made, whether on the *Olympic* or elsewhere, ended with some sort of logo appearing on screen, whether government-related or from a private communications company, but nothing came up on this call.

He walked back and slumped onto his couch, not enjoying the way his interaction with Bennett had left him feeling. He had always been part of a chain of command and never been troubled by being a cog in the larger mechanism, but at least he had always known something what the mechanism was. He felt out of control now, and just as keenly felt that he needed to get on top of the situation that was in front of him.

Arnold got up again and crossed over to his desk, bringing up information about Enceladine. He would, of course, have to talk to Franklin very soon, but perhaps he could arm himself with a little understanding first. He asked the computer to bring up a list of minerals found on Enceladine by highest occurrence and cross-referenced it with what was known to be present in the area around where the mine was, which was also close to two of the largest settlements, something that he wondered about. Perhaps relevant, perhaps not.

A list appeared on the screen, and, in a particularly helpful mood today, it seemed, the *Olympic's* system also attached some early, public-access reports on Enceladine. Arnold scanned them, reading between the lines a little bit to see them for what they really were—a typically human assessment centred around the idea of whether or not it might be worth insinuating a strong presence on this barely industrialised planet. Not exactly an occupation, Arnold understood, for he had been in the military for long enough to know much of how it approached the exploratory side of its role, but a friendly-faced, "bringing civilisation to the natives" attempt to take control of all their valuable minerals. In the event, it had been decided it wasn't worth the effort. Apparently Enceladine had little of great value and so had been allowed to remain relatively free of human influence, save for a boom in its tourist industry.

What the heck were the Koru after among this list of mostly very familiar minerals that was worth the risk of causing a major incident over? There were, not unusually, a few findings that were either unknown or assumed to be variants of other—essentially unremarkable—minerals and ores. But their properties would have been looked into at the time, it was the way things had always been done. He was going to have to speak to Franklin, as the bar owner and former pilot had actually been there, as well as to their notable new guest, the one-time star of UTC politics, Vikram Shah.

If ever there was a man who should have been an enemy to Arnold, he was it. He had been among the loudest voices in the movement for independence from Earth for Proxima and the other colonies. Had been at the centre of things during the war and in the immediate aftermath. Yet here he was, an outsider again. The lunatic fringe espousing mistrust of the same Koru race that had won the war for the UTC—an organisation which, to Arnold's mind was as centralised and empire-like as Earth had been, only centred a few light-years from where it had been before. Now this Shah man—the husband of his favourite bar owner's ex-wife, if ever the galaxy could be said to be a small place—was on his ship and espousing views that much more clearly aligned with... well, at least some of his own.

Arnold leaned back in the seat at his workstation and let out a long sigh. Yes, he needed to go and talk to them soon, but another thought came to him, something that had been nagging at him almost since the moment that Bennett's mostly unseeable face had appeared on the projected display in the middle of his quarters.

He got the computer to patch him through to the *Olympic's* security and surveillance system and, remembering as best he could, pulled up the footage for the time when he met first met Bennett. Arnold found himself and the organisation representative where they had been sat in a small alcove off one of the *Olympic's* thoroughfare corridors, having their initial chat.

What he found came as no surprise. His own image was plainly there to see, that familiar-yet-not-familiar aging face, because we are always a little different when not aware of being on camera—even though he was always on camera on the *Olympic*, save for right now, in his quarters—but nothing could be seen of Bennett's face at all.

He rewound through the surveillance footage, tracing Bennett's path through the ship before their meeting and then, not getting what he wanted, he went the other way and followed Bennett after their meeting.

A deep shiver ran down Arnold's spine as he got confirmation of what he already expected. There was no point in all of the footage where Bennett's face could be made out clearly, as if the man knew the position of every camera on the ship. Even more worryingly, he seemed to vanish both in the rewind and as Arnold moved forward through the camera footage. There was a point when Bennett just turned a corner and suddenly wasn't there anymore, as if he knew of a blind spot and how to exploit it. *Dammit,* Arnold had been captain of the ship for years, thought he knew it better than almost anyone else, yet he would struggle to know how to pull something like that off.

A kind of panic began to seize him, and Arnold started going into logs and into more of the ship's footage, the morning quickly disappearing on him. His idea to find Franklin and Vikram Shah temporarily forgotten, as he continued to be unable to find any other trace that Bennett had been on the *Olympic* at all.

The last thing he did before leaving the terminal was to finish the job, wiping the images of his and Bennett's meeting from the record.

SEVENTEEN

At first, Franklin thought the chiming sound was his alarm clock, and opened his eyes to realise that he had overslept by some order of magnitude. He was usually an early riser, although had never put it down to not being able to shake off the habits of military life, as some might. He had always risen early, unable to lie in bed, even if he had wanted to. Today, however, he had slept most of ship's morning away and someone was at the door to his quarters.

He had the feeling that the long sleep was probably something to do with his body's need to heal after suffering through a somewhat rough couple of days down on Enceladine. But, then again, there was another nagging feeling that he just didn't want to get up and face the consequences of that trip to the alien planet, a trip that looked to have thrown him right back into the middle of conspiracies and potential conflict with the Koru, over a decade after he thought he had left all that ridiculousness behind.

"All right, all right," he complained at the soundproof door to his quarters, despite knowing that whoever was on the other side could not hear his complaints. "It's not even midday yet," he added.

The door slid open to reveal his captain, one-time military commander and friend, Arnold Philby. Arnold looked Franklin and his state of undress up and down, with just a mild hint of amusement on his otherwise stoic features. "Morning, Mr Franklin, not interrupting anything am I?"

"It's many years since you would have been interrupting anything," Franklin quipped wryly, instantly recovering a little of his poise. He turned and waved for the *Olympic's* captain to follow. It did occur to him to wonder why Arnold—both as a friend *and* captain of the ship—had taken so long to turn up. Perhaps he had anticipated Franklin needing his rest.

Franklin found something that wasn't a bed sheet to dress himself in and then returned to find Arnold had settled himself into the only free spot on Franklin's sofa, between various piles of dirty clothes. His bar was spotless and well organised, and Franklin did have the virtue of being an early riser, but a tidy single man he was not. His quarters were mostly one long room, a kitchen at the far end and the bedroom off to one side, with a small en-suite shower room. He had never changed the regal blue and red colour scheme, even though he could have.

"So...?" Franklin began, inviting the questions he was sure were coming. "I would offer you a drink but, believe it or not, I don't have anything to offer you."

Arnold cast one raised eyebrow around but didn't pass any further comment. "So, I'm going to ask things as informally as I dare," Arnold began. "How do I put this...? Oh yes, what the hell happened down on Enceladine that has parts of the planet blowing up and Koru fighters chasing you?"

"All good questions," Franklin replied, trying to think of the best way to answer the man's questions. Perhaps he should have done more thinking and less sleeping before the captain of the *Olympic* had walked into his quarters. He wanted to be respectful of his friend, but Arnold was also responsible for the ship. "Remember my wife?"

"Yes, I saw her just a couple of days ago," Arnold answered, "and since then your life seems to have taken a bit of a left turn."

"Also a fair point," Franklin had to admit. "Well, she needed help finding her husband."

"Not usually the job for an ex-husband."

Franklin shrugged and nodded at the same time. He wanted to point out that, as far as he was concerned, they were still married. It did not, however, seem to be the time.

"Especially when that husband happens to be still one of the more controversial and influential figures within the UTC political system," Arnold added. "And this led to said explosions and potential diplomatic incidents?"

"Well, that's kind of the short version."

"And what else?" Arnold pressed.

Out of the corner of his eye, Franklin glanced over to where he had, rather carelessly, left the all-important piece of ore on his desk next to some half-eaten noodles. Then, having glanced once, he tried hard not to look again. "They were holding him at a mine," Franklin said, trying to figure the best way to give some of the truth, which he found to be the best way to lie.

"Okay," Arnold sighed, leaning back in his seat a little, "a couple more pretty important questions... What are they mining down there, and why the fuck did it blow up?"

Franklin chose his words carefully, "Well, we were there to get people out, rather than to ask questions."

Arnold's eyes narrowed suspiciously.

"But hands up to the other bit, we did blow some shit up on the way out."

"Blow some shit up?" Arnold repeated back to him, a little incredulously.

"There were a lot of explosives just lying around," Franklin told him, as if this in itself was just an invitation to set the stuff off. "So, there was a ship and, um... a few deaths."

"Are you just trying to start another war?" Arnold growled at him.

"A war," Franklin bristled, "the bloody Koru shouldn't have been down there in the first place. If anyone's starting someth-" He stopped, realising that Arnold was deliberately trying to get a rise out of him, hoping he might let something else slip. Cunning old fox.

Arnold got up, as if about to leave, but instead paced the small amount of space between the two of them in the centre of Franklin's quarters. After a few moments, he sucked in a breath and turned to look at Franklin. "I'm not sure how I feel about having that man on my ship."

"Which man?" Franklin asked a little stupidly. He knew which man.

"Vikram Shah. I would not usually be well disposed towards him, whoever he was, on account of him having married your ex-wife. ... Friends and all that." Arnold did this sort of informal camaraderie poorly at the best of times, but Franklin could feel that there was something heavier weighing on him. "But I'm afraid my mistrust of that man long predates his association with Sarah."

"I don't know," Franklin found himself arguing, surprised too, in a way, to be defending the man, "you might find that nowadays you have more in common than you would have thought. For one thing, he's quite mistrustful of the Koru."

Arnold raised his eyebrows. "I never exactly said I was, er... mistrustful." As captain of the ship, Arnold was very good at not extolling strong opinions, but Franklin had served with the man and spent many subsequent years around him. He knew.

"But you're right," Arnold went on, "like any sensible ex-military man who saw what they were able to do in the latter stages of the civil war, *of course* they worry me. It's not like they are humanity's most fully engaged neighbour, peace treaties notwithstanding."

Arnold's jaw set as he meandered back towards the door. Then he stopped, turning to Franklin again, his eyes piercingly hard all of a sudden. "You would tell me, wouldn't you?"

"What do you mean?" Franklin replied, again playing a little dumb.

"If you knew what was going on down there, on Enceladine?" Arnold said to him. "If you knew what they were mining for, what it meant, you would tell me, wouldn't you?"

There was something strange in the way Arnold asked the question, a kind of neediness that Franklin could not ever remember him appearing to display before. Like he would be genuinely hurt if Franklin withheld something from him.

"Of course I would," he spluttered out, a barefaced lie that seemed to come almost too easily, like he believed it just a little too much. "But, to be honest, I really don't want to know either way. I can't believe I got dragged into this business with Sarah in the first place. I don't know what's wrong with me."

Arnold laughed at that, a reassuring chuckle that sounded genuine to Franklin. Arnold Philby did not laugh very much, but it was an infectious sound when he did. However, as Franklin watched, the smile melted off his face in a slow, almost chilling way. "You know what?"

"What?" Franklin snapped back too quickly, unable to stop himself, yet he had an eerie feeling that he didn't want to hear whatever was coming.

"I just feel like we'd all be a lot safer right now if Earth still had more of a say in things. The UTC is too content to sit on its laurels."

Franklin held his expression carefully neutral, his eyes started to sting as he held Arnold's piercing gaze.

"Don't get me wrong," Arnold continued, "I know there was plenty wrong with our old empire, plenty wrong. But we *were* strong. Don't forget that Earth would have won the civil war were it not for the Koru. We were a mighty military power, and we knew an awful lot about mistrust. Still do."

He raised an eyebrow as if those words contained a heap of subtext that he felt sure Franklin would understand. But, worryingly, he did not. With that, the *Olympic's* captain turned and stalked out of the room.

EIGHTEEN

The first thing that Franklin did when Arnold left his room was to get up and grab the piece of ore, shoving it safely away on his person.

Then he waited ten minutes before he left and took a circuitous, indirect route to the cabin rented by Sarah and Vik. When there was no immediate answer at the door, he quickly rang a second and a third time, suddenly desperate to see and talk to the two of them, irrationally fearful for their safety.

"What's going on?" Vik asked when he answered the door, failing to mask a certain amount of irritation. He looked in a state of undress, husband and wife evidently being even slower about getting going this ship's morning than Franklin had been. He could not help but feel a tinge of jealousy.

"Something's not right," Franklin said, pushing past Vik and into the room, where Sarah was hastily putting on a robe. Despite the urgency of what he had come to say, Franklin felt a slight clenching around his stomach and chest, and he momentarily lost what he had been about to say. The air was riddled with the scent of two people sharing what was not a huge space, the scents at once familiar and unfamiliar to him in a way that felt like it was curdling in his gut.

"Yes?" Vik prompted, the door now closed behind him.

"The captain's just been in my quarters asking questions."

"But that's hardly unexpected," Vik told him. Then his eyes suddenly went wide, and he sucked in a worried breath. "You still have the ore, of course, haven't you? You haven't gone and done anything stupid like handing it over to him?"

"No, of course I haven't!" Franklin snapped back. "But there were things he was saying, they were getting me nervous."

"Nervous in what way?" Sarah asked worriedly, coming over to join them.

"I dunno, just being a bit odd. Talking about…" He paused for a moment, realising that blurting out their discussion to these two would be a betrayal of his friend, whose last thoughts in the conversation, if not exactly treasonous, were not befitting the captain of a starship. Considering the stakes, however, what they were dealing with, he could not keep potentially important things to himself. "He's talking about how much safer we would be from the Koru if Earth was still in charge."

Sarah raised a fierce eyebrow and huffed out her displeasure, while Vik only bit his lip. "So, you've got the ore here?" Vik asked. "With you?"

"Of course," Franklin replied, bringing the ore out from his pocket, although it was wrapped in one of his old, slightly smelly T-shirts.

"Does anyone know yet why they came back for us?" Sarah asked.

"I should have asked in my quarters," Franklin admitted. "Naively, I initially thought he was just worried I was in danger and came back to check."

"He brought a liner with thousands of people on board back for you?" Vik asked sardonically.

"Alright," Franklin blushed. "Exciting things were happening, I didn't really give it a proper thought."

Sarah looked to Franklin. "Do you think we should get off the *Olympic*?" There was something in the way she asked, he had to admit, that warmed him a little. The trust there, the belief in him, the need that she had to tell both her and Vik what they needed to do.

"Well, if we want to do that," he answered, "the mining planet, Regus, is not too far away. We were planning to go there, anyway, and the *Mutt's Nuts* will get us there just fine under its own power, a fair bit ahead of the *Olympic* if we want."

Vik frowned at Franklin. "You really think this captain friend of yours is going to betray us or something?"

Franklin shrugged. "I don't know anything for sure. I just know he was acting strangely and, like you pointed out, as much as he is my friend, I don't think he would have turned the *Olympic* around just on the wishful thinking that we were done with what we were doing and desperate for his help. And on Enceladine still.

"I mean, we were all of those things, but that why it's so weird. If you ask me—and this is a pure guess—someone sent him back to Enceladine. Someone who knew or had a good reason to think that we might have stumbled on something important."

"The Koru?" Vik asked.

Franklin barked out a harsh laugh. "No, I don't think so," he answered. "He's got no more love for them than you do."

"So what?" Sarah interjected. "Someone in the UTC? Someone else?"

"I'm only guessing," Franklin reiterated. "But isn't it just a little bit strange how the Koru have been able to run that mine on Enceladine without anyone noticing?"

"We're not exactly in the heart of things out here," Sarah pointed out. "But if Arnold knows something he isn't telling you... If I were in your place, I'd wonder why that was."

Franklin watched Sarah's expression change suddenly, turning inwards, retreating. "Look, Mark, maybe we've taken up too much of your time with this," she suddenly went on. "Maybe just me, Vik and Engee should take things from here."

Franklin felt a complex set of emotions crash in with Sarah's words. Panic and relief, the possibility of loss and the lifting of responsibility. The worrying idea was that he was not standing where he was for only altruistic reasons.

"You know what," he answered after what felt like an age, "there is still a big part of me that would like to just leave this to you, I'll admit that. But, if Gus is our best link to Regus, then I'm not letting him go with you and not coming along myself. No offence, but if he's getting into the middle of whatever this is, he'll be my responsibility." *Yes, Franklin, just keep telling yourself that. No other reasons.* "So, I'm in still, at least until after we've seen if we can get the rock analysis done there.

"And maybe the best thing to do is just get it over and done with. Jump on the ship and get to Regus as soon as we can. Although, if all of this with Arnold is nothing and I shut up the bar for no reason," Franklin added a little ruefully, "he is going to give me shit about all the annoyed customers who won't be able to get a drink."

Both Vik and Sarah smiled at that. "Should we try and get hold of Gus and Engee now?" Vik suggested.

Franklin and Sarah both nodded, each bringing out a T-Slate. After several long moments without answers from either of them, Franklin could see that Sarah and Vik were both looking as tense as he was beginning to feel. Finally, Gus picked up. He looked like crap. Franklin also noticed that he wasn't at the bar as he had promised he would be. "What time is it?" Gus groaned.

"I thought you were going to open up for me?" Franklin said. "You overslept?" Gus was usually an early riser and annoyingly chipper with it.

"I still can't get Engee," Sarah complained, sharp tension evident in her voice.

On Franklin's screen, Gus looked around, his unseen arm perhaps grabbing at an unseen tabletop. Finally, his hand came up, a small T-Slate in it. "Sarah's calling Engee," he remarked back towards Franklin.

"You've got Engee's slate?" Franklin asked, confused.

In the background a head snapped into view, as if suddenly sitting up.

"Engee?" Sarah screeched out, surprised. Her head had suddenly appeared over Franklin's shoulder, and she was peering down at the rather compromising scene on his handheld's screen.

"You didn't..." Franklin said, sounding appalled.

Gus glanced behind him and then back to the screen again. "It's not what it looks like. We just got a bit drunk, and..."

"That's exactly what it looks like!" Sarah raged at him, grabbing Franklin's T-Slate.

"No," Gus protested, "she was just too drunk to walk back to the ship, and it was much too far to carry her, so I let her crash here."

Sarah shot an evil glare and Franklin. "This is what happens when we leave her alone with one of your friends for a night?"

Franklin sighed, snatching back his T-Slate. "Look, Gus, I don't want to talk about it now, but I need the two of you to get down to the *Mutt's Nuts* as soon as possible. We'll meet you there."

"I don't see why we have to go this way," Sarah complained, "I thought getting the fuck off this ship was urgent."

They were heading along a corridor with a faded red carpet that was almost worn through in places. Reaching the door to Franklin's quarters, he took a final look up and down the corridor and thumbed his print onto the door scanner before it slid open.

"I had to come here for something," Franklin told Sarah over his shoulder as Sarah and Vik quickly followed him into the room. He pretended to ignore both husband and wife as they looked around at the mess with a certain level of distaste.

"You've got the ore," Vik said, "and we can pick up anything else we need on Regus. So what is it you need so desperately?"

As if in answer, Geoff the cat came running out to meet his owner, curling affectionately around Franklin's legs before allowing himself to be lifted onto a shoulder, where he balanced like an oversized, furry parrot.

"I'm not leaving without this little fella," Franklin said with a grin. "Who knows when we'll be back?"

"You came back for your cat?" Vik growled.

"I'd save this little guy before I'd save either of you two," Franklin said with a grin, then they headed back out into the corridor.

It was the middle of the day and plenty of people were moving around, although most of the people they passed were just passengers aboard the *Olympic*—sightseers or those with other reasons for taking the giant, almost opulent, bus that was the *Olympic* around the McMurdo neighbourhood.

They came to a fairly inane-looking door, painted the same blue as the surrounding wall and even with a latch handle built into the door, virtually invisible at first look. Franklin swiped a crew ID badge—something he got as the owner of the bar, even though he wasn't technically crew, which gave him access to parts of the ship that passengers were not usually allowed in, such as the emergency routes.

The door opened on a narrow metal stairwell, a service route that was rarely used by crew and only opened to the public during emergencies, the latch unlocking as part of an automatic procedure when the alarms sounded, a way to move around the ship if the lifts were down or unsafe to use.

Also, quite critically, there were no surveillance cameras in them. Entering them, Franklin felt, was like peeking behind the proverbial curtain, except that the *Olympic* was no longer all that magical, so there, the analogy sort of fell apart.

They descended the five floors to the hangar level and came out on a corridor leading up to Bay 4, where the *Mutt's Nuts* was berthed. Franklin started to relax a little, but just as he did so, he saw a member of the security team coming the other way.

"Franklin," Hultz said, a wary note below the forced cheerfulness. At that moment, Franklin knew that it wasn't by chance that Hultz was walking along the corridor. They were looking for him, which meant that Arnold was looking for him. A cold chill ran through. Why would his old friend, his old commander, be sending members of the ship's security team after them?

Dammit, he liked Hultz, and not just because the man was a regular at the bar. He was ex-military and, having twenty years on Franklin and with a little extra spread around his midriff, Hultz had an almost grandfatherly air about him. *Shit, why was it Hultz?*

"Captain says he needs a word with you," Hultz said, all smiles and with a posture that was desperate to look relaxed. Shit, maybe Hultz was hoping this was all nothing, but Franklin was starting to worry that it really wasn't. Franklin noticed his hand drop to the ballistic concussion gun at his side. He wasn't quite touching it, but the fingertips were only half a hand's breadth away.

"I doubt it," Franklin bluffed, playing for time, trying to think of a way this might not end in violence, "I only just saw him in my quarters less than twenty minutes ago."

"And I just spoke to him myself," Hultz answered amiably but firmly, "said you needed to be brought straight to him." Hultz coughed out a nervous, unconvincing laugh. "Not sure what the hell you've done,

Franklin. Not watering down the beer, I hope?" He eyed Vik and Sarah nervously.

Franklin thought he could see Vik fumbling with something in his pocket. He hadn't even noticed if either Sarah or Vik were carrying a gun and had left the little Black Arrow pistol that had served him so well during their time on Enceladine back on the *Mutt's Nuts*. He didn't really know Vik, didn't know how likely the man was to shoot this security guard who was only doing his job. The man was nothing to Vik. He had not sat on a seat at his bar day in and day out for years now.

Thinking quickly, Franklin lunged forward and punched Hultz in the face, sending him staggering backward, blood spurting from his nose. As Franklin had hoped, it took him a shocked couple of seconds to bring his ballistic concussion gun to bear, disbelief as much as pain probably playing its part.

Franklin darted forward again and grabbed Hultz's arm, twisting his wrist so that he let out a yelp of pain and dropped the concussion stick. "Point your gun at him, Franklin barked at Vik, "but don't pull the trigger unless you have to." *Don't bloody pull at all*, he thought with a sickening sensation in his stomach.

Vik fumbled to get the weapon out of his pocket, and what did emerge was quite a surprise. Projectile weapons were a rarity, although perhaps a little more common in the older, more remote part of human space, but the revolver that Vik held was positively an antique—or at least a pretty accurate copy of one.

"We need to take him with us," Franklin added, "or we'll never get the *Mutt's Nuts* out of the docking bay."

Franklin had known from the moment they had started dashing to get to the Mutt's Nuts and off the ship that, if Arnold Philby did not want them to leave, they were going to have to take some sort of action to get the bay doors open. Moments later, having used Hultz's thumbprint to get into the control room for Bay 4, Franklin, Vik and Sarah ordered the operator to set a rapid opening sequence ready to go.

A terrible feeling gripped him, the sickness in his stomach spreading through his whole body. Punching Hultz and forcing him along at gunpoint had been more than bad enough, but forcing a bay to open against the usual procedure was one step below space piracy. He saw his life slipping away from him and he still didn't really know quite what for. He would lose the bar, most likely become a fugitive and end up in jail.

Looking down into the bay, they saw Gus and Engee entering the bay and heading across towards the *Mutt's Nuts*, then ordered the controller to set the sequence going. The inner bay doors would be locked to entry in around thirty seconds from the start of the rapid opening sequence. In half a minute, they would be safe from pursuit.

With that, there was one more thing to do. Franklin turned towards Hultz, the ballistic concussion gun in his hand, and pointed it at his customer's head. "Sorry, man," Franklin said and Hultz started to raise his arms in protest just as Franklin pulled the trigger. The air rippled slightly in the low light of the control room, before the disruptive wave of energy knocked the security guard out cold. Then he turned to the control room operator, a woman who, thankfully, he did not know too well. "Right, now it's your turn."

Moments later, they were crossing the bay with the alarms of the release sequence screeching in their ears. Something slammed into the side of Franklin, almost knocking him from his feet and nearly causing him to drop Geoff, who was now tucked under his arm. The force of it set his head ringing and he looked over to see that two more members of the security team had made it into the bay before the inner door's one-way lock had cut in. He had been hit by a blast from a ballistic concussion gun, but luckily the extreme range had saved him from the worst of its effects.

The three of them dashed up the ramp into the cargo hold of the *Mutt's Nuts*, Sarah slamming the emergency close button as another wave of concussive energy hit the back of the ship. "They need to get the fuck out of the bay," Sarah said as she saw an external camera pick up the security team as they approached the ship, looking for a way in.

They rushed out of the hold and up towards the cockpit at the front of the ship, where Engee had picked up on the importance of the opening sequence alarms and was beginning to start the engines. "We are leaving?" she asked Sarah.

"Yup."

Another display in the cockpit showed the security men head back across the bay, glancing up to the control room while the alarm sound increased in pitch and rapidity as they entered the final thirty seconds before the doors would open.

"Strap in," Franklin advised Gus, who was hovering behind Engee. Ahead of them, the bay doors finally started to slide open.

"*Mutt's Nuts*," came a familiar voice through the comms system—the *Olympic* broadcasting direct to the ship in its bay. "This is Captain Philby. I am ordering you to power down your engines again. We are beginning the close sequence from the bridge. For your own safety, do not attempt to leave."

Anger suddenly filled Franklin and he leaned forward, pressing the button to open the general cockpit mic. "Fuck you, Philby," he said, "you've no authority to keep us here." It wasn't strictly true; the captain had every right to decide whether the bay doors were open or not. If he hadn't had any genuine authority to arrest Franklin ten minutes ago, the unconscious bay controller and security men up in the booth had certainly changed that.

"Don't be a fool, Mr Franklin. You'll get yourself and your friends killed."

The doors were still opening, now about the height of the *Mutt's Nuts*, just as the engines gained enough power to start moving the ship.

"Or we'll blow the shit out of the bay as we go, maybe even this side of the ship," Franklin growled back, knowing in his heart that it wasn't what he wanted for many reasons. He noticed Gus look over at him with a raised eyebrow.

Sarah got into the pilot's seat and strapped in. "Let's go," she said, pushing the power up a little too fast and lurching unsteadily forward. Ahead of them, the bay door stopped and, after a second's pause, started to close again.

"This is your last-" Arnold Philby began over the comms before Sarah slapped it off.

"I'm trying to fly here," she complained and dipped the nose as they reached the closing door. Then, a moment later, there was a terrible, almost apocalyptic scraping sound, and they were free of the bay, gliding out into space.

Sarah stood up and turned to Engee. "Can you take over for now?" she asked. "I'm going to go and see if we still have a cargo hold."

NINETEEN

Franklin had spotted Commander Harris as the ship touched down on the landing pad at Regus' main mining facility. The hangar bay was a huge space, shaped a little like an upended barrel and with three raised circular pads of varying sizes within it, connected by walkways that all eventually led towards the main door out of the bay. Among the security team and the landing pad operators, Commander Harris was the only one without a breathing mask to aid him while the environmental system worked to return the air pressure to normal now that the outer doors were closed.

Commander Harris was Luna stock, Gus had told him that on the way, which meant he was tough and, most likely, a no-nonsense kind of guy. He had worked his way up to his current position, having "arrived as a young man with only the clothes on my back", as he had apparently been fond of telling Gus in the past.

They let Gus disembark the *Mutt's Nuts* first. While Franklin had been down to the surface of Regus several times before, he had never met the station commander—nor the station commander's daughter, for that matter—so he decided to trust his friend to set the tone, as they were in town to ask for favours, and these favours were the type with no questions asked. Also, they might need some sort of asylum when the *Olympic* arrived... There was that too.

"How far can we trust this guy?" Franklin asked Gus as they stood at the top of the gangway leading down from the rear of the *Mutt's Nuts*. The ship had descended onto an internal landing pad because of the thin—if just about breathable—atmosphere, which, for most people, would lead to the beginnings of hypoxemia in less than a minute. Apparently, not for Commander Harris.

"The station commander is as straight as they come," Gus answered. "Perhaps straight enough to tell us to piss off with our secret tests and then hand us over to Philby when he turns up to inform Harris that we fought our way off the *Olympic*."

"Point taken," Franklin replied with a grimace.

"It's one of the last facilities of its type for light-years around here," Gus went on, "they're only scraping by, finding just enough useful deposits to get from year to year. Tourists coming to see the old mining town from the *Olympic* are a small but important part of what keeps them going."

Franklin raised his eyebrows. "Be a shame if that were to stop."

Gus inclined his head in agreement. "He's a good, fair man, Commander Harris, but he's got a whole colony to be responsible for." The big man's eyebrows—along with a bit of goatee, the only hair on his entire head—furrowed. "You sure we can't be a little more honest with him? It might make things go a lot faster. For one thing, he'd be appalled by the Koru presence on Enceladine. If they can just turn up there..."

Then they can turn up here. Franklin finished Gus' thought in his head. It was a strong argument, but he shook his head. "Not yet, at least."

The commander was waiting for them just inside the entrance to the landing pad. "Moreau, you big, bald bastard," Harris called out in a thick, working-class accent when Gus was still twenty paces away, "you're here and the *Olympic* is late. What the fuck is going on? I need my tourists!"

Commander Harris was a thickset, ruddy-faced man of at least fifty. Short but stout, he had a pock-marked face, full eyebrows and thick hair that stood on end and swept slightly backwards, like bristles on a broom head. He made a show of peering around Gus where, with Franklin at the head, the rest of the current complement of the *Mutt's Nuts* walked along the slightly raised path away from the ship. "I recognise this man," rumbled Harris at Franklin, "although I've never had the pleasure. And this one," he added, pointing at Vik. His eyes glided past Sarah to Engee at the rear, who was moving slowly as she still nursed a hangover. "And a Koru. You're not trying to start up a modern-day version of the Village People, are you?"

Franklin arrived to see Gus screwing up his face in confusion.

"Never mind," Commander Harris said with a wave of his hand, "although I can't wait to hear this one. You always bring us a little fun, Moreau."

"I've brought you something interesting, at least," Gus said, finding somewhere to hang his opener.

"Interesting's only good when it brings in income," Harris replied. "Otherwise, it's just trouble in my experience."

"That's a narrow way to look at things, " Gus observed humorously, and Harris raised an eyebrow.

"So, it's the latter then. Still," the station commander swirled his finger around to loosely indicate Franklin, Engee and Vik, "you've turned up with a Koru, one of the UTC's biggest Koru-sceptics and the man who killed a whole, city-sized spaceship full of Koru. So, I'm guessing clandestine negotiations of some kind?"

Behind Gus, Vik half-raised his hand, as if protesting at the commander's label for him. Franklin wanted to do the same but, in all honesty, knew that he couldn't. However, before any objections could be raised, Commander Harris had turned and stalked off. Gus hurried after him and Franklin, along with the others, did the same.

Regus Main Station—nowadays, just about all of Regus that mattered—had the air of somewhere that was well-run on virtually no money. Like a mech stripped of its paint but well-oiled underneath, it didn't look pretty but worked just fine... mostly. There was an overriding feeling that the station was only a bad month or two away from things starting to go properly wrong. The *Olympic* was a faded beauty, Enceladine the epitome of "rustic," yet neither felt as precarious as Regus. The main part of the facility didn't feel different from the hangar, with exposed struts crossing overhead and everything down to bare materials—no artifice, no sense of "decoration."

Franklin watched Gus as he followed Harris through the atrium and corridors, much of which was lined with an almost seamless combination of alloy and rock. He reached out a hand here and there, fingertips brushing a wall or a door frame in an affectionate way. Franklin remembered how, although he rarely bothered to come down to Regus himself—especially as it so quickly followed the breathable air and open spaces of Enceladine on the *Olympic's* route—Gus almost always did, at least until about six months ago. Franklin felt like a lousy friend, realising that he had never pressed Gus on why.

Suddenly, Commander Harris veered left through a set of automatic sliding doors, giving one a shove and a glare when it seemed to get stuck halfway. Gus gave a lingering glance up and down the corridor, as if looking for someone, before following inside. "Come on in, all of you," Harris bellowed, "let's see what this is all about."

"We need to use your mineral analysis lab," Gus said once they were all inside, the doors reluctantly closed behind them. The slightly maudlin look from before was gone, and at once he had become all business. They stood in a small office, a desk between them and the commander, although Harris made no move to take his seat, and there were no seats for his guests.

"To analyse what?" Harris replied evenly, his steely gaze matching Gus.

Gus flicked a look at Franklin, then onto Vik and Sarah. Franklin didn't know what expression to give back, hoping that his friend somehow intuitively understood the balance between trust and secrecy, necessity and carelessness, with information that was already proving very dangerous. He remembered that Arnold Philby—an older friend than Gus—was on their trail with his own agenda that may well involve this little piece of rock. The commander and Regus were already involved, merely by their coming here.

"Well," Gus tried, "that's what the analysing is for."

Franklin cringed, getting the sense that Harris would throw such an obviously evasive reply back in Gus' face. Instead, the older man's eyes just narrowed, and, after a moment, he spoke again. "Where did you get it? Is it dangerous? Radioactive?" He moved his neck around, peering at his guests, looking them up and down. "Did you just waltz straight into the middle of my station with it?"

"It's on the ship," Vik lied hurriedly from behind Gus—perhaps a little too hurriedly. Franklin was still holding onto it and suddenly hoping it really wasn't radioactive. Franklin studied Harris as he expected Vik was doing. Was the man going to order a search of their ship, ready to relieve them of whatever they found so important?

Instead, Commander Harris kept his eyes fixed on Gus. "And this rock is why the *Olympic* is late, I suppose? Why you've arrived ahead of it? Who's after you? Is it Philby?"

Damn, but this man was too perceptive. He asked questions like he already knew the answer to them, like the mere act of asking was, in fact, his way of telling those gathered in the room that they weren't going to get away with hiding anything. After what Gus had said earlier, Harris was not going to want to upset the Captain of the *Olympic*. Franklin's heart sank; this was a lost cause.

Commander Harris rubbed his chin thoughtfully for a long moment, then took them all in with one swift movement of his head. "You never used the labs, understand? In fact, if anyone asks, I never even knew you were here. If the *Olympic* turns up and you're still here, I'll turn you over if that's what I'm asked to do."

"Sounds fair," Franklin answered.

"And if whatever you've got turns out to be worth a fortune," Commander Harris added, "don't forget your friends on Regus, eh?"

The initial chemical scan analysis had brought no surprises. Although it appeared reminiscent of coal and was similarly brittle, the ore's makeup had calcium carbonates in it, and, admittedly, a couple of heavy metal traces that the equipment was only around fifty percent certain about.

A tall, thin laboratory assistant with an enormously long forehead had shown them how to use the equipment and offered to stay and help them read the results, looking gravely offended when Vik and Gus had escorted him from his own workplace. "Commander Harris..." he had mumbled as some vague protest or threat of retaliation as the door closed behind him. The laboratory felt only the barest bit more sophisticated than the rest of the facility. Its surfaces were mostly metal with some sort of self-cleaning veneer on top that probably had not been capable of cleaning itself for some time. While most laboratories that Franklin had ever been aware of were well-lit by an almost ubiquitous light level, this one had several long strips of a greenish-yellow hue along one side, with pull-down spotlights here and there, all of which made the place feel like somewhere one artificially stuck body parts together and attempted to reanimate them.

They moved through the various tests, slicing off small pieces to try burning the ore, mixing it with a number of different acids, and even melting some to see if they could separate out its component elements —maybe isolate those uncertain traces. The hours passed, the *Olympic* likely getting ever-closer, but they could not be sure what made this boring-looking rock so desirable for the Koru.

The secret files that Engee could not remember accessing had said something about shields for ships, and Vik had jumped straight onto the possibility that this ore was a part of that. It seemed reasonable to Franklin that the Koru's rather flagrant breach of Enceladine neutrality and independence had to be about something important, and which military didn't want to cover their ships with more than just reflective hull plating? But the idea of energy shields was fanciful, like actually making teleportation work. Surely not even the Koru were *really* that advanced?

There were other reasons that the Koru could have decided to mine on Enceladine without permission, right under the UTC's noses. The detaining of Vik, the kidnapping of Engee, the pursuit by Koru fighters... all of it could be explained as the actions of a sovereign race who—like any other—wanted to keep hold of its secrets and have control over it subjects.

"Maybe we should give this up for now," he suggested. "Keep moving and just tell what we know to the UTC authorities. If we go to them now, maybe they'll even forget the way we left the *Olympic*, not pursue any charges."

"Let us burn it again," Engee suggested. She was staring closely at the diminished chunk of it with her opaque eyes, seeming like she hadn't heard a word Franklin had said.

"We need to keep some of it intact," Franklin complained. "We don't really know what we're looking for, what we're expecting it to do."

"Shields," Engee and Vik both answered at once, no hint of doubt in their two voices.

"Well, unless you can put a whole fucking wall of the stuff around a ship," Franklin snapped back, "then I'm not seeing it."

"Indulge me, Mr Mark," Engee pleaded, and Franklin heard the desperation in her tone. "I cannot be here for nothing, an exile from my people."

He stepped back with a sigh, indicating that—for now—his resistance to this whole fruitless act was being put aside, although he couldn't help one parting shot. "You heard what Harris said, if we're here when the *Olympic* turns up."

"Just let us capture the gas again," Engee insisted and set about taking another slice.

"We know what is in the smoke that it gives off, Engee," Sarah said, but the little Koru held up a hand in a particularly human gesture, and Sarah fell silent.

They watched as Engee took a separate container and drew off some of the vaguely yellowish smoke that the burning ore gave off. Then she took two electrical clips, a positive and a negative, and connected them to conduction points at either end. They had already run current through the ore itself, but Franklin found himself not wanting to question the determined-looking Koru again until she was finished.

Watching as the current was turned on, the swirling grey-yellow smoke didn't look any different as the electricity passed through it, although a readout showed that it was acting as a good conductor.

Engee turned up the current and the smoke seemed to slow a little in its movement. She went into the safety settings and took off the current limiter before turning it up some more.

"Careful now," Vik warned her, "none of us have any protective equipment on if you blow the thing up or something."

"Take cover if you wish," Engee answered without a beat. It seemed dismissive, but Franklin could see the focus on her face. She was going to see this to a conclusion of some sort.

"Engee…" Sarah tried as Vik took her suggestion, at least a little, tugging his wife a couple of steps back as Engee turned the current up again, the container now beginning to hum like a nest of angry hornets. Even Gus took an involuntary half-step away, but Franklin found himself fixed in place, looking between the transparent container and Engee, who had a desperate need for answers to the mysteries of her wrecked, mostly missing life in the experiments they were conducting.

The smoke seemed to thicken, now solidifying like some sort of dirty-looking cotton wool and tiny little veins of lightning started to move across its surface, the whole cloud occasionally glowing momentarily from within. It was like a storm cell in a bottle.

That was when the alarms started to sound.

For a moment, Franklin thought it was their fault, that somehow their experiments had set off some sort of emergency, perhaps the miniature storm cell having drained power to the base's electrical grid or... Well, no, that was a dumb idea.

Gus opened the door to the lab and stuck his head out to see what was going on, flagging down a passing security officer. "What's happening?" he asked.

Perhaps only in his early twenties, the security officer looked almost as confused as they did. "We're under attack, I think."

"Attack?" Gus repeated back, sounding as incredulous as Franklin felt. Franklin wondered whether the *Olympic's* arrival was causing chaos, although he had hardly expected it to warrant an alarm. The liner had no weapons, for one thing, but perhaps the *Olympic* had come closer than usual to the planet and had set off some sort of proximity drill, as it was such a large, non-terrestrial ship.

"I want your gun," Engee barked at the young security officer, emerging from the lab next to Gus, standing just over half the fitness instructor's height but showing more presence than usual.

"What?" the security officer replied in what was most definitely a squeak, his hand going protectively to the weapon strapped to his belt.

"I need to shoot at something," she told him, matter-of-fact but impatient.

The security officer started to back up a little. "Er... *no*."

"You shoot then," Engee said in what was, Franklin guessed, an understated show of Koru exasperation. "Quickly, before we are blown up."

The young officer pointed the way he was going, presumably wherever he was supposed to station himself in an emergency, sidling away a couple of steps, his mouth making shapes that were probably reasons he needed to be elsewhere, although no actual words came out.

Gus stepped forward and gently took his other arm, guiding him back into the room. "It'll only take a moment."

The officer started when he saw the glowing, crackling container of semi-solidified gas in the middle of the room. It had become slightly less opaque in the past few moments, so that the bursts of tiny lightning within it could now be seen, bright and intricate like the blood vessels seen in a picture of the back of someone's eye. The whole apparatus hummed dangerously.

"Shoot that," Engee told him. "I need to know."

Suddenly, there was a distant noise, a thump that could be felt through their feet, through the walls, that even seemed to pulse through the inside of the container, the gas and flow of electricity pulsing like a miniature Mexican wave.

For some reason, this finally saw the security officer pull his weapon. "Stand back," he said grandly and fired his compressed energy pistol. The red beam shattered the glass but, for just a moment, seemed to slow as it passed through the yellow, lightning-filled gas. It was a brief moment, a mere fraction of a second, then the beam seared through and began to burn a great mark in a metal cupboard a couple of metres behind it, before the security guard released the trigger. The lightning faded, and the gas started to drift apart, now free of the container.

"You saw that?" Vik cried. "Everyone saw that, right? It worked!"

The security guard looked at his weapon for a moment, then back to where the container had been. "The gas..." he began.

"For a moment," Sarah finished for him, "it absorbed the beam. Just like a shield might."

Another distant thump brought them all back to the fact that there was an alarm sounding, that something which definitely wasn't the *Olympic* had come to Regus.

TWENTY

"You!" roared Commander Harris as the group ran back into the central atrium that they had passed through earlier, which led back towards the docking area in one direction and, in the other, through to what served as the base's town centre and to other points around the station, most importantly the mining.

The whole group came to a stop—the man had quite a fearsome roar—and the young security officer looked over at the station commander sheepishly, although Franklin had a feeling that Harris was pointing at him.

"You're not getting out of here yet," Harris growled as he crossed the atrium towards them. "I did you a favour and look where it's got me." He threw a hand skyward, although only distant girders and composite ceiling arched overhead.

"Who's attacking?" Vik demanded. "Has that bloody Philby lost his mind?"

"It's not the *Olympic*," Harris corrected him, "those are Koru ships dropping ordinance on my station. They haven't actually hit anything yet, only because I don't think they've meant to, but I'm getting a feeling that their generosity won't last long. Has this got anything to do with your little science project?"

Franklin's heart sank. It was bad enough when he thought it was the *Olympic* coming for them. "Turn us over to them, if you need to," Franklin blurted out. "Or get us to our ship, we can try and outrun them."

"Have you got any weapons on that little rust bucket of yours?" Harris asked.

"Hey!" Sarah tried to protest, although they, indeed, had no weapons and Harris looked directly at Franklin before speaking again.

"I thought not. There's fighters and a fair-sized military vessel up there, they'll shoot you down or capture you before you're even out of the atmosphere." Harris turned and pointed out of the atrium's one large viewing window, which looked over several outbuildings, beyond to a rocky plateau and, in the distance, the vague outlines of abandoned buildings that had once belonged to a whole town that had lived independent of the mining colony, back in Regus' heyday. On the left of the view, a long, low throughway led to another squat, trapezoid-shaped building covered in thicker plating than the rest of the facility. "We do have a defensive canon. Never been fired in anger, not even during the war, but we maintain it with as much love and care as we do everything else here."

On cue, a Koru fighter craft flashed across the view, an intimidatingly close flyby, near enough that various aerodynamic fins and other protuberances could be seen, giving the craft a slightly insectoid feel.

"The targeting system is ancient and will be no good against those fighters, and no one else here will have your experience, Mr Franklin. Perhaps they might think twice if we start fighting back, though."

"Or they blow the whole station up," Gus protested, looking incensed by the idea. "You said you weren't going to stick your station's neck out for us, and you shouldn't."

"That was where the *Olympic* was concerned," Commander Harris replied grimly. "This is an act of war by a foreign power."

Franklin was already moving towards the door that led towards the connecting corridor and the defence cannon. He could see that Harris knew his mind, even before he heard the man add behind him. "And, back in the civil war, those bastards took my son from me."

Franklin closed his eyes for a split second when he heard those words. The universe kept putting him into a position where he had to try and take more Koru lives; he had already been responsible for the death of so many. Yet something in Harris' voice and the sight of the Koru fighter flying so brazenly above the old mining facility had his legs pumping painfully hard to get him to the cannon.

One of the security team was waiting for him at the entrance to the cannon and gave him a headpiece connecting him to Harris, then coded him into the interface.

"You there?" Harris asked.

"Here," Franklin answered, coming into a half-spherical emplacement that felt like being in a small observatory.

"I'm at the comms station now," Harris went on, "I'm hailing their ship on every frequency we know, so let's see what these bastards want."

Settling into a bucket seat that was suspended from the ceiling, Franklin looked at the readouts before him, noticing that one of them said "Rounds" on it. "What the hell does this thing fire?"

"Good-old depleted uranium rounds," Harris answered. Then, after a snort of disbelief from Franklin, he added, "They don't need a huge power source like a large compressed energy weapon and have a much better rate of fire than plasma rounds, yet they'll go through all but the thickest armour."

Oh well, they were what he had to work with, anyway. He was sure that they could do for the little fighter craft, but as he magnified the image on his display and looked up at the cruiser-sized Koru warship that must have launched them, hanging in the upper atmosphere of the planet, he had to wonder at the thickness of their front armour.

"Any word from our friends up there yet?" As Franklin watched, one of two Koru fighters arched through the sky between where he was and its carrier, turning to again bring itself on course to pass over the base. "Maybe I should loose off a few warning shots, let them know that we're not defenceless down here?"

"Nothing from them yet," Harris replied. "As far as I'm concerned, if they've dropped bombs on my planet already, even if they didn't drop them anywhere they can actually kill someone, then you've got a right to shoot back."

Franklin wasn't quite sure if that was an invitation to target the Koru fighters, but he wasn't quite there yet. He aimed a little to his left of the fast-approaching fighter and squeezed the trigger, sending a short burst forward of maybe no more than ten rounds. He saw two yellowish tracer rounds amongst the burst, streaking up and past the approaching ship.

The shots didn't deter the approaching fighter, which continued on its current flight path—looking very much like an attack run—towards the base. Franklin started to track it, wondering whether to fire again, knowing he had only a couple of seconds to make a difference if the ship genuinely was going to shoot at the base this time. But then, in the back of his picture, he noticed a tiny flare of light much further away, up towards where the Koru cruiser was sitting.

It was only there for a brief moment and then was gone again, but it caused fear to take hold inside his stomach. Franklin magnified the targeting view again, the Koru cruiser appearing slightly grainy with distance, and he spotted something between them... what he had suspected to be the case.

"Missile!" he shouted into the comms. "They've bloody launched a missile at us, and I bet that's targeting something more than the fucking ground."

"Shoot it down, man," Commander Harris urgently ordered into his ear. "We've got nothing else to protect us from it."

Franklin centred the missile within his targeting view—a tiny dot heading at supersonic speed towards them, seeming within the view to move and dance around. Franklin knew that it was his efforts and those of the defence cannon's ancient stabilisation system to track the missile at extreme range that had the view shaking all over the place. Still, there was a lot of ammunition, and now that the fighters knew he was there, he might not have long to try and save the station from what was coming for it. He started to squeeze off some long-range shots.

After a couple of short bursts, he stopped, unable to determine if he was even getting close as the tracers either burned out or were too small to see.

"Give yourself a few more seconds," Harris advised, perhaps watching the feed from the weapon display, "then blaze it like hell."

"Got you." Franklin quickly swept about for the fighters, although he could not see them, and there was no radar readout available. He shifted back to targeting the missile, waiting for some terrible sound to be the last thing he heard before one of the fighters scored a crippling hit on the cannon. Several more seconds passed, the missile now much clearer in his view and, still alive, he began firing again.

This time, he could get a better sense of where his shots were going from the tracer fire. They seemed again to dance around the missile, and it took Franklin a few moments to realise that the missile itself was now taking evasive actions, swinging this way and that in small, graceful, but quick movements as it sensed the defensive fire coming in. His shots became more frantic, his movements wilder, at one moment way off target, the next streaking right across the missile as he tried to catch it out at its own game. Two times, three times he was sure he must have hit it, yet still it kept on towards them.

Shit, it must be so close now.

Everything suddenly went white on Franklin's screen. "What?" he screamed in frustration. Watching the overloaded visual sensors slowly bleed back their picture, he saw the tell-tale shape of a fighter's behind, rising up and away, disappearing from the shot, and then moved the cannon to again pick up his target, now coming in low across the landscape, using it for cover. But too close now, he hoped, to effectively dodge the incoming rounds.

"Die, you fucker," Franklin spat as he centred it on the target, no longer having to account for trajectory as the missile was now only a matter of a few kilometres away. He squeezed the trigger, but nothing happened.

"It won't fire," he screamed to Harris on the other end of the comms connection, although he was screaming it at everyone and anything—the people who lived on Regus Mining Station, his friends, his ex-wife, all who would die if the missile hit them. "They've taken out the cannon."

"External sensors show it is intact," Harris replied, his voice different now—the high-pitched tones of a man who was staring not only his own death in the face, but the deaths of all those he was responsible for, perhaps all those he loved.

The same security team member who had let him into the cannon's tight control booth suddenly appeared next to Franklin again. "Reset," was the only word he caught, the blood now rushing through his ears, but the man's lips moved to say much more than just that. A couple of seconds later, he stepped back, and Franklin squeezed, again spewing forth depleted uranium slugs, although they were wildly off-target, disappearing far into the dead landscape behind where the missile now was.

Franklin yanked hard on the controls and found the missile again, now speeding across the last open stretch of plateau before the base. He fired, fired again, was sure he had winged it as it suddenly skipped to the side, but then guessed it must have somehow dodged once more as it came ever onwards. They were a few seconds from a strike, and Franklin took a deep breath, his mind leaping back through the years to a man whose eyes and arms were as good as any computer tracking system. Then he fired one more short burst.

It seemed almost surreal when the missile pitched forward into the ground, but Franklin was brought straight back to reality when it exploded, the shock wave visible through the cannon's view of the scene, before it shook the station a moment later, rattling everything like a not-too-small earthquake.

They were saved, at least for the moment, yet a cold rage now burned within Franklin—in his chest, choking his throat. "Fuckers," he growled, swinging back to find the ship that had fired the missile in his sights. They must have many more missiles aboard the cruiser, and perhaps he should have been worrying about how many more he could shoot down while the fighters harried him. What happened if the Koru ship fired two or even three missiles at once? He should be worried, but he wasn't.

"Fuckers!" he growled again—more of an animal snarl—as he followed the targeting system's suggested adjustment for distance and gravity. Now in a zone he had not been in for over a decade, not even when they fled Enceladine, he found that shot didn't feel right, and he tilted it upward just a little more. Then he didn't just squeeze, he held the trigger down.

The tracers arced away, soon invisible to him, although he kept the display on the Koru cruiser in full magnification, waiting to see any evidence at all that his shots were landing. If the front armour wasn't thick enough and his shots did find their mark, this was a good weapon, however old it was, and even a big cruiser like that would feel it.

Then something unexpected happened, something unforeseen and yet, in the end, perhaps not surprising. The shots hit a shield.

....

"Did you see that?" Franklin called excitedly. "Those shots just hit something. It's exactly like we thought, they've got a shield!"

"That's great that you proved your theory," Harris replied. "But doesn't that just make us more screwed?"

The commander had a point, and Franklin doubled his concentration, firing again. Several more bursts raced away towards the ship, which, at least as it looked from the ground, just hung there in the sky. He studied the zoomed-in image for the precise moment—the flash—when the rounds he was firing hit something that wasn't the hull of the ship...

There it was. A dirty yellow flicker. Did he see something branching through it in that fraction of a second, something a bit like lightning? Or was he just imagining it, because surely he could not make out such detail on the distant, grainy image? Franklin kept firing, the fighters—wherever they had got to—forgotten for the moment, even the fear of another missile launch not foremost in his mind. Almost like a curious child, he was prodding. *Yes*, he was prodding an alien warship sitting many kilometres away in the atmosphere with a gun emplacement, but he was remembering the gas in the laboratory. It was undoubtedly a crude, weak version of whatever was on that ship, but surely it, too, had a stress limit.

"You want to save some ammo for point defence, Mr Franklin?" Commander Harris reminded him over the comms.

Franklin barely heard him, firing off rounds, the ammo counter a blur that he wasn't paying much attention to. As the shots hit home, the dirty yellow colour of the shield came more and more into view, and now he fancied he really could make out the white-blue capillaries spreading through it. Then, coming in from the left side of his zoomed-in view, Franklin saw what had happened to the two fighters—they were returning to the ship.

"I think it's giving," Franklin said, sending burst after burst skyward, the shield now an almost opaque presence in front of the Koru cruiser, but that was when the rounds ran out. Franklin squeezed and squeezed the trigger, like it would make a difference. "Ah... bollocks."

"Is it coming closer?" Commander Harris asked, the question sounding a bit like an accusation. But, worse than that, Franklin could see something else in his view. They were launching another missile.

He let the view zoom back out and turned to the security officer, who was still stood behind him. The man's face had gone pale, and Franklin glanced up to see that he was watching a secondary viewer

"How long to reload this?"

The security officer just shook his head.

Franklin started to rise, not knowing exactly what he was going to do but feeling a pullback towards those he had come to Regus with, when something else on the display caught his eye. It was a bloom of light, flaring momentarily on the extreme right edge of the view until the auto-balance damped it down. Even then, it took him a moment to understand what he was seeing—a ship, an extremely familiar ship, lifting up and away from the station.

"Where the hell are they going?" he asked aloud, the security officer giving a small, fear-filled shrug, even though Franklin had been posing the question to himself. Belatedly, he realised he was still connected with Commander Harris.

"They haven't abandoned you," Harris informed him. "They came through to ops after the first torpedo was launched, felt that if they fled the station then the Koru might call off the attack." Franklin could hear the tightness of the man's inner conflict in his voice. "I couldn't very well deny them. But it looks like their sacrifice might now be too late for us. I don't suppose there are any weapons that might take out a ship to surface missile on that old cargo vessel, are there?"

"Sorry," Franklin answered, although his thoughts were with the ship that was quickly becoming small in the zoomed-out view, burning at an angle to try and make it past the cruiser. He wasn't angry that he had been left behind, possibly to die, but rather he found himself disappointed that he could not see this thing through.

"Oh well," Harris said with a sigh of resignation, an oddly understated reaction to their terrible situation, "I will give the order to brace for impact."

A moment later, a klaxon-like alarm began to sound, and the security man who had been with Franklin since he had come into the emplacement rushed out of the room. Franklin stayed, however, watching the *Mutt's Nuts* as it burned hard, still turning away to starboard. *Please*, he thought to himself, *please let them get away.* He knew that somewhere out there a missile was less than a minute away from striking the station, perhaps from striking the emplacement he had been using to fire at the Koru ship, but he didn't even try to search it out.

As he watched, the *Mutt's Nuts* suddenly began to move strangely, turning and moving through the atmosphere at maybe a twenty-five, even thirty-degree angle, compared to moving straight. Then, the ship turned even more, so that he could clearly see the starboard side of the ship, even as it continued to travel directly away from him. Franklin was sure that it was rolling side-to-side as well—tiny little tilts... left-right-left in quick succession.

Franklin quickly zoomed out again, trying to make sense of what he saw. He saw that the Koru cruiser had manoeuvred surprisingly quickly onto an intercept course. At this wider angle, he thought he could just about see the dot of the missile heading towards them within the viewer. It was less than thirty seconds away. He knew what he was seeing now, watching as the incredible thrust of Sarah's cargo ship was overcome.

It was barely even moving away anymore, was perhaps already being reeled back in towards the Koru ship, which held the *Mutt's Nuts* in the longest-ranged, most powerful gravity beam that Franklin had ever seen or heard of. Gravity beams—known as tractor beams by many, because apparently that was what they had been called long before they were ever invented—were most commonly used as docking aids or ways of moving cargo about in the vacuum of space without having to give every little container its own thruster or creating some other complex system of rails or something. This Koru ship had used it over a distance of tens if not hundreds of kilometres to stop a ship that was burning hard to get away from it.

Franklin's heart sank as he watched his friends being reeled in by an invisible fishing line and waited for the missile to hit.

TWENTY-ONE

"We are under attack, mam," the young, serious-looking guard in front of the docking bay informed Sarah, her jaw set tightly, "no one goes in or out."

"But they are after *us*," Sarah argued, feeling her rosy cheeks begin to turn even redder than usual. She clenched her fists. "If we go, they might stop."

Vikram Shah quickly stepped in front of his wife.

"Please," he pleaded with the guard in a way Sarah recognised as not pleading at all, like he was simply pointing out the best course of action, "call up Commander Harris. Get his permission; I expect he will be pleased to have us off his station."

The security woman looked reluctant, like she thought doing so would most likely result in her getting chewed out—which, strangely enough, seemed like a bigger concern to her than the death currently threatening to come from above—but eventually she sighed and tapped her earpiece. "Commander Harris, sir," she said, "This is Patton at the docking bay. I've got the crew of the *Mutt's*

Nuts here wishing to defy the lockdown and leave." Sarah saw the security guard wince as she said the last bit, as if pre-empting some sort of tirade from the other end of the comms link.

"This is Harris," came the reply. "we've got one of their number on the defensive cannon," he said, "so they can't leave yet."

Sarah nodded towards the security guard, who took the hint and tapped to open the channel for her to speak. "We will leave him here. We need to go now before that cruiser fires any more missiles at the station."

"Do it," Harris shot back immediately. "You heard that, Patton? I want them off my station as soon as possible."

Less than a minute later, Sarah, Vik and Engee were running across the slightly raised walkway in the docking bay, wearing masks as the doors above them were already opening and the less breathable atmosphere outside the station was coming in to fill the space. One of them had been left behind, although he had been far from pleased about it.

Gus had looked crestfallen when Sarah pointed at him as he made to grab a mask before entering the docking bay. "Not you," she had said, her haste perhaps making the words sound a little harsher than she had intended.

"What?" he asked, more confused than angry at first.

"This isn't your fight, Gus," Sarah had said. "We're going out there to get captured or killed, almost for sure. I can't let you come." She glanced back in towards the station. "And I need you to stay here and explain this to Franklin."

"No!" Gus protested. He looked at Engee imploringly. "I can help. I came out here to help."

Suddenly, Engee darted forward and, more than a little awkwardly, she kissed Gus on the cheek. "You have helped, Gus Moreau," she went on. "So, I am kissing you as humans do, to let you know that you are liked."

None of it really seemed to be an argument that should necessarily keep Gus from the *Mutt's Nuts*, yet it worked nonetheless, and he stepped back, an odd mix of frustration and shock pulling at his features.

"Are you sure we should be doing this?" Vik asked several moments later as the three of them reached the *Mutt's Nuts*, his voice distorted and muffled in the mask, which didn't have any sort of comms system incorporated. "We're sure to be captured or killed, but we don't yet know the fate of Regus. We could have fled the base and out onto the planet's surface instead."

Sarah looked at her husband, aghast. "There's a small city's worth of people here," she shot back at him, perhaps exaggerating the mining colony's population just a little, but with an important point to make.

"And this is why you could never have done my work, Sarah," Vik shot back a little harshly. "You don't want to make the big, difficult decisions. I'm not concerned for our safety, but we are the only ones who can really let the UTC know what's going on."

Sarah stopped two steps up the ramp into the *Mutt's Nuts* and glanced back towards the doors into the docking bay, which led to the rest of the station. "We've left Franklin here, and Gus," she answered, "I wasn't being altruistic about Gus. We needed to leave him here in case those fighters shoot Franklin out of the gun emplacement."

Vik regarded his wife, and Sarah liked to think there was at least a little newfound respect for her somewhere inside the mask, that she was still capable of surprising him. But, when he spoke, whatever spell she had been imagining was broken. "You know they're probably gonna blow the whole station either way, right?" he told her. "It would be the sensible thing to do."

Just about the first thing to happen once the *Mutt's Nuts* had cleared the docking bay, rotated to light its rear thrusters and started the serious business of breaking the planet's gravity, was that an alarm started sounding. It was an oddly unobtrusive alarm, which politely seemed to say: "This may or may not be of interest."

"Proximity alarm," Engee noted efficiently. All of Sarah's attention was already given over to pulling a shallow, hard-angled burn, sending the *Mutt's Nuts* above and across the surface of Regus in the vain hope that they might catch the Koru cruiser napping and have half a chance of getting to a position where they could power up the interstellar drive.

"The proximity of what?" Sarah snapped irritably. The alarm was primarily a warning for space debris. Technically, Regus could be argued to be one great, big bit of space debris, but it probably wasn't that.

"I think it's another missile coming from the cruiser," Engee answered.

"Shit." Even in the middle of her difficult and dangerous manoeuvre, Sarah couldn't help but glance back at her husband in the seat behind Engee, who at least had the good grace not to look smug about being right.

He managed a weak smile. "Perhaps Franklin will shoot it down."

"Either way," Sarah said, turning back to what she was doing, "let's distract these bastards by making them chase us."

The *Mutt's Nuts* kept on its slow, shallow climb, the whole craft vibrating in what seemed like a very definite complaint about the long and extended hard burn through the planet's atmosphere as they tried to put the planet's curvature between them and their pursuers.

"They have turned towards us," Engee said in an inappropriately emotionless tone.

"The missile?" Sarah asked. "Still heading towards the station?"

"It is. About a minute until impact."

Sarah nodded grimly, then looked down at her controls, her eyebrows furrowing into their own question. She looked out of the front viewport, as if it would have some sort of answer to whatever her current predicament was, then down again at her controls. She pulled hard on them, yet it felt like the ship was pulling back in the other direction. What had already been a violent vibration felt throughout the cockpit suddenly became so hard it seemed like everything in Sarah's head was rattling. All around her, the *Mutt's Nuts* was complaining loudly. Creaks and groans and other—even more worrying—noises could be heard over the noise of the vibration.

"What the-" Sarah began, but Engee interrupted her.

"That will be a tractor beam," Engee offered up matter-of-factly.

"Oh great," Sarah complained, "they've got those too."

"The UTC military do not?" Engee asked.

"No!" Sarah replied, "I'm pretty fucking sure they don't. Not ones that reach across half the distance of a fucking planet, against its fucking gravity well." She glanced back at her husband and didn't like the look on his face. "You knew about this?"

Vik shrugged. It was a shrug of admission.

"Perfect," Sarah snapped, "everybody knows this but the pilot. I don't suppose there's any way we're getting out of it?"

The *Mutt's Nuts* seemed to answer her itself with another loud groan and a sudden shudder that had everyone in the cockpit lurching forward against their seat restraints.

"I would bring down the thrust," Vik advised his wife, "or you'll risk tearing us apart."

"Would that be so bad?" Sarah croaked back at him, her voice breaking.

Vik tried to reach out to his wife from his seat behind Engee to comfort her but was too far away, and his hand stopped awkwardly in the air between them. "Things are never lost," he told her. "Your recent rescue of Engee and I taught me that."

"And the missile?" Sarah asked Engee.

Sarah glanced across and saw Engee find the missile on a radar display at her co-pilot's station. She tapped on the display to bring up a rear-facing camera view that quickly zoomed in toward the missile as it sped across the last part of the open plain towards the Regus Mining Colony. Sarah suddenly realised that this was the last thing she wanted to see right now and was about to tell this to Engee when, less than a kilometre from the station, the missile suddenly exploded.

TWENTY-TWO

Although irony was not exactly a thing for the Koru, Engee had some sense that the people she had thrown her lot in with were—if not quite "Koru haters"—then at least they were Koru sceptics. That and her actions working against the interests of her people might be referred to as "heroic," or something similar. Yet she still felt like she was the one in the room taking on the burden of the things the Koru did. It was like they expected that she might have an explanation for the things that happened or be privy to some intimate knowledge of anything and everything Koru.

Yet, the size of the cruiser that swallowed the *Mutt's Nuts*—reeled in as they were by its tractor beam—shocked her as much as the rest of them. The ship was, as Sarah would probably say, fucking huge.

The noises that sounded from within and just outside of the *Mutt's Nuts* once they were inside the belly of the huge beast were loud, echoing and as terrifyingly disconcerting for her as for the others, she was sure. All the same, Vik and Sarah were both looking at Engee as if she knew what would come next. As it happened, she didn't see the gas coming either.

THUMP.

Engee woke up in an inimitably Koru room. Whereas during her incarceration on Enceladine her captors had been doing their best to make rooms—particularly cells—as plain as possible when working hurriedly within the rock and dirt of the landscape, this was an example of what happened if you give a Koru full control over the materials and the environment. What you got was the blankest, most boring-looking room possible. *This* was something that Engee knew. It was also something that Engee guessed she probably wouldn't have appreciated before spending some time living in human spaces. Even when humans built and decorated to be as uniform and unremarkable as possible, it was a riot of design and individuality compared to—for instance, case in point—the utterly white room in which she had woken up.

Engee was lying on a bench which, seen from certain angles, would have just blended into the whiteness of the rest of the room, a rectangular cuboid of—she did not doubt—precise angles and edges that came to the finest of almost razor-sharp points. They were white to the point of glowing, although the idea that any light might emanate from within the surfaces—as surely it did, because there were no other light sources—seemed almost to be a trick of her opaque, light-sensitive eyes.

She felt groggy and her head hurt, but she managed to turn her head and saw that Vik was laid unconscious on another cuboid protrusion, like her own, while Sarah was similarly unconscious on the floor. Something within Engee's chest tightened for a moment as she was worried that the Koru-designed knockout gas might have been too much for their human physiology. Then, with a lurch and an unsteady step that nearly saw Engee fall right on top of Sarah, she made her way over to her captain and checked for signs that she was breathing.

She was, and Engee's touch caused Sarah to come around as well. "Ow, my head," Sarah groaned as she half-opened her eyes. That effect, then, was the same for both of them.

"We are in a holding cell," Engee explained, probably needlessly.

Sarah stared blinkingly at the ceiling for a moment, and then back at Engee. "That explains the decor, then. I thought there was just something wrong with my eyes."

Gingerly, Sarah tested sitting but only got about halfway up before deciding to pause. She looked about the room, her eyes going wide. "Where the fuck is the door?"

"It's probably there somewhere," Engee answered. "Just not available to us."

Sarah frowned at her. "You Koru do know some cool shit." She rubbed her head again. "And your drugs are damn powerful too." Looking over at her unconscious husband, Sarah gave him a disapproving look. "Someone's sleeping like a baby."

"You have the same saying?" Engee asked. "Are your children also raised in torpor pods?"

Sarah looked strangely at Engee for a moment. "Er, no."

With a small hydraulic hiss, a thin, dark line appeared in one of the walls and the door moved inward and to one side. Three Koru walked into the room, two of them built slightly larger than the other one and carrying weapons. Although it clearly wasn't the same Koru, the third figure nonetheless bore a striking resemblance to the officer that they had taken captive on Enceladine. An interrogator, Engee supposed.

"Designation NG-972," the interrogator barked. "You have given us quite some trouble. Even memory correction has not proved effective in reigning in your deviant activities. You cannot expect such a lenient approach this time."

"Lenient?" Sarah repeated, clearly in disagreement with the interrogator's description, Engee suspected.

The interrogator glanced over at Sarah and gave what Engee recognised as a thoroughly disdainful sneer before her gaze drifted over to Vik's unconscious form. "And it is good to have Mr Shah back in our custody." The interrogator looked thoughtful for a moment. "I shall have to seek guidance on what is to be done with him." And then, with a dismissive gesture in Sarah's direction, "And this one. But you, NG-972, have outlived any potential usefulness to the nest. You are too dangerous to be kept alive and will need to be terminated once interrogation is complete."

Sarah glared up at the interrogator. "You don't tell someone that *before* you interrogate them. Is this your first time?"

TWENTY-THREE

"It's been a pleasure," Commander Harris said, shaking Franklin's hand as they stood by the entrance to the docking bay next to the one that the *Mutt's Nuts* had left from less than an hour before. There were, indeed, only two docking bays on Regus Mining Station, as the six berths they provided were at least twice as many as were ever needed nowadays. "Now," the commander went on, "please leave and never come back to my station again."

The corner of Franklin's mouth curled up just a little at that. He liked Commander Harris and suddenly wished that he had chosen to spend more time on the station before, that perhaps he might have known the dry-witted administrator a little better. "Understood," he answered, then turned and followed a young, blonde-haired pilot called Taylor—which was her first name or her last name, he wasn't totally sure—into the bay, while Gus quickly shook the commander's hand as well.

Gus had looked utterly forlorn when Franklin found him, seemingly haunted by the fact that he had not joined the others aboard the *Mutt's Nuts*, that he had not shared their fate in being snatched up by the Koru cruiser, even though being made to stay on Regus had almost seen him blown up by a ship-to-surface missile.

In the bay, they boarded a blocky, almost trapezium-shaped, dull grey shuttle. While the pilot went into the front, Franklin took a worryingly flimsy fold-out seat almost directly behind her in the combined passenger and cargo section and Gus sat next to him, silent and haunted still. It only now occurred to Franklin that Gus might have stayed on Regus, that it was mainly Franklin who Arnold Philby would be after.

The *Olympic* had arrived above Regus less than fifteen minutes before, and must surely have been aware of the Koru cruiser, which had left in the direction of Enceladine. For all Franklin knew, they could have passed right by each other although, of course, the passenger liner would not have wanted to attract the warship's attention. Although Harris had not divulged to Franklin the full extent of the conversation he had shared with the *Olympic*, his first words afterward had been, "They want you back." Those words had made Franklin feel like a possession to be traded, but he hadn't complained. Harris, after all, had been quite clear about where they stood right from when they had all first arrived at the station.

"What sort of a welcome do you think is waiting for you on the *Olympic*?" Taylor now asked as she completed her pre-flight checks. Above them, the roof doors slid slowly open and let the more breathable air inside mix with the planet's much thinner atmosphere. It seemed like the news that Franklin and his friends were fugitives of a sort was making its way across the station.

"I don't know," Franklin admitted glancing across to Gus and finding his big friend staring at the floor between his feet. Arnold Philby's wrath was not what concerned him right then, except for the ways that the captain of the SS *Olympic* might prevent him from heading after the Koru cruiser and rescuing those on it. The idea was insane, of course; for all he knew, they were already dead. Yet the thought was still there, firmly lodged in his head and heart. Like a hunting dog, this particular rabbit was speeding away through space, and all he could think of was getting after it.

"Well, I think you're a hero," Taylor said. The way she said it made her seem younger than he had initially thought, the cropped blonde hair, steel-blue eyes and almost military air all adding age to what he could now see was a youthful face. Franklin hadn't been feeling much like a hero because a hero would not be stuck where he was, at the mercy of others. Perhaps a little unheroically, the words brought a slightly warm, swelling feeling inside him. "You were on the cannon, weren't you?" She went on. "You saved us."

Franklin snorted. "I used up all the ammo," he protested as Taylor lifted off and they began to rise towards the gap above them and the grey sky beyond, "that's what *I* did." There were no clouds, but the daytime sky on Regus was a sort of dirty colour, like much-worn, faded white overalls.

Taylor was quiet as they passed out of the station and the shuttle tilted to fire its main thrusters, Franklin's fold-down seat creaking heavily as the acceleration pushed him back into it.

"And you're him," Taylor said once they were clear of the station, speaking as if there had been no break in their conversation. "The one who saved Earth. I'd heard you were on the *Olympic*, of all places, but didn't believe it." She glanced backward briefly, smiling at Franklin as they sped upwards. Through the front viewport, Franklin could see the *Olympic*, sitting much closer to the planet than usual, so that it was a lot larger in the sky. The old luxury liner—his home—looked oddly "other," like the moon seen from the Earth during the daytime, a sight that Franklin had not seen in a very long while... Familiar, and yet utterly alien too.

"I thought you'd be too young to remember or care," Franklin answered, almost reflexively.

"You made me want to become a pilot," she enthused, making Gus glance up briefly too. "I can't believe I'm really flying you, of all people." On the one hand, Franklin was in no mood to be hero-worshipped. Yet, there was a tiny devil on his shoulder, one that was flattered by the young woman's attention, who thought he could almost hear an invitation in her voice, who remembered that Sarah—his damned ex-wife—had chosen to walk into *his* bar to ask him to rescue *her* husband. And that devil was mightily pissed off that all he could think of now was pale skin and flame-red hair. All he could feel was that he had somehow let her down and that, worst of all, he would never see her again when, only a few days ago, he had never expected to anyway. Add to that, his cat was still on the *Mutt's Nuts*.

He glanced across at Gus, who hadn't known any of them before the last few days, and was struck again by just how tired and traumatised the big man looked, and how grimly his jaw was set. "You okay?" he asked.

Gus managed a smile that he didn't look like he meant. "I just wish..." he trailed off and looked down at his feet again, never finishing the thought. All the while, the view of the SS *Olympic* grew in the front viewport.

Franklin stood outside the SS *Olympic* Cocktail Lounge looking at a printed sign below the currently inactive neon-style one, which read "Closed Until Further Notice." It wasn't his sign, as they had left the *Olympic* in far too much of a hurry for signs, but someone had thought to put it up. He took it off the door and entered. All the chairs were on the tables in the middle of the space, and much of what was behind the bar had been put away. Somebody really thought that he hadn't been coming back. Not knowing what else to do, Franklin started taking the chairs down, as if getting ready to open again.

He had been expecting to find a welcoming committee waiting for him at the docking bay, from where he had imagined he would be taken straight to a cell. When that hadn't been the case, he and Gus had wandered in an almost dazed state through the corridors until Gus had turned to peel off towards his own quarters. "What are you going to do?" his friend had asked.

"I don't know," Franklin admitted. "I should talk to Arnold, I guess, beg with him to go after the others, or to call the military or something, although who knows how far away the closest ship is. Of course, he might remember that he wants to throw me in the brig."

"He's your friend," Gus argued.

"So maybe he won't throw me in the brig. Either way, he's not going to chase after a warship for us."

"You said yourself that he was interested in what went down on Enceladine," Gus pointed out hopefully.

Franklin had tried his hand at a reassuring grin before turning and heading off. He found himself walking towards his bar without really thinking about where he was going. His mind was occupied with whether there was anything currently parked in the bays of the *Olympic* that might be suitable for going after the Koru cruiser; he was fairly sure that there wasn't.

"Does anyone drink absinthe anymore?" a familiar voice now asked as Franklin was halfway through putting the chairs back out. He froze and looked up as the captain of the SS *Olympic* walked out from his storeroom, holding a blue-tinged bottle. "It's the one you set fire to, isn't it?"

"One of them," Franklin replied, turning to face the other man.

"I didn't know how long you would be," Arnold said, an odd cheeriness in his voice, "so I came in while you were gone, tidied up a bit." He gestured to the sign on a table close to the door. "Made a sign."

"Are you angling to take over the bar as a second job?" Franklin remarked drily. "Captain not paying enough?"

"If you were just a renting landlord, I might be considering finding someone more reliable," Arnold replied smoothly, like a schoolteacher good-naturedly ticking off a usually well-behaved pupil whose behaviour had been slipping.

"Why did you try and stop me from leaving?" Franklin shot back, suddenly taking the gently sparring subtext out of the conversation.

"I didn't," Arnold replied, blinking indignantly, shock arching his thin eyebrows. Franklin wasn't buying it.

"That wasn't the way Hultz saw it. Seemed real determined not to let us leave."

"You need clearance from the duty officer to disembark between stops," Arnold answered with a weary sort of patience, "you know this, Mr Franklin. Had you asked for it?"

No, he hadn't, but Franklin was fairly sure that wasn't the point.

"Instead," Arnold went on, "you went about attacking the security and docking staff like some half-crazed madman, dragging poor Moreau along on your crazy exploits. Jesus, man, I'm bloody-well worried about you. This ex-wife of yours has got you acting crazy."

"Bullshit," Franklin seethed, "what was all that bollocks in my quarters before I left? 'Earth having more of a say in things'?"

For the first time in the conversation, Arnold Phiby's cool slipped a little, and he took a couple of lanky strides forward, his chin jutting out as he spoke. "Well, something needs to be done. Now there's a bloody Koru cruiser zipping about as it pleases, as I'm sure you've noticed."

"My friends are being held captive on it," Franklin put in, although he had a feeling that Arnold already knew that.

"I asked you what happened on Enceladine, that's all," Arnold said, then gestured in the direction of the ship's, which Franklin knew was to the left as one entered the bar, "so I could understand. And now I wonder even more so when the Koru have kidnapped your friends and even fired weapons on a UTC facility." Franklin had known that Arnold would have grilled Harris about what had been going on. "This is where I operate my ship, Mark," he went on, using Franklin's first name in a way he almost never did, "so I feel I have a right to know why these things are happening if you do. I'd hope our years of friendship and our shared past might be worth that at least."

"You pointed bow-wards."

"What?" Arnold blinked, this time in confusion.

"When you spoke about my friends, you gestured towards the bow," Franklin explained, "but that's not our direction of travel... or is it?"

Arnold had the look of someone who had just been busted. After a long moment of silence, he finally answered. "We're going after them."

Franklin put a hand to his mouth in an uncharacteristic gesture. "You'll have a riot on your hands from the passengers. You'll lose your job." This was what he wanted—to be heading back after Sarah and the others—but he was still appalled that Philby was doing it, and without him even having to plead.

"Tell me," Arnold hissed, "what am I putting my ship and my career in harm's way for? I know you'd want to go after them and, dammit, so do I. Just tell me why I'm doing this, Mark?"

In his heart, Franklin knew that Arnold had his own agenda that went beyond the safety of these three people that he didn't know, and beyond simple concerns about the safety of the sector in which the ship operated. But, then again, what did it matter? This was his only hope to get Sarah back and, given the uncertainness of what lay ahead, maybe someone else should know about the shields and what the Koru had been up to on Enceladine.

TWENTY-FOUR

"It just occurred to me," Vik said as he slumped to the floor in the sparse cell, sweat soaking his shirt, "that I have no idea what happened to Geoff."

Sarah saw that he was gasping as he spoke, having just been deposited into the cell by two Koru guards after nearly an hour away. They had come and grabbed him almost as soon as he had woken up, the knockout gas which had rendered all of them unconscious back on the *Mutt's Nuts* seeming to have had a much greater effect on him. She rushed to his side. "Geoff?" she asked, thrown by these first words to come out of his mouth. His absence had seemed like an eternity and Sarah had started to succumb to the panicked feeling that she might not see her husband again.

"The cat." Vik winced as she tried to help him sit up. "Franklin's cat. The little blighter wouldn't leave me alone on the way over to Regus. I wonder if he's still on the ship or if they found him." He glanced over at Engee. "Do your people have cats? Would they know what to feed Geoff if they found him?"

Engee looked at Sarah, then spoke almost as if Vik wasn't there. "I think they must have used the same neural reordering equipment used on me. It has made a mess of your husband's brain, I am afraid."

"I'm fine!" Vik snapped. "But they did plug me in, and they were looking for something in here," he went on, tapping a forefinger to the side of his head. "So, I kept thinking about Geoff to stop them from finding what they might be after."

"Did it work?" Sarah asked.

Vik shrugged. "They didn't really talk to me about what they were doing with that machine, but they didn't seem very happy."

Sarah managed a brave smile and leaned over to kiss her husband's head. "If we get out of this, let's find somewhere as far away from trouble as possible, hey? Can we just do that? Leave the saving humanity to someone else?"

"I could get a job on your ship," Vik offered. "Have a weird crush on my boss."

"Hey," Engee put in, "there is already a co-pilot who has a weird crush on her boss, so you will have to be something else. Can you cook?"

"Er... do you know what a crush is?" Sarah asked Engee.

"Is it not when you think your boss is a fabulous person?" Engee asked, her face now concerned.

Vik nodded. "Kind of."

Sarah leaned back against one of the benches, her back finding the hard, white surface that blended into the rest of the cell. The even whiteness of the room was beginning to hurt her brain. She kept losing all sense of being anywhere at all, felt detached from reality, suspended in a sort of nothingness, and so found herself turning inward. All three fell quiet, and the time passing could have been minutes or hours. Sarah was truly beginning to lose the ability to tell.

As she sat there, she thought about Mark. They were complicated feelings. On the one hand, she thought about how she should never have dragged him into all of this, although she was relieved that the Koru had shown an unwillingness to destroy the Regus mining station. She could not know for sure that they hadn't turned around to finish the job once they had safely knocked out the crew of the *Mutt's Nuts* but had a strong feeling inside that they hadn't. He might be on the *Olympic* now—perhaps in trouble because of how they had left it—but whatever Philby had been up to that had so spooked Mark before they left the cruise liner, she was at least sure that he would be alive and well, and that was enough.

On the other hand, as absurd as it might seem, she also held out a small hope that he was still coming after them, that he had found some way to try another rescue. That was a selfish thought, but there you go. Mark Franklin might not realise it, but even all these years later, so long out of the military, he still had that doggedness about him, that determination and sense of "right" that had led him back to Earth during the war and effectively ended their un recognised marriage. Sarah did not love him anymore, but she knew him and trusted that heroic streak within him. If there was a way, he would come.

The door opened, pulling Sarah from her thoughts and she felt momentarily dizzied by that sensation of not knowing how long had passed. The two guards from before came in, while the interrogator stood by the door and pointed to Engee.

"Take her," the interrogator said, "her sentence is to be carried out immediately."

TWENTY-FIVE

Franklin thought he could hear the *Olympic* creaking, groaning and complaining almost as much as its septuagenarian and octogenarian passengers, who at this time of the year made up a significant portion of the fares on the old liner, as the three-week trip around the McMurdo Rift was a cut-price cruise compared to many other destinations. They were not, he had gathered, in the slightest bit happy about heading towards Enceladine for the third time.

He could feel the ship's acceleration like a gently insistent hand pushing him towards the aft of the ship, and that was something he had never felt before on the *Olympic*, which, built for comfort, hardly ever felt like it was moving at all.

They were burning hard after the Koru cruiser as it headed back towards the only planet with a breathable atmosphere in the sector. Why that was had been a matter for debate between Franklin, Arnold and Gus, the latter having joined them in the bar while they tried to decide what to do. The *Olympic's* captain felt that the cruiser had plans to lay waste to Enceladine, perhaps trying to erase any sign that they were ever there. Franklin and Gus were more hopeful, thinking that maybe they were planning only to retrieve the ore that powered their shields. Either way, the cruiser would likely have to stop and stay above the planet for some time, so he hoped to find the opportunity to get on board and try to rescue his friends... if they were still alive.

"You know they could take out the *Olympic* well before we get anywhere near them if they wanted to?" Franklin said as they sat around a table in the Olympic Cocktail Lounge, each with a shot of the absinthe in front of them. The craziest of drinks seemed to suit this particular situation.

Arnold nodded. "That's why we're going to keep our distance, at least a little bit. It won't be far enough away from their weapons if they really do object to us, but..."

"But what...?" Franklin asked, his eyes narrowing at the captain's tone. He wasn't usually this reticent about anything.

"I have an idea."

"I'm going to die a really shitty death," Gus complained as he zipped up his suit just inside the airlock. While the rest of the ship was faded blues, reds and whites, with a little chrome, brass and gold plating here and there, the airlock was gunmetal grey, aside from a thin, defiant strip of red about halfway up, intersected by the airlock number. Gus glared at Franklin. "At least you've done this sort of stuff before."

"Not like this," Franklin protested, although he didn't want to protest too much and cause the other man's confidence to falter even further. It was a long time ago and involved the odd maintenance walk on the *Mutt's Nuts* back when he ran his own business with what was now Sarah's ship. Like Gus, he felt that he was about to die a really shitty death, but the other man didn't need to know that. He should make the gym instructor stay on the *Olympic*, force him out of the airlock and back into the ship—although Gus was quite a bit bigger than him and that was easier said than done. For all the fear in his friend's voice right now, Gus had been determined to come along on this crazy mission that Arnold—conveniently not on said mission—had suggested. Seeing his best friend's face when he had been left behind on Regus, Franklin just couldn't do it to him again. The whole thing made him feel quite a swell of admiration for the other man.

Yes, Arnold had, indeed, had an idea. The problem was that it was an insane one that involved the *Olympic* speeding towards the Koru cruiser, launching the two of them out of the airlock while they were still thousands of kilometres away and then veering off before the other ship decided they were a threat... hopefully. Then—and this was the best bit—Franklin and Gus would use the very limited supply of oxygen in the suits as a propellant to adjust their path and slow them down, so that they didn't shoot right past the Koru ship or get splattered all over its hull. Assuming it didn't spot them or just happen to fly out of the way first and, of course, that they didn't misjudge things and run out of breathable air on the way over.

Yep, Franklin had never done anything even remotely this stupid.

"Are we ready, gentlemen?" came Arnold Philby's voice into their helmet comms once they were fully suited up. Suddenly, Franklin was back in the military, taken there by Arnold's words and voice. The man had sounded almost jealous, as he always had when sending his pilots into war.

"On three we will blow the hatch from here," Arnold went on. "You've got six seconds from the hatch blowing to the ship turning, and we'll be turning fast. The passengers will definitely be feeling this one. You want to be far enough away from the ship by then, as you do not want to be caught in our drive plume. That would make it a very short mission."

"Great," Gus grumbled.

Franklin didn't add that if even any of the attitude thrusters caught them they would likely be irretrievably blown off course and condemned to asphyxiate when their air ran out. The big man was probably fine without that knowledge. That said, there wasn't enough room for them both to get through the airlock opening at the same time and Franklin was having to lead the way, with

Gus doing his best to stay a good distance behind him, reacting to all of Franklin's small course changes and, hopefully, matching his breaking when the time came. "Just make sure you are out that door as soon after me as you can," Franklin said in a way that he hoped sounded reassuring. "Then you can let the gap stretch out a little once we're clear. Just a little, though."

Gus didn't answer.

"Just a reminder, gentleman," Arnold cut in again. "Although your friends are the primary mission, a very close secondary mission would be finding out everything you can about their shield technology."

Franklin knew that Arnold really held the shield as the primary mission. Maybe he would have agreed to help retrieve Sarah and Vik—and even Engee—without the knowledge of the shield technology, yet his enthusiasm increased five-fold when he learned about the Koru's new technological advantage and the mine on Enceladine. Still, of course, a military man at heart.

"Right then," Arnold said, "it's time."

TWENTY-SIX

"Captain!" Yelland snapped behind Arnold as the *Olympic* pulled a tight turn that its motion suspension system completely failed to deal with. His second-in-command stumbled sideways and had to grab the edge of a console for support, satisfyingly—so Arnold felt—interrupting the righteous tirade that Arnold was sure he had been about to launch into, as Yelland stumbled across the raised command platform and had to reach out and grab the captain's chair for support.

Life aboard most ships was relatively flat, with only combat ships usually needing to pull the sort of manoeuvres that would overwhelm the environmental controls' ability to keep things feeling flat and level. Despite her age, the SS *Olympic's* motion suspension was better than many newly built ships, but right now the bridge listed worryingly as they turned hard away from the distant Koru ship, so that Arnold couldn't help but fret about what was happening throughout the rest of the ship. How many glasses of champagne and plates of lobster thermidor were currently further spoiling the already aged carpets?

They could barely see the cruiser that they had been heading towards, although the planet, at least, was a fair-sized ball behind it—more a blue-grey than the blue-green that most life-sustaining planets appeared to be from space. They would retreat to a safe distance and begin hailing for military help, still available if Franklin and his friends found a way to them. Ready, hopefully, to take possession of the secrets of this Koru shield system too.

Yelland had spent most of the last few days on the bridge, whether or not he was on shift, and looked—for the first time since Arnold had known him—decidedly strung out. Arnold drew in another breath to bat aside the latest of the Lieutenant-Commander's objections but stopped short when he saw a familiar but unexpected face, whose accompanying hands were clinging desperately to the back of a chair just inside the bridge entrance. "Dame Hatherleigh has requested an audience with you," Yelland told him, nodding to the overdressed older woman.

Arnold looked down at Yelland, but the man refused to wilt under the captain's most piercing glare. "And you let her straight onto my bridge?" he fumed. The woman behind Yelland, who was the most honoured guest of this particular tour had, until her retirement not all that long ago, been one of the most influential members of the parliament on Proxima.

"Technically, Sir," Yelland pressed, who should right now have been the duty officer, "it's my bri-"

"Be quiet, you child! Get her off my bridge, now. And if you try to undermine me once more-"

"Captain Philby!" Dame Hatherleigh screeched, regaining her balance as the *Olympic* completed its turn. She was dressed in a cream-coloured satin ballgown that contrasted nicely with her light-brown skin—Arnold hadn't even registered that it was the evening of the weekly gala, an event at which he should have been present—and was tall with long, grey hair and a sense that age became her, even empowered her. "I demand to know what is going on at once."

Arnold bristled. He would have struggled with her presence if she was still a serving member of the parliament, would have felt no compunction to recognise her, yet she had no more genuine authority than any other person on the ship. Of course, what she did have in buckets load after a career of so-called "service" as one of the ring leaders in the Proxima Parliament that first rebelled against Earth control—then a seat at the centre of what came after—was influence.

Arnold squared his shoulders, straightened his back and forced a mask of civility onto his face. "Dame Hatherleigh," he purred politely. "I'm afraid that guests are not really supposed to be on the br-"

"Don't talk down to me, Philby," the dame roared, the breath from her tirade lightly blasting Arnold's face with the sweet scent of Champagne, made slightly fetid by the woman's breath. *Halitosis, nice.*

Arnold decided not to point out that she was the only person on the bridge he *physically couldn't* speak down to. And she was powerfully built, too. He could imagine that she must have been formidable when debating on the house floor.

"We've been crossing back and forth on the same piece of space for over two days, accelerating hard for hours now and then..." Dame Hatherleigh spread her arms wide to indicate, he supposed, the recent bout of unusual manoeuvring. "Are you trying to kill us?"

"He's chasing down a Koru cruiser," Yelland put in around the ex-politician, who the snivelling runt literally seemed to be hiding behind.

"He's what?" Dame Hatherleigh exploded, rounding again on Arnold, who couldn't help feeling at least a little intimidated. "Are you a military ship?" she raved, taking most of one of her long strides towards him. This time the blast of bad breath was all sulphur, the sweetness of the lingering champagne now lost. It took an effort of will to hold his ground.

"We're doing our duty in tailing a trespassing military ship," Arnold argued. "For hundreds of years, civilian ships and sailors have done their part-"

"We're not at fucking war!" the dame bellowed, showing that she likely argued as well in a bar room debate. "These aren't your glory days, Philby. You're putting everyone's life at risk. I want you to resume the ship's proper course at once."

Doing what he should have done before the conversation started, Arnold turned to the bridge's security officer. "Zhao," he beckoned. "Would you remove Dame Hatherleigh from the bridge?"

Zhao, broad-shouldered and with a very military-looking haircut, moved to obey, then faltered as Dame Hatherleigh spun and turned that laser glare—of which Arnold was becoming quite jealous—on him. "Don't you touch me-" she began, balling her fists, although it was now Arnold's turn to interrupt.

"And put her in detention if she resists."

Yelland—along with half the bridge crew—gave Arnold a shocked look.

"This is my bridge," he went on.

"But I don't think it should be anymore, sir," Yelland said. "You've abandoned your duty to the *Olympic* and its passengers and crew in chasing this ship, showing a dangerous allegiance to your old friend, the barman. You've put us in danger and put the ship unnecessarily behind schedule."

Ah, the schedule, Arnold thought, *the worst crime of all for a ship that runs the same bloody loop every few weeks.* "And if you could call assistance to ensure Mr Yelland enjoys a trip to the cells, as well, Ensign Zhao," Arnold added, as smoothly as if he were asking for the man to make him a cup of tea. Zhao, for his part, had one hand outstretched towards the dame's upper arm, cautious, as if he might be about to lose a finger or two.

Yelland looked back towards the bridge entrance and nodded towards one of the junior officers who stood close to it. He opened the door and three more security officers walked in. Arnold would have loved it if every would-be prisoner were so accommodating.

"Take the Captain," Yelland told them, "and Ensign Zhao, if he resists. Along with anyone else who would rather carry on with this current insanity than resume course and take the more than one thousand passengers who are currently relying on us to safety."

Oh, Arnold thought, *bollocks.*

TWENTY-SEVEN

Franklin's breath was like a howling gale inside his helmet as he hurtled through space. It was the only thing that gave him any real sensation of movement, as the Koru cruiser remained barely more than a glinting dot in his vision as the seconds passed.

After the initial moments of acceleration, which were needed to be sure of clearing the *Olympic* and the ship's super-heated wake as it turned, he had kept the oxygen-supplied thrusters turned off, saving them for heading adjustment and the whole heap of braking that needed to happen if he wasn't to become a smear against the side of the Koru ship. *Fuck*, but that was just going to be one great big guess.

The oxygen was needed for breathing as well. EVA suits usually kept the thrust and breathing supplies separate, with some allowing thruster oxygen to back up the breathing supply. However, so much was going to be required for braking—EVA suits were not usually used for travelling great distances at high velocity between ships—they had needed to open the partition in the other direction. If Franklin and Gus didn't manoeuvre and slow down correctly, then a few minutes' extra oxygen was not going to matter either way.

"You okay back there?" Franklin asked, suddenly remembering that he should check on the fitness instructor, who had virtually no EVA experience.

No reply came for several moments and Franklin was about to ask again—as there was no way he was going to be able to turn around and check—when Gus' strained, crackling voice sounded over the speaker in his helmet.

"No," his friend answered. "I'm not okay at all."

"What's the problem? You still behind me?"

"The problem is I'm hurtling through space at... I don't even know how fucking fast, and I'm not in a spaceship, Franklin, like I should be."

"But you're still behind me, right?"

"If you're that vaguely blank bit of space quite far ahead of me, then yeah, I'm still behind you."

It was true, the only EVA suits that the *Olympic* had were a dark grey colour which, once away from any good light sources, was essentially black. However, Franklin realised that he might have failed to explain the one really simple piece of EVA usage to Gus.

"You're using the HUD, right?"

"...Maybe. What's a HUD?"

His friend was going to fucking die. "Shit, man. It should have come on once you were in the suit and it was active. A display that shows important shit like your air, suit pressure and all that?"

"Oh, yeah, I've got a display with some numbers."

"And you can't see me on it?"

"I get a hint whenever you fire a thruster," Gus added.

Mother- Franklin was amazed that Gus was even still following him. "Okay, lift your hand in front of your visor. Yep?"

"Uh-huh."

He could hear the barely contained fear in Gus' voice, probably inherited from his own panicked exasperation as they needed to get this sorted quickly. He couldn't believe he hadn't made sure that Gus knew this stuff, however basic. *Get your head in the game, Franklin.* "Right, next time I fire, tap me with your finger and it'll ask you if you want to track. You've got to be accurate with your finger, though, so it can identify me as an object. This is usually done when you're right in front of each other, not a few hundred metres. Ready?"

Gus did as he was told and moments later confirmed that he was tracking Franklin, who then began to breathe just a little easier. Once things had calmed down again, the silence, the strange emptiness of it, came crowding back in. Franklin had been on spacewalks before, mostly minor maintenance work on the *Mutt's Nuts*, although there were one or two stupid examples of spacewalking that had happened during drunken get-togethers with friends. They had involved challenges and bets and were nothing that Sarah had ever needed to know about. Those stupid examples were, strangely, coming in handy right now, although nothing had ever been quite like this. He was a piece of space debris, speeding quiet and unseen through the cosmos. Never had he felt so small, so insignificant, so lost among all of it.

From this distance, with all this space around him, he saw how the Koru ship was, like him, such a small, distant part of the whole. So small that it barely seemed to be getting any closer, and Franklin found that his mind kept getting drawn towards the murky majesty of the planet beyond. It was only partly lit from this angle by the star that it orbited, yet still a vast oasis in an infinite universe. It made everything man-made —even Koru-made—seem like a tiny little joke. Maybe he would feel different those last few moments, however, with the ship rushing up at him as he tried to slow on his approach to it.

"Why are you doing this?" Gus' voice—still sounding much more frightened and breathless than Franklin now felt—shocked him out of the odd moment of serenity.

The pertinent question seemed to be, "Why was Gus doing this?" They were friends, yes, but he had no deep ties to anyone on the Koru ship, and he was not the best prepared for this... Never done a spacewalk, never been in the military, maybe never fired a weapon in anger. But the question had been asked of him, not Gus.

"Someone has to; we're here."

"Would you be doing it if it wasn't her?"

Franklin was quiet for a long moment. "Probably not, but then we wouldn't be in any of this shit if it wasn't her, would we?"

"And if she wasn't your ex-"

"Ahem."

"Your wife, I mean. As well as being the wife of that other guy." After a few more moments of silence on Franklin's end, Gus changed the subject. "Do you think this is it? Do you think the Koru are starting plans for some sort of invasion or war? Do you think it's happening out here first?"

"If you'd asked me a week ago, I would have said the Koru were about as utterly alien as any intelligent race could be to us. I never minded the Koru, despite my history with them, but I never understood them either. And that meant I would never have trusted them as a people. Never felt that they didn't have their own motives and agenda.

"I mean, why sit peacefully on our borders when they could have rolled over us at any time, then get involved in a war that wasn't theirs to fight? *And then* retreat away again while asking nothing from the peace, from the victory they helped to win?"

"Ask a UTC patriot and they'll tell you it was because they saw the rebellion was the right side, the good side," Gus put in. A second later, he added, "I got you good now, by the way, less than a hundred metres right behind you."

Franklin grinned wryly inside his helmet. "If there's one thing I'm sure of, it's that the Koru never saw it that way. I don't think they care about our rights and wrongs. To his credit, Vikram Shah is sure of that too. And, like I said, a week ago I would never have thought of the Koru as anything other than unknowable. Then I met a Koru rebel."

"Engee," Gus breathed. *Yeah,* Franklin knew that their friendship and "the right thing to do" were not the only reasons that Gus had insisted on coming along. He had developed a fondness for a particular little Koru.

"Go figure, eh? A Koru rebel. Engee makes me feel that maybe they aren't so unknowable, so alien. But, if they are more like humans... I'm not sure if that's an even scarier thought with their motherships and shields. But no, I have no fucking idea what they are doing, or if there's a bigger plan for them beyond getting the raw materials for their shields. Technically, Enceladine is not UTC space, but I don't think they care either way, and that in itself is worrying."

The Koru ship was beginning to take form and shape in front of him now, they were getting close. "I don't know if they've turned since we launched," Franklin told Gus, "but our angle's too close to the thrusters. We can't risk coming in close to them, so we'll need to do a hard burn to the right, then a hard one to the left. Even then, we'll be coming in at an angle, so we'll have to be careful not to glance straight off the surface, yeah?"

"Is that going to screw with the oxygen reserve?" Gus asked.

Franklin waited for an all-too-obvious beat before replying. "Let's see. Now, on three I want you to activate the left suit thruster-"

"Left," Gus asked. "I thought we were going right?"

Oh my fucking God, Franklin thought again, *this man's going to die*.

"The left thruster sends you right," he said, failing in his efforts not to sound impatient. "Just... just press right, the suit knows which thruster to operate. Then switch to left burn when I call "left." Okay?"

"Which is the right thruster?"

Argh! "Then release thrust when I say stop."

"And go on three, not after three?"

"Yes, on three."

"Got it."

"It'll be fine," Franklin said, trying and failing to be reassuring because he realised that the stupid questions were probably a result of extreme terror on Gus' part. Then it occurred to him how the military training was still with him, that ability for adrenaline and fear to bring concentration, rather than panic. "Ready?" he added.

"Ready,"

"One... two... three!"

Franklin fired his left thruster on full power and saw the oxygen gauge begin to move visibly.

"Ah, I was fucking slow!" Gus screamed into his helmet.

"Don't worry, adjust after... Now, left!"

"I missed that one too!"

"It'll balance out... probably. STO-O-OP!" Franklin cried. Then, "Brake, brake, fucking brake! We're coming in too hot!"

TWENTY-EIGHT

"I know that is too late to save my own life, but if I show you where the ore and some of the other information I stole is, do you think it will help my friends?" Engee was addressing the interrogator, as the two guards with her would have no opinions of their own on the matter, beyond carrying out their current orders. Such was the life of a soldier.

Fragments had finally been coming back to Engee as she sat in the cell, memories of a life before the last few weeks. Some of it was random scraps of knowledge and little moments, but much of it was better described as general "feelings." For instance, she was glad that she was not a soldier, that the set of generic characteristics that would have naturally pushed her in that direction the size and strength, the quicker reactions—were not who she was. She knew that with those genetic traits came a natural propensity towards mental conditioning, something that was stronger for the soldier than for any other Koru—not to think independently, not to have opinions or ever seek knowledge beyond the very slim perimeters of your role in society.

Her inclination for independent thought as a technical drone had landed her where she was—about to be executed—but she could still not bring herself to regret it. Which, ironically enough—she knew this as Sarah had been keen to teach her about irony almost since their first association—was very much a Koru trait. No regrets. Perhaps it was better that she should be removed, for she was far too rare an aberration to be able to truly affect change with the others. Yet—and this was a detail that would not come back to her—she felt that, when she hacked the central memory, she had not been working completely alone.

The interrogator snorted derisively. He stood in front of her in the interrogation room, which curved overhead and gave the feeling of being within someone's torso. Engee had noted that all of the ship she had seen beyond their cell was like this—gently curving—the spaces seeming to fit together like some sort of squashed cellular structure. "We have already searched the ship you came in and found nothing of interest," the interrogator said." Are you playing for time? That is a worryingly human trait."

Engee shrugged, an intentionally non-committal and very human gesture. "That is up to you. Your loss, bud-dy."

"Budd-y?" the interrogator growled back.

"Bud-dy," Engee corrected.

"B-u-d-d-y?"

"Close enough."

They walked in silence for a moment, then the interrogator looked over. Engee could feel a suspicious eye like heat on her cheek. "You can show me?"

"*If* it will help my friends."

The interrogator laughed. "Friends! You truly are a lost cause, NG-972. But we will take you to the ship before we take you to your death, and maybe you can live a little longer."

When they got to the bay, Engee led the interrogator up the ramp and into the rear of the *Mutt's Nuts*. Her heart sank as the two guards followed them. She had a plan, but it was a very, very stupid plan. It had just the tiniest chance of succeeding if she was left alone with the interrogator, but with the soldiers there as well...

"We checked everywhere in here," the interrogator said with a sweeping left-to-right gesture, indicating the *Mutt's Nuts'* fairly small cargo hold. "If you are just trying to prolong the time until your execution, NG-972, then it is a feeble effort indeed. Your death is the only gift you can give to your people now, you should take it well and redeem yourself a little, not waste my valuable time."

"I did not hide them here," Engee said in what she hoped Sarah would think was a cutting tone, "I am not of the stupid type."

"Where then?" the interrogator asked impatiently, lifting an eyebrow.

Engee pointed mysteriously to the metal steps that led up to the gantry above the bay, then into the galley through an airlock.

"Come on, then," the interrogator growled, and they started up the steps. Engee went first but, halfway up, the other Koru paused. "Wait there," the interrogator barked back towards the two soldiers, "I don't think this little one will give me any trouble."

He squeezed her shoulder then with a strong hand, his fingers slipping to the back of her slender neck in a way that no Koru should touch another without consent. Engee shivered and forced herself to keep going.

I can do this, she made herself think, all the while feeling that there was no way she possibly could. Reaching the top of the steps and continuing through, they came into the ship's galley area, which was more of an all-round social space where everything important that happened on the *Mutt's Nuts* that didn't involve *actually flying* the ship seemed to happen. Humans and their obsession with food. Engee realised that she was incredibly happy to be back on the ship, despite the circumstances. If she really was about to die, then it was good that she could be on the *Mutt's Nuts* one more time. She had felt free here, and yet like she belonged. It had only been a matter of weeks since she had first set foot on the ship, yet the metal and composite that surrounded her right now had witnessed some of her happiest memories—and that wasn't just because of the whole memory loss thing.

The interrogator looked around the space disdainfully, sneering at the personal items that were fixed in place around it. At the food preparation area that would probably see the ship shut down if a health inspector ever went anywhere near it, at the detritus of Sarah's life and, more recently, Engee's. "I've never seen such a disorganised mess, NG-972," he spat. "You lived in this?"

"I did," she answered evenly, shuffling as incongruously as she could manage over towards the far side of the right-hand wall from where they had come in. She cast a hopefully casual eye up at a nearby vent, remembering how a certain miniature member of the crew had taken to hiding there.

The interrogator continued casting his own eye distastefully around the room. Even by human standards, Engee had come to understand, Sarah was, perhaps, a little messy, but by Koru standards the place was a cluttered nightmare, apt to bring on a panic attack. Or at least an extended bout of cleaning. It was amazing, Engee mused, how in a few weeks living in it had gone from causing mild panic to a sort of affection... Well, affection soaked in disinfectant, perhaps.

"No wonder we could not find anything," the interrogator commented. Finally, his attention came back to Engee, and she felt his eyes slide up and down her lasciviously. "Once you've told me where the ore and the information you stole is kept, we could prolong your sentence a little longer if you would like?" He stepped towards Engee and reached out to touch her neck, which she found repulsive.

Of course, that's why he had made the soldiers stay behind.

"I think I will jump out of the airlock myself," she shot back unwisely.

The interrogator's eyes went wide, genuinely taken aback for a moment by the sharpness and directness of her response. The anger quickly followed, and a hand shot out, not caressing her neck but instead clasping around it hard so that she immediately felt herself choking.

"Why you stupid little-" The interrogator stopped suddenly and looked about. "What was that?"

Engee had heard it too. A metallic, scraping, scrabbling noise and something else, something like a "hiss."

"Hiss-s-s-s," Engee said, panicking, trying to get his attention back on her and away from the sound, "it turns me on to make you angry. H... Hiss-s-s-s. Yes-s-s-s. Come on then... Big... Interrogator." She was terrible at this.

The interrogator shoved her back, a look of disgust crossing his big, bold features. "Forget it," he said, "living with those humans has made you very unlike a Koru female should be, NG-972. It repulses me. Go on and get me what we came for, or I will make sure that your friends suffer after you have gone."

"I..." Engee pointed towards a grill that joined the ship's environmental system high on the wall on one side, intentionally looking nervous.

"What?" the interrogator snapped impatiently.

"I need your help. It's up there. Can you get it for me?"

The grill was clearly far too high for Engee to reach and, indeed, too far for the interrogator, even though he was tall for non-soldier designation. *Please don't get them*, she thought, thinking that he might order the soldiers to come and help. Hopefully, his pride would stop him from doing so. As it turned out, there was a third answer.

"Here," the interrogator said, grabbing a small refrigeration box and bringing it over, "stand on this."

Engee stood on the box reluctantly. *Fuck*, as Sarah liked to say; she was now tall enough to reach the grill. She put a hand up, three of her slim, still greenish-brown fingers wrapping around to the inside of it. She pretended to pull, jumping slightly when something soft quickly tapped her fingers—once, twice, three times in quick succession. Even though she had been half expecting it, she jumped and almost pulled the grill off, which would have ruined her whole plan.

"I can't do it," Engee said, "I'm not strong enough to get the grill off." She shook her fingers for effect, which was a natural reaction, as something sharp had caught the end of one of them as she had taken her fingers away.

"Well, I don't think you've really tried." The interrogator shook his head with a growl and roughly pulled her off the refrigeration box, stepping up to take hold of the grill. "Just let me-"

The grill came off and a ball of hissing fur erupted from behind it.

"Oh, the Nest, oh the Nest, get it off my face!"

The interrogator fell from the box, landing heavily with a tabby cat still attached to his face, which was somehow managing to stay on there as he jumped and shook and slapped at his face.

When Geoff finally leaped free, the interrogator had two hands clasped over one eye as he began to climb to his feet. "NG-972, what is that crea-"

The interrogator was cut short as Engee used the only thing handy to batter her captor—the rather hefty refrigeration box.

Knowing that she might not have long if the sound of the interrogator's screams—or the following "thump"—had carried down to the bay, she quickly turned the unconscious Koru over and located his weapon but was only halfway back up to standing when the first of the soldiers came through the door.

No! Another couple of seconds and she could have found cover. The soldiers had turned up too quickly and she was about to die, because she could not stop now, could not throw her hands up innocently. She had at least try and shoot them, as this moment was her one and only plan. It was all Engee could do to force her eyes open as she straightened fully and started firing.

"What the...?" said the first soldier.

"...Is that?" the second soldier kind of finished as he barrelled in behind. Both of them had fixed on Geoff, who was now trotting over to see if those things they were carrying dispensed food. Horror and fascination warred in the two soldiers' faces and, in the following split second, two of the three weapons in the room were discharged.

TWENTY-NINE

"What are you going to do?" Arnold asked Yelland as the two security officers had marched him from the bridge, calling back over his shoulder to where the Lieutenant-Commander and Dame Hatherleigh stood in the middle of the room, right next to each other like the actors in some coup—as if the retired politician was now the acting second-in-command of his ship.

It was both vaguely ridiculous—almost to the point of surreal—and devastating. He had been among those commanding the defence of Earth and now his brown-nosing whelp of a second-in-command and Dame Full-of-Herself were in charge of his passenger ship.

"I'm going to turn the ship around and resume course, obviously," the ship's new commander replied haughtily. Arnold wanted to strangle him with his bare hands. Watch the smugness drain from his face. "I'm going to put the safety of the people aboard it ahead of my friends and some vainglorious notion of recapturing my past."

"But they're expecting us to be here," Arnold protested, more for the rest of the bridge crew's benefit than Yelland or Hatherleigh's. "You condemn them to death!"

Yelland gave a sharp nod and Arnold was dragged from the bridge, although at least the two security officers had the decency to look abashed as they did it. Ensign Zhao hadn't, as it turned out, resisted—which, given the odds, Arnold couldn't blame him for—and so was not being dragged away with his erstwhile captain.

Some way along the corridor he gave up fighting, which was undignified, and let them take him towards the holding cells without having to drag him. Not the "brig" or the "jail," not even the "detention centre." On a ship like the *Olympic*, they were rarely used for more than letting a drunk cool off for a few hours, so the least threatening terminology tended to be used. Arnold had even once joked that they might call it "Time-Out." Well, who was getting a time-out now?

Arnold looked up just as the hand clasped around his right arm released, its owner falling limply to the floor, and found himself looking at a grim-faced Hultz. The elderly security man held his ballistic concussion gun and still had a swollen, red-looking nose from where he had been punched in it as he had tried to stop Franklin and friends leaving the ship. Now, less than a day later, he was helping out his captain again—who was, in turn, helping Franklin this time. Things had certainly become more exciting on the *Olympic* recently.

Arnold turned the other way to see a scuffle happening to his left, where Ensign Zhao and—was that Petty Officer Stanley, the sensor operator?—were wrestling the other officer to the ground. Arnold turned back around again.

"Do you mind?" he said to Hultz, holding out a hand and receiving the ballistic concussion gun. "Very good of you." Then he aimed, catching the look of horror on the guard's face before he fired and the man was knocked out cold. *Satisfying.* Arnold smiled at the three men who had come to aid him. "Promotions for everyone, hoorah!"

A mixture of trepidatious joy and outright confusion came back to him in the looks of the other three men. "Only joking. Let's take back our ship, shall we?"

THIRTY

"Get his gun!" Vik screamed at Sarah as he wrestled the solitary Koru guard who had come in to bring them food. This had not been planned or discussed, not even theorised. Instead, Vik had suddenly jumped the guard, who was fortunately small for one of their soldiers and almost half a head shorter than Vik, who was now half-hanging off his back like some overgrown child who still liked getting a "piggyback."

Sarah darted clumsily forward. The cell doors that had been closed to them all these hours suddenly slid open—perhaps somehow coded to the guard's presence—and all three of them spilled out into the corridor. Sarah stumbled and fell to her knees, while the struggling pair careened to the other side of the corridor—which, as was the Koru way, was vaguely circular, like a tube running through the ship—Vik hitting the wall with an "oomph" as the guard's weight thumped into him.

It was enough to cause Vik's grip to loosen and he began to slide down the wall. The Koru guard staggered upright—the front of his uniform now stained with the greenish sludge that apparently passed for food in the Koru military—and made for his weapon. Sarah reached up from her position on all fours, like she might have the telekinetic powers to wrest the weapon from his grip and had time enough to briefly wonder if it was to be her or Vik who would die first. Perhaps their valiant effort to escape and save Engee would have been in vain, anyway, as it had been far too long since the soldiers had taken her away to carry out the death sentence.

Several CEW beams suddenly lit the space in front of her, one the menacing purple of a Koru weapon. Interestingly, the other two were not. Two struck the guard and he tottered sideways, briefly aflame before he fell, dead before he hit the ground. Sarah's eyes met her husband's, then they turned to see who or what had just saved them. The answer to that question was "a barman, a fitness instructor, her first mate and, running between their legs, was a cat."

Sarah's great swell of joy was suddenly dampened when she saw that Engee was moving awkwardly, holding one arm against her side, and she ran over to her.

"You're hurt," Sarah said.

"I was very heroic," Engee told her, the words typically lacking any ego or guile. "And I escaped the interrogator with Geoff's help, but..." She lifted her arm to show that there was an area on the left side of her torso where the cloth of her jumpsuit was both blackened and slicked through with blood. Engee glanced around at the rounded corridor. "This ship is... not very Koru."

"Oh my God," Sarah exclaimed as she took in Engee's wounds. She looked up at Franklin and Gus. "How do we get off this thing and get her a doctor?"

Franklin pulled a face. She knew that face; they weren't going anywhere. "Now we're on here, we can't just leave. We need to see what they've got in store for Enceladine." To his credit, he sounded as disappointed about it as she felt. "And this might be the only real chance to look at their shield tech before they start using it on UTC warships."

"What are we going to do, take on a whole cruiser?" Sarah shot back, exasperated. She was tired of heroics, of sacrifice. Sooner or later, heroics were going to get them all killed.

Vik stepped up behind her. "Franklin's right," he said, looking down as Geoff came over and wrapped himself around his legs. "We need to find out as much information as we can about how this shield technology works. We need to safeguard Enceladine, *and* we need to live to report all of this to someone who can make use of it."

Sarah found herself looking back at Franklin. "What was your plan to get off of here?"

Worryingly—although perhaps not surprisingly—Franklin shrugged. "Steal a ship, I guess. The *Mutt's Nuts* if it's going. I'm kinda fond of that ship."

He grinned, but she wouldn't let him get away with just a cutesy remark.

"Hey, it was hard enough to work out how to get on here in the first place. Are you not hugely impressed by that bit?"

"I would have been halfway to Enceladine by now if Franklin hadn't grabbed me," Gus put in a little too cheerily.

"Okay," Sarah said. "I will take care of the 'way off' bit. I'll take Engee and we'll get back to the ship, see if we can find the bay controls and kill anyone who doesn't want us to use them. The rest of you do the other thing and meet us back there in…" Sarah looked at her watch, as if there really was some way to coordinate this insanity. "Fifteen minutes, twenty tops."

"And then you'll leave us," Franklin told her.

"We'll wait, of course we'll fucking wait," she snapped. "I was just trying to give you men a sense of urgency."

Vik stepped forward and put his hand on his wife's hand. "It wasn't a question, my love. If we're not back or if it gets too difficult to hold onto the ship, you leave and get back to the *Olympic*."

A lump forced itself into Sarah's throat and she shook her head. If she had been about to protest, then her attempts were cut short as they heard movement at the far end of the corridor.

"Gus!" Franklin called. "You get them back; Vik and I have got this." Gus started to protest, but Franklin cut him short, getting off an early shot to keep the enemy's heads down. "Engee's too wounded to fight properly. *I know* you'll get them back." His tone brooked no argument.

"Go!" Vik encouraged them as exploratory purple beams streaked down the corridor. They turned and ran, rounding a slow bend to the right at the far end, the ship's corridors seeming not to do harsh angles—unlike the damned uncomfortable cell they had been in—instead sweeping gently this way and that, so that it quickly became hard to work out whether they were heading towards port or starboard, to the bow or the stern. Sarah glanced back and caught one last sight of her husband, suddenly scared to be separated from him again, too late wishing that she had made him come with her too.

As they went, a Koru occasionally crossed their path or came out of an adjacent room or corridor, but none that they came across tried to hinder them. In fact, most tried to get out of their way, perhaps something to do with the fact that Gus was near twice the height of some of them—having to stoop in places not to strike his head—and that all three were carrying weapons. Although, many seemed to be running from Geoff, who occasionally darted ahead as they went. Cats, perhaps, were not a Koru thing.

"I have never thought much of the drawbacks of the Colony System before," Engee observed between increasingly laboured breaths.

"Colony System?" Gus asked, keeping his weapon well into his shoulder as they advanced along a particularly slow, long left-hand curve. He was, Sarah noticed, keeping his Koru rifle—more a carbine than a rifle in his large arms—up and tucked well into his shoulder. Now looking much more a soldier than a fitness instructor, she briefly wondered about that.

"We are chosen for our roles in adolescence," Engee explained, "and from that time we grow to become that and only that. In the same way our skin over time changes to our surroundings, our bodies change to fit into our roles. Our senses, our instincts, all of it." She threw out a hand to indicate the smaller Koru who had been scattering before their progress throughout the ship. "As it is not the nature of a soldier to do anything other than fight or guard, it is not in the nature of a technician or a service worker to fight unless someone of command level is there to direct them. To impose their will."

"Lucky for us," Gus said as they passed another Koru who kept her head down and shuffled past, as if trying to pretend they weren't there.

"Exactly. Although it does mean that a soldier will always fight to the death. They have no other purpose."

"Nice," Sarah said, looking at her first mate as she helped her along the corridor. The wound was bleeding again, the dark stain now having reached her hip, yet she managed to talk and keep up a good pace. There was something else pressing at Sarah's thoughts, though. "Has your memory come back now?" she asked. "Do you remember everything from before?"

"I do," Engee answered simply.

The space ahead suddenly opened out, the end of the corridor flaring almost evenly like the end of an artery. They arrived on a gantry above an open space. Several ships sat on the floor of the space below them, the biggest of them had the familiar rusty colouring of the *Mutt's Nuts*.

"That was surprisingly easy," Gus observed, and it was, of course, just like a man to go and curse their good luck.

Shots came at them from the gantry opposite. The space was vast, and the shooters must have been nearly fifty metres away, yet the first shot came dangerously close, and Sarah felt the searing heat of the beam almost painfully as it passed only a few centimetres clear of her left side. She and Engee lurched to the right as the soldier tried to use the beam to track and slice into her. For the first time, Engee cried out in pain.

Gus dove the other way and returned fire, although his shots were way wide, hitting the gantry supports some way below their attackers. Sarah brightened a little to see that there were only two of them, then cursed her optimism as two more arrived on the opposite side of the gantry. Then two more.

"We need to get down there now," she told Gus, "before we get overwhelmed."

"You two go, I'll cover," Gus replied heroically. *Bless him.* However, as Sarah watched him return fire again, only getting a little closer than the last time, she realized that his form back in the corridor might have been misleading. He was a terrible shot at anything over about five metres.

"I've got a better idea," she told him. "You give me one minute, yeah? Then you grab Engee and haul ass onto the ship." Then she turned to Engee, whose eyelids were drooping— something that they never did. "I might not be able to join you," Sarah told her. "You'll know if that is the case, and I want you to go. Don't wait for me and put yourself at risk. Are you still able to fly the ship?"

Engee nodded weakly, and Sarah briefly wondered if her first mate even understood her. There was little she could do about it either way.

"Cover me," she said to Gus, hoping that his inaccurate shots would be better than nothing. The first of the Koru soldiers were starting to move around to the side, and a beam went straight over her head as she ducked and began to descend the steps down onto the docking bay floor.

Sarah leaped and darted from side-to-side, not heading not for the *Mutt's Nuts* as their enemies might have expected, but for a ship that was sitting much closer to her—right at the bottom of the steps, in fact. It was a lot smaller than her ship, yet a little larger than its UTC equivalent—a fighter. Unlike the ship in which it was sat, the fighter had a more familiar Koru design—all angles and with a faded white exterior. While the UTC design still saw a pilot getting into a cockpit that sat in front of the engine, the Koru fighter was more like a small shuttle that the pilot stepped into, and the door on this one, she had noticed from the gantry, was open.

Unfortunately, just as she reached the bottom of the steps, its pilot appeared in the doorway—unadvisedly coming to check on what the racket was about. Sarah got her weapon up just in time to shoot him in the chest, sending him staggering back into the craft. Another time, she wouldn't have chosen to shoot an unarmed adversary and, if she lived through the next few minutes, she expected that she might be revisiting this moment in her—

Oh, bollocks.

Somehow, the little pilot had not been stopped by the shot directly in his chest. He rebounded off the far internal wall and suddenly they were grappling. He was strong, despite his size, and surprisingly bitey, but Sarah had once done four classes of Jiu-Jitsu several years back, and it flooded back as she somehow managed to roll him over the top of her and out of the hatch. Then she thumped an obvious-looking panel next to the door, closing it with great relief.

Sarah rubbed at her shoulder, which likely had Koru teeth marks somewhere below her jumpsuit, and turned to the control panel, hoping it would look familiar. It did not, but at least the lights were on, and that was a start. There was no joystick or column in the traditional sense. Instead, the panel in front of the pilot's chair was a flat surface with various highlighted areas. Sarah started experimentally moving her hands over them.

Nothing happened with the first few, then she heard the gratifying whine of the engine powering up. Sarah could see out of the front viewport that four of the soldiers had reached the floor and were charging towards the craft, so she quickly went back to experimenting with the other controls, which seemed to have come to life now that the engines were on. The craft leaped several metres into the air, then wobbled left and right as she played with something that felt like a trackpad.

Right, now to find those weapons, she thought, still needing to deal with the soldiers. She slid her hand over the panel; they had to be there somewhere. Suddenly the power dropped and the craft fell sharply. In her panic, she moved the trackpad and drifted quickly forward, still dropping, and landed on four Koru soldiers

Well, that was one way to deal with the problem. She still needed to find those weapons, though. There was the small matter of some blast doors and a tractor beam to deal with…

THIRTY-ONE

Vik was definitely not a soldier, Franklin could see that, but there was something in the way that Sarah's husband—the man who had replaced him, there was no getting away from that—threw himself into combat. He had this wild abandon that involved a lot of shouting and firing his weapon wildly. It reminded Franklin of something he had once heard about running into a bear in the wild and making lots of noise while waving your hands in an attempt to startle the dangerous beast.

This was the spirit in which Vikram Shah fought the professional, life-long soldiers of the Koru cruiser.

While—unbeknownst to the two men—the other three had enjoyed a trouble-free route to the docking bay, for Franklin and Vik, it seemed that every new section of corridor brought with it more people trying to kill them. So far, they had made quite a good team—Vik drawing their fire with his shouting and shooting and somehow not yet dying, while Franklin continually rediscovered what a good marksman he could be.

Franklin would have worried that he didn't have a plan or any idea where they were going, but there wasn't any time to worry, as just staying alive was keeping them quite busy. Maybe crazy Vik had a plan, as he had seemed even more certain than Franklin that this was what they had to do. They now reached a slightly more expanded—if not exactly open—area around twenty-five metres across, with smooth walls that curved overhead in a rough sort of shallow dome, perhaps reaching about two-and-a-half times the usual ceiling height at its top. Franklin had the feeling that they were right in the middle of the ship, deep within its heart.

The centre of the space was filled with what looked like tubing that expanded out evenly from a smaller dome in the middle of the room, like the dome was the top half—or maybe just a third—of the sun in a child's drawing, and the tubes represented light beams heading out in every direction, each one disappearing into the outer wall. He could see that, a little way to his right, narrow, spiralling steps led downwards.

"What do you think this place does?" Vik asked, moving his head about as he strained—just as Franklin had been doing—to look between the gaps in the tubes and see if he could spot anybody coming to kill them.

"I've never seen anything like it, on a ship or anywhere else." It was the first thing they had come across that didn't seem in some way familiar—the same as a piece of human technology but different. He stepped cautiously forward to peer closely at the tubing which, he now realised, was semi-transparent, its surface sort of like a milky-misty glass. "Is that-"

He was cut off by the clunking sound of three soldiers arriving at the opposite end of the room. By way of reaction, Franklin lifted his weapon but hesitated in firing, struggling to find a way to aim past all the tubing, which was like a forest on its side, the trunks jutting out at varying angles. One of the soldiers lifted a weapon in response and Franklin's chest tightened, but then the soldier next to the first one put a hand up and gently pushed the barrel of his comrade's weapon back down again.

O-kay... *That* was interesting.

Next to Franklin, Vik belatedly lifted his weapon. If Franklin didn't feel confident that he could shoot through the pipes, then he didn't fancy Vik's chances. Who knew if the shots might rebound back at them or something? "Wait," Franklin said, "they're not shooting."

Vik looked at Franklin and then at the pipes around them. On the other side, the soldiers were beginning to move towards them, trying to pick their way over, under and between the pipes.

Vik took a step back. "Should we find another way around?"

"No." Franklin pointed at the spiral staircase that disappeared below floor level. "I want to see what's down there."

Vik eyed him doubtfully but did not protest, so Franklin crossed over to the stairs. The Koru soldiers were nearly halfway across the room, and it seemed that their opaque eyes glared at the two men as Franklin and Vik crossed temptingly in front of them, the soldiers' laboured movement around the obstacle course of tubing giving the whole confrontation the feel of happening in slow motion—interpretive dance or something.

The ceiling was low on the next level down, so that the two men had to hunch slightly to avoid hitting their heads. It was dimly lit by a soft, yellowish glow, which Franklin saw was coming from the centre. Moving closer, he realized that it was a continuation of the dome from the centre of the room above, like the middle section of a sphere. Seeing another spiral staircase on the other side of the room from where they came down, he quickly crossed over and looked to the level below. Sure enough, it was the underside of the dome, again with the myriad lengths of tubing extending from it.

Turning back to the room they were in, Franklin noted the lack of tubing in this middle space.

"Those soldiers will be here any moment," Vik told him. "Maybe we should keep moving.

"You know what this is?" Franklin asked, indicating the central portion.

"Fucked if I know," Vik shrugged impatiently.

Franklin shook his head and pointed again. "This is it," he said, crossing back to the middle of the space and using the screen on his T-Slate to shine a little light on it. The surface, as with the tubes, was a kind of milky glass but, putting his face close to it, Franklin could make out what was inside. A familiar yellowish gas, swirling about, and, like lightning in a cloud, there was the occasional electrical flash. "This is the shield generator."

Just then, the sound of boots could be heard coming down the spiral staircase behind them. Vik spun to face the soldiers, weapon at the ready, but Franklin stayed where he was and slowly raised his weapon at the strange construction in front of him.

"Do-not-do-it!" called out one of the soldiers in halting English.

"This is how it works," Franklin said, as much to himself as to anybody else, glancing up towards the floor above, where myriad pipes spread out from the central device. "The whole ship is built around it, and the electrified gas spreads out to the exterior." He cocked his head back towards the soldiers. "And what happens to it there?" He did not expect them to answer. "How does it make a protective shield around the ship?

Three more soldiers came down the steps, close to them in claustrophobic space.

"Franklin?" Vik prompted nervously.

"Don't worry," he answered, "they won't shoot us here."

Vik looked between Franklin and the soldiers. "Does that really help us?"

Franklin understood what Vik was getting at. Even if they didn't get shot, they were not getting out of this room with six Koru soldiers between them and the exit. Especially not when he kept demonstrating his growing knowledge of their prized shield system. "Seems there's only one thing to do," he said, scaring himself by how eager he was. He was still a crazy bastard, after all. Still that idiot who flew alone into a Koru mothership.

The answering grin that Vik flashed back in return made him realise that, in some ways, they were kindred spirits.

"No!" one of the soldiers screamed, catching on and starting to lift his weapon just a moment before Franklin pulled the trigger. Time seemed to hang as the beam struck the surface; briefly, the glass-like casing held for a second, like it was made of a much harder substance—or some sort of shield itself—but then it gave way.

The casing shattered and the beam continued slowly onward, even after Franklin had released the trigger. The effect was underwhelming yet seemed to be enough to get the soldiers behind them to turn and run, no longer worried about killing their intruders. It was almost insulting. Vik and Franklin looked at each other, then back at the beam as it continued to slowly move through the gas, which kept its shape instead of floating out to fill the room.

"Should we run?" Vik asked.

The beam was now reaching what was surely the centre of the construct, the heart of the shield system, or so it looked. Suddenly, there was a great flare of blinding light from somewhere in the middle of it and the rest of the casing began to crack.

"Yup," Franklin answered. They both turned and ran like men ducking for cover, hunched over as they made for the steps in the corner of the room. When they got to the next level up, Franklin could see that the top dome of the casing had also ruptured. Lightning cracked and arced from it, spreading along the floor towards them, shooting up into the ceiling and snaking along some of the tubing.

"It looks really bad," Vik said, and Franklin realised that Vik was having to shout, that somehow the background noise level—which had been little more than a static hum when they first came into the space—had leaped dramatically and was now an incessant howl.

They moved carefully as the lightning continued to reach along the floor towards them, its vein-like strands coming ever-closer to their feet, until they were back out into the corridor, the same one they had first entered the room from. It now seemed that everything around them was shaking.

"Back to the ship?" Franklin suggested.

"I think our work here is done."

The ceiling just behind them suddenly exploded, showering parts of it into the corridor, then strands of lightning erupted from it, hitting the floor right behind Franklin and causing a great shower of sparks.

"I think we might have broken the ship," Franklin shouted in a shrill voice. He was wide-eyed—alive and terrified, and unsure of the wisdom of what he had just done. It was some mad part of him that had fired that weapon—something destructive and vengeful—although perhaps he hoped to convince himself that he was destroying some prototype, sending the Koru shield program back several years, yet he knew better than that.

No one tried to stop them as they sprinted towards the docking bay, all thoughts of caution and tactical movement abandoned in favour of speed. At the same time, around them, it seemed as if the whole ship periodically shuddered, like someone with a terminal illness in their final hours or minutes letting out terrible, wracking coughs.

Close to the docking bay, as Franklin vaguely remembered it, they came along a curving corridor and saw panicked crew members cross in front of them and step into egg-shaped openings that contained a seat with restraints. *Escape pods?* Franklin wondered, noting that they had not been visible earlier. *They are abandoning ship.* But then the last one he ran past opened to show a small Koru female who was already strapped into the seat and looking terrified as she continually punched a button, like the pod was not doing what she hoped it would.

However, Franklin had no more time to consider her, as then they were in another, straighter corridor and moments later coming out above the bay. He could see the strands of tell-tale lightning writhing across the ceiling here and there. Sparks erupted as some circuit or system was overloaded. The *Mutt's Nuts* was still in the bay, and there were the smoking ruins of several shuttles or fighters, and another fighter was lying on its side. There were the bodies of Koru soldiers, too—the whole thing looked like the aftermath of a terrible fight—and fire was beginning to spread from one of the downed fighters. Scanning about, his chest tight, he could not see the body of anybody he knew.

Glancing to the left, beyond the *Mutt's Nuts*, he could see that the blast doors protecting the bay on the outside of the ship were mostly gone, their broken edges still glowing orange and smoking in places, while a large section of wall just above and to the right of them was again black, orange and smoking. There was now a hole in the blast doors easily big enough for the *Mutt's Nuts* to pass through. Some sort of gravity shield—this one a translucent blue, not orange—held the atmosphere in the bay and kept the lethal vacuum out where it belonged.

"Are they in the ship?" Vik wondered out loud.

"Let's hope so," Franklin answered. Based on what he could see, it was possible. He found himself feeling proud of the other three. Whatever had happened here, they had caused some heck. "Let's get down there."

As they arrived at floor-level and ran towards the back of the ship, the smaller crew access ramp opened towards the back of the left side. At the same time, Franklin heard the engines come to life with something between a whine and a roar. Above and behind them, several soldiers ran out onto the gantry and these ones—the first since the shield generator—paid them lots of attention, unlike all the other crew they had passed. The first shot to come down from the gantry was accurate and glanced across

Vik's left thigh, causing him to stumble over with a shout of pain.

"Leave me!" he called as Franklin stopped and turned to come back, then ducked as another shot streaked over his head to hit the back of the *Mutt's Nuts* in a shower of sparks.

"Shut up!" Franklin growled as he scrambled over to Vik and aimed a quick shot up towards the gantry level, causing at least some of those shooting at them to duck back. The whole bay spasmed at that moment, this one at least twice as violent as any previous ones, and a soldier above them toppled over the railing and fell headfirst to land on some ship wreckage. Behind them, the *Mutt's Nuts* also seemed to groan in protest.

Gus appeared at the top of the ramp and began to fire wildly in the general direction of the soldiers, giving Franklin the opportunity to half-pull Vik the rest of the way to the ship. Once inside, Gus slammed a button, and the ramp came up. He hit a second button and spoke into a wall comms unit. "Good to go, Sarah."

Franklin looked down at Vik. Although a glancing shot, the burn on Vik's leg was quite visible. He could see by the way the other man clenched his teeth that it was extremely painful. "I'm going to get you a painkiller," Franklin said as Gus helped Vik into a bucket seat by the wall, "we don't need you going into shock."

Franklin headed to a medical box at the opposite end of the cargo hold and Gus went with him. A loud, metallic clunk seemed to vibrate through the floor and the two of them to shared a worried look. When nothing exploded or collapsed, Franklin shrugged. "All good?"

"Yes," Gus answered, "although Sarah's a bit knocked about. You should have seen her, Franklin. She stole a fighter, blew shit up, crashed it. It was awesome." He went to head back up the steps but paused. "All this...?" he asked, swirling a forefinger around in a circle that pointed towards the ceiling and the bay beyond, indicating the larger, more general destruction that seemed to be happening.

"Us. Well... me, I guess," he added, feeling the need to shoulder the responsibility. "It seems that their shield generator might also be their Achilles heel."

They felt the ship's movement as it started to rise the first few inches off the bay's deck, then the slight tilt as it moved forward, and...

There was a sudden stop and a moment of recoil, not unlike being in a vehicle and hitting something or slamming on the brakes at slow speed. Imagining the whole of the docking bay—maybe the cruiser itself—having started to collapse around them, Franklin hit another comms panel located close to the medical box. "Sarah?"

This panel had a small screen above it and the screen flared into life, showing Sarah and Engee sitting in the pilot and co-pilot positions in the cockpit, "Fucking docking clamp or something!" Sarah raged. "Someone must have just activated it. We took care of the tractor beam already."

Franklin remembered the loud clunking noise that had sounded as he crossed the Nuts' cargo bay and sighed, realising that it was a last desperate attempt to keep them in place. There would be a manual release, he was sure of it, as such clamps were a safety measure for during capital ship combat or other emergencies, not manacles to shackle an unwilling ship. It was as important to be able to release it manually, if necessary, as it was to keep it there in the first place. He turned to Gus. "Can you get this pain killer to Vi-"

He stopped, having turned to indicate Sarah's husband at the back of the bay and seeing him instead standing by the ramp, which was already most of the way down. "Vik!" he cried out, and both he and Gus started for the back of the bay, but the other man—hobbling though he was—quickly went out and half-fell from the still descending ramp. Franklin saw streaks of the purple beams go past as Vik disappeared out of sight, and everything had that strange quality of happening fast yet also seeming to be in slow motion.

As soon as he stepped out onto the ramp, a beam raked the hull not more than six inches from Franklin's head, and he ducked down and returned fire. Glancing back, his heart sank to see that there was a smoking hole on Vik's back and that he was crawling across the floor. Yet the seemingly tireless and unstoppable older man had got to the huge, gunmetal-grey shoe that enclosed the base of one strut of the *Mutt's Nuts*' landing gear. A hand reached up and pulled a thick lever on the side, making the clamp let go, which in turn caused the ship to jerk upwards.

Franklin fell backward onto Gus at the top of the ramp. While Franklin clambered back to his feet, Gus reached for the comms unit next to the door. "Sarah, stop!" he cried. "Vik's outside!"

The ship thumped back down again, but that was when the gravity shield protecting the whole of the docking bay from space let go.

Franklin watched as the thin, see-through, blue energy screen that separated the bay from the harshness of space blinked once, then vanished. The air in the bay rushed towards the vacuum and Franklin saw Vik spin around on his front and manage to grab the clamp release handle. Their eyes met for a moment and Franklin, himself having to hold onto the ramp's hydraulic strut to stop from being pulled out into space, thought he saw Vik try to say something to him, but the rush of noise made by the evacuating air was blocking all sound out.

He was fixed on the other man's eyes and his lips. Their eyes met, and he could tell that the other man understood what was coming as the clamp—now having released the ship— continued to recede back into the deck. Vik's lips kept moving, although Franklin could not read what they were saying. Then the clamp handle dropped too low, Vik's fingers slipped, and a moment later he was gone, leaving Franklin screaming, reaching his hand out uselessly, his own fingers getting weaker and weaker as they kept him in place, the air around him turning to vacuum.

The next thing, Gus' strong arms were around Franklin's chest, and they were falling back into the cargo hold, the ramp closing again behind them. There was screaming, screaming coming from somewhere—not him anymore. His head swam and he struggled to stay conscious. *Oh God*, he had never heard her scream like that.

THIRTY-TWO

"We need you, Captain," Admiral Maxwell told Arnold as they spoke via the projection terminal in the captain's quarters. "The UTC does not know it yet, but it needs as many men like you as possible, those who will have the stomach for what is to come. They are blind to the threat the Koru pose and too willing to look the other way, even with the evidence of what has been going on in the McMurdo Rift recently."

"I can't say I'm entirely surprised, Admiral," Arnold answered. He had hoped for more, although the destruction of the Koru cruiser without a single survivor had left them with little evidence of what the Koru had *actually* been up to, only an unimpressive-looking piece of rock and a barely successful science experiment which—by UTC technological standards, at least—was not very scalable and still did not make for an implementable shield system.

Chills still went through him when he remembered Franklin's report of passing escape pods on the Koru ship that did not appear to be firing. *Everyone* was to go down with the ship, no one left to talk. He also remembered Franklin's haunted look. The ex-pilot had killed another whole ship's worth of Koru—at least that was how he would see it—and witnessed the final moments of his ex-wife's husband to boot. Too much for one man who had come out to the McMurdo Rift to disappear and find a quiet life.

For Arnold's part, he had to admit that he had only felt a thrill throughout recent events, a sense of coming alive again after being dormant for so long.

"And there's more going on out there, I know it," the admiral went on. "Now we've got reports of phantom ships that no one sees coming, or so the rumours have it. Ship disappearances and unexplained losses to a worryingly high level."

"Oh, that's long been a legend out here, Admiral."

"This is more, Philby," the admiral insisted gruffly. "Believe me. And the Koru have something to do with it, mark my words. It's been good to have you on our side and in the area."

"Thank you," Arnold replied, although he doubted that he could get away with treating the *Olympic* like a spare military vessel too often. Things had turned out well, and he felt quite sure of keeping his job, but there had still been a lot of complaints, not least from the influential Dame Hatherleigh, whom he thought it wise to release after only a short stint in captivity. Yelland was not getting the same leniency.

"However, I think you've done all you can do there," Admiral Maxwell went on, almost like he was reading Arnold's thoughts. "You'll still be a useful pair of eyes, of course, but you'll be much more useful here with us."

"Pardon?" Arnold's stomach lurched.

The admiral gave a self-satisfied grin. Arnold knew that his poker face had gone out of the window. "I mean that I've found a position here for you, if you'd like it?"

....

Franklin pulled out a bottle of gin from underneath the counter at the bar and took it over to the table where Sarah, Engee and Gus were all sat. The bar was still closed, and the chairs were up on all the other central tables, as the ship's hour was past the time that it would have been open. Aside from the four of them, only Geoff was in the bar, sprawled across one of the comfy booth seats against the wall, licking his private area. Perhaps the cat equivalent of having a good, stiff drink after his adventure on a Koru spaceship, helping Engee to escape the enemy's clutches. Franklin was proud of him.

As nice as it was, in some ways, to be back, for the first time in almost a decade of ownership, the SS Olympic Cocktail Lounge seemed a little small—and quite a lot less significant—than it had been not much more than a week ago.

"Vik's favourite," Sarah remarked sombrely as Franklin placed the bottle and three glasses down on the table.

"Have you got another glass there?" came a voice from by the door. Franklin looked up and saw the man who was—after a brief lull and now with a larger number of people than usual occupying the holding cells—the ship's captain again. He went back to the bar and Arnold wandered over.

"You're up late," Franklin remarked. "Thought you would be tucked up in bed after all the excitement, old man."

Arnold scoffed. "Still got it. And I'm not the only one who thinks so."

Franklin gave him a questioning look but didn't, for now, ask what he meant.

They crossed with the glass over to the table and took their seats, Franklin pouring them each a shot. "To absent friends," he offered.

"To Vik," Sarah said, and they all drank. She was even paler than usual, her eyes red-rimmed and haunted. As they escaped the dying Koru cruiser, she had watched on the external camera feed as her husband was sucked into the cold vacuum of space, vanished and untraceable in the vastness before she could even fly after him.

"What will the UTC do now, Captain Philby?" Engee asked Arnold once her face had recovered from the various shapes it had screwed up into after drinking the shot of gin.

"I hope they will send someone out," he answered. "There will be interest in what was being mined on Enceladine, I expect, especially with your discoveries about the properties of the resultant gas and Mr Franklin's account of the machine itself giving at least some clue to how the technology might work. Although I think we may be some way from replicating it. Perhaps the most important thing, for now, is that your... *the Koru* seem to have abandoned their mining operation on Enceladine. A military presence to at least make them think twice about re-establishing it would be nice." His expression did not look hopeful. "But..."

"They sacrificed everyone aboard their own ship," Franklin remembered.

"So no one could talk," Gus put in grimly.

"Hey!" Sarah's voice was soft, if firm, her smile strained but there in her eyes. "They don't have the shield material from Enceladine now, and we don't know how important that might yet prove, especially if the UTC can work out the technology. You did what you had to, and Vik gave his life to get us off that ship. Let's not regret any of it."

Let's not regret any of it. "I'll drink to that," Franklin said, swiping up the gin bottle and gesturing to see who wanted another shot. Everybody did, even Engee.

"Not regret," Engee giggled as she placed down her emptied shot glass for the second time.

"No regrets," Gus agreed.

Franklin had been running from his regrets for too many years, and they had just damn well gone and caught up with him anyway. Maybe he needed to work on not having any in the first place. For tonight, however, he was just going to focus on getting stupidly drunk.

Arnold Philby tapped his shot glass twice on the table. "Come on, Mr Franklin, keep them coming."

Franklin, Sarah and the crew of The Mutt's Nuts will return in THE MCMURDO TRIANGLE

Also In Series

Want to find out how Vik ended up on Enceladine?

Sign up for the newsletter at

www.BradleyLejeune.com to download the short story "Withdrawal."

Acknowledgments

Thanks are due to Laura and Lorraine firstly, and also our Beta readers Bethany, Chris, Alex, and Dickie.

About The Author

Bradley Lejeune is the ingeniously abbreviated combination of writers Malcolm Bradley and Martin Lejeune.

Malcolm has worked for eight years as a freelance ghostwriter, while Martin has a background in filmmaking and visual effects.

They figured that attempts to forcefully join their various talents with one another might result in some good books. Or crimes against nature... Only time will tell.

Martin loves graphic design, reading sci-fi, and he dreams of one day writing a spy novel.

Malcolm is a total fantasy nerd with a leaning toward horror, who identifies a little too strongly with zombies. They met far too many years ago while working in a cinema together. Except that they talked about movies and never did any work.

Printed in Great Britain
by Amazon